"The Nauti series is one that [...] The characters are brilliant, sexy, [...] tion and soul-gripping plots have y[...] it!"
—Fresh Fiction

"Completely blown away by this surprising story. I could not put [it] down . . . and before I knew it, I had read this entire novel in one sitting. . . . A smoldering-hot tale of secret passion and erotic deceptions."
—Romance Junkies

"Wild and thrilling."
—The Romance Studio

"The sex scenes are, as always with Leigh's books, absolutely sizzling."
—Errant Dreams Reviews

"Heated romantic suspense."
—*Midwest Book Review*

MORE PRAISE FOR LORA LEIGH AND HER NOVELS

"Leigh draws readers into her stories and takes them on a sensual roller coaster."
—Love Romances & More

"Will have you glued to the edge of your seat."
—Fallen Angel Reviews

"Blistering sexuality and eroticism. . . . Bursting with passion and drama. . . . Enthralls and excites from beginning to end."
—Romance Reviews Today

IN ISABEAU'S EYES

LORA LEIGH

BERKLEY ROMANCE
NEW YORK

BERKLEY ROMANCE
Published by Berkley
An imprint of Penguin Random House LLC
penguinrandomhouse.com

Library of Congress Cataloging-in-Publication Data

Names: Leigh, Lora, author.
Title: In Isabeau's eyes / Lora Leigh.
Description: First Edition. | New York: Berkley Romance, 2023. | Series: Kentucky nights; 1
Identifiers: LCCN 2022026272 (print) | LCCN 2022026273 (ebook) | ISBN 9780399583872
(trade paperback) | ISBN 9780399583889 (ebook)
Subjects: LCGFT: Novels.
Classification: LCC PS3612.E357 I5 2023 (print) | LCC PS3612.E357 (ebook) |
DDC 813/.6—dc23/eng/20220627
LC record available at https://lccn.loc.gov/2022026272
LC ebook record available at https://lccn.loc.gov/2022026273

First Edition: March 2023

Printed in the United States of America
1st Printing

Book design by George Towne

For my little Pied Piper.
Gammy loves you, girl.
Always.

And for Darryl and Maxine.
Thank you for your friendship.

IN
ISABEAU'S
EYES

ONE

SHE'D ALMOST DIED. AGAIN. AND THIS TIME, THE NEAR miss had nearly taken someone else as well.

Isabeau Boudreaux sat still and silent in the front seat of the pickup she'd been led to, the door open, fighting the misty blurriness of her eyesight and her own fear.

For ten years she'd been fighting to live, and for nine of those years it seemed bad luck was determined to kill her where her father had failed.

If it was bad luck, as her brother, Burke, was wont to say.

"Goddammit, Angel." A new voice, filled with anger and disgust, rose amid the others that had arrived at the site where Angel's truck had nearly gone over a sheer cliff after the tire had exploded. "What the bloody fuck is going on here? That was no convenient blowout. That tire was shot out, and you and I both know you're experienced enough to see it."

Isabeau froze, her fingers tightening on the handle of the cane she carried as the accusation drifted to her over the distance between the truck she sat in and Angel's truck a good fifty feet away.

She was guessing the unknown male was one of Angel's brothers, most likely the eldest brother, who they called Tracker. She'd met the younger one, Chance, and rather liked him. But even angry, his voice wouldn't sound like this.

She couldn't hear Angel's response, but the male didn't care if he was heard or not.

Rough, dark, and raspy, it was a sexy sound, despite the anger filling it.

"And you damned well know that woman is a walking target and has been for years," he snapped again. "Why didn't you stay the fuck away . . . ?"

Isabeau flinched; the pure fury in the man's voice and his words whipped across her emotions, pulling at the guilt she already felt and a fear she'd fought for years.

Unfounded fear, she was told often, but a fear all the same.

Of all her accidents in the past ten years, law enforcement hadn't found a single shred of evidence that they were anything more than bad luck. Even her brother, as strong and suspicious as he was, and the friends he surrounded himself with, couldn't find so much as a rumor that they were anything more than accidents.

She was blind. Shit happened. Right?

Her blindness hadn't been an accident though. The bullet she'd taken to her head when she was fifteen should have killed her. Instead, it had somehow lodged in her skull, taking her sight rather than her life.

And her memory of that night.

"Dammit, Tracker, I said shut the hell up." Angel's demand had come too late; the words had already been said. "Stop being an asshole just for the sake of it."

"I'm never an asshole for the sake of it, little sister," he countered with a snarl. "And you damned well know it. It comes naturally."

Isabeau heard the heavy sigh next to her where the door had been left open by the young woman keeping her company.

Annie Mackay was eighteen, and very sensitive for her age. That sound was heavy with sympathy, and Isabeau hated it. The girl felt sorry for her, when that was the last thing Isabeau wanted.

"Tracker is Angel's brother," the young woman told her. "Sort of. He and his family raised Angel after Aunt Chaya thought she'd been killed in a hotel bombing. He's like her foster brother."

"Angel told me," Isabeau said. "He has a right to be angry. She was almost killed."

"But it wasn't your fault," Annie stated, her voice soft. "Tracker's just really worried about her. He always worries more now that she's pregnant. And that would have been a really bad accident."

Isabeau tightened her fingers on the cane once again, the all-too-familiar feeling of helplessness, of dependence, strangling her. She couldn't even leave, not without asking someone to take her home. And how could she do that, after Angel had nearly died driving her to the remote location where the weekend gathering hosted by the few friends she made was being held?

The invitation to the Mackay reunion weekend had filled her with such excitement when Angel had extended it and told her she could ride to the property with her. Three days and nights at the lake house getting to know the rest of the Mackay family amid good food, music, and bonfires.

Now she just wanted to hide in the small house she owned in Somerset, Kentucky, and decide if she should call her brother and tell him about this latest incident.

One more time, he'd warned her, and she was returning to the ranch with a bodyguard. He was tired of the accidents that made no sense and defied explanation. He'd protect her himself if he had to lock her in the ranch house to do it.

A miserable existence.

She didn't want to go back to Texas.

She loved her brother, Burke, and his father and stepmother. His half sister, Kenya, was fun to be around, but Texas wasn't home. It was dusty and too hot in the summer, too cold in the winter. The sound of cattle filled the air constantly, along with the shouts of the cowboys on horseback who worked them.

But she didn't want anyone else hurt because of her either. This accident had been too close. If the truck had gone over the cliff, she, Angel, and Angel's unborn child would have died.

"It was an accident." Annie broke into her thoughts with the assurance, but Isabeau heard the doubt in her voice.

An accident.

Like the truck that nearly ran her over in Beaumont, the attempted abduction outside her college dorm, the gas explosion in the empty apartment next to hers when she'd moved to Dallas—and those were just the highlights of her bad-luck adventures, as she'd been calling them.

Just an accident.

But evidently, this one hadn't been.

Tracker Calloway had told his sister that she had enough experience to know that the tire was shot out. That meant it had been deliberate. Someone had shot it as Angel rounded the sharp curve in the narrow mountain road.

It was no accident, Isabeau thought as she fought back the sudden terror that wanted to rise inside her.

Had someone really been causing the "accidents," and had they finally grown tired of failing and decided to use a bullet?

She rubbed at the side of her head, her fingers finding the scar beneath her hair that marked where the bullet had struck her the summer she turned fifteen.

"Uh-oh, here comes Tracker," Annie murmured. "And Dad and Duke."

Dad being Rowdy Mackay, and Duke being Angel's husband.

"Annie, go with your mom," Rowdy directed his daughter, his tone warm and caring when he spoke to the teenager, but Isabeau heard the undercurrent of tension. "We're going back to the lake house now."

"Okay, Dad." Annie moved back, the blurred shadow of her form hesitant as she moved.

"Isabeau, this is Tracker Calloway with me," Rowdy told her as Annie left. "He'll be driving you back to the lake house."

Isabeau's felt the lash of trepidation as it rushed through her.

"Ms. Boudreaux," Tracker said as he opened the driver's side door and slid in.

She jerked, flinching away from him a second later as the huge shadow suddenly moved closer, his arm reaching across her.

"Seat belt," he seemed to bite out as he grabbed the latch and pulled it across her.

The complete lack of respect the move indicated was like a slap in the face.

"I'm blind, not incompetent." The words burst free from her before she could hold them back. "And I can buckle my own damned seat belt."

It snapped into place even as she spoke.

"Tracker." Duke spoke from behind Rowdy, his voice holding a warning. "Politeness counts."

It seemed to be a repeated order, if Duke's tone was anything to go by.

"As does common sense," Tracker snorted. "Now close the damned door so I can get her to the house. Hopefully without either of us going over a cliff."

Isabeau barely stilled a gasp at the not-so-subtle accusation in his tone and her own surprise at how deep it seemed to hurt.

"Why don't you let someone in possession of that common sense drive instead," Rowdy snapped as the tension shot up by several degrees.

"Because the rest of you actually give a damn if you live or die," Tracker growled, his voice deepening, becoming more graveled as Isabeau felt anger beginning to burn between Tracker and Rowdy. "Looks like me and Ms. Boudreaux are the only two here who don't give a flying fuck. Now close the goddamned door so I can leave."

"Like hell . . ." Rowdy snapped, his body shifting closer to her as though he intended to jerk her from the truck.

She actually wouldn't have put it past him.

"Rowdy, I'll be fine," Isabeau hurriedly injected as she lifted a hand helplessly, looking between the two men, the fiery tension building around them too much for her to take in or to deal with.

The shadows of both men standing beside her suddenly seemed far more dangerous as they'd stepped closer to where she sat.

"Get out of the truck, Isabeau," Duke ordered. "Some of us aren't nearly the asshole Tracker's making himself out to be. . . ."

Making himself out to be?

"It's not an act, Duke. You of all people should know that," Tracker snorted, the complete assurance in his tone almost amusing as he voiced her own thoughts.

Amusing if the situation hadn't had the potential to be so disastrous.

"I'm certain it isn't," Isabeau assured him as she did the unruly students she occasionally dealt with. Despite his gruff words, she sensed he wouldn't hurt her. "And you do it very well." She turned back to Duke and Rowdy. "Mr. Calloway and I will get along fine, I promise. Tell Angel I'll talk to her later."

Reaching past Duke, she felt for the door handle, gripped it, and eased it toward her slowly. She was rather surprised when the two men shifted back and allowed her to close the door.

The truck slid into gear and moments later began backing along the road, only to swing into what she assumed was a wider spot to turn and continue along the steep incline of the mountain.

Folding her hands in her lap, Isabeau faked composure. She'd learned how to do that years ago, after first losing her sight, to appease Burke, who had been enraged for more than a year because of their mother's murder and Isabeau's father's attempt to kill Isabeau as well before he'd killed himself.

That was what the official police report concluded, as had the coroner. That her father, Carmichael Boudreaux, had killed his wife, Danica, and believed he'd killed his daughter, then turned the gun on himself.

Her gentle, laughter-filled, loving father had seemingly found some reason to believe they should all die.

There had been no suicide letter, no indication that he harbored such darkness inside him. Friends hadn't noticed anything unusual in him, no hint of depression or financial worries. Yet he'd killed his wife and attempted to kill his daughter.

Isabeau's accidental survival had amazed the doctors and surgeons. The fact that she'd recovered, with only the loss of sight, had astounded them.

"I'm not one of your teenage students." Tracker's voice interrupted her thoughts. "I don't like being patronized, Ms. Boudreaux."

She'd known all that offended male pride would escape soon. Most men dislike being talked to as though they were teenagers. Especially when they were acting in that age group.

"Then don't act like a schoolyard bully," she suggested calmly. "As I understand it, you know both Duke and Rowdy fairly well. Infuriate their protective instincts, and fists are going to start flying. You should be old enough to realize that."

Not to mention experienced enough. According to Angel, he specialized in rescuing hostages and protecting high-level clients. He should know when to put aside the more prickish aspects of his nature.

"Wouldn't be the first time with either of them," he assured her, the dark, brooding tone of his voice deepening. "Neither of them should have allowed Angel to transport you to the lake house. If I'd known what was going on, I would have brought you in myself."

She glanced over at him. For some reason, the dark form of his body was easier to distinguish than others that day. She wished this were one of those times when her sight was a bit clearer and hints of color could actually be seen.

"If I had thought anyone would be in any danger, I would have kept my ass at home." She reminded him of his furious words as he'd spoken to Angel earlier. "My bad luck has never involved anyone else before. I never imagined it would now."

Which left her wondering how the hell she was going to have a normal life now.

"Lady, did that bullet you took at fifteen shear off the simple-logic-forming brain cells or what?" The cold, furious snap of his tone had her freezing. "That was no goddamned back luck; nor was it an accident. A bullet took that fucking tire out. The fucker that shot it out just didn't know who he was dealing with at the time. But he's getting ready to find out."

She shook her head. What reason would anyone even have to try to kill her?

"That's crazy, Calloway." She turned to him, glaring at his dark profile, her fingers curling into fists as she fought her own fears where his suspicion was concerned. "Who would want to kill a blind teacher? Hell, who would have to go to such extremes to do it? I'm about the easiest target to kill that I can think of."

"Evidently you're not." That dark tone too closely resembled a growl. A dangerous, far too sexy sound for her peace of mind. "A bullet to the head didn't take you out, whoever tried to run you over in Beaumont was foiled at the last second by some drunk cowboy, an attempted abduction was countered by two party girls walking with you, and you barely escaped a gas explosion in the apartment next to yours when you made an unplanned visit to a neighbor downstairs. Did I miss anything?"

"Well, you hit the high points at least," she muttered, actually trying to hold back her sarcasm. And failing.

"Lady, you're not a bad-luck magnet. Quite the opposite. Your guardian angels are haggard and exhausted trying to keep your ass alive. And because my sister has become so damned attached to you, it looks like they're finally gonna get a break at least. Because I intend to find the bastard trying to kill you and put him out of his misery."

Arrogance. The level of this man's arrogance absolutely astounded her.

He intended to do all this how, exactly? Multiple police detectives and private investigators had tried to solve that very question. God only knew how much money her brother had spent over the years, and every report came back the same.

An accident. All but the attempted abduction anyway, and in that case, several other young women had nearly been taken as well that night. The officer investigating it had concluded that the two men were part of a human-trafficking ring.

What made him think he'd find anything they hadn't?

"And just how do you intend to do that, Mr. Calloway?" she demanded, certain he had to be wrong. Because if he wasn't, then she'd have no choice but to return to the ranch. "No one else can find so much as an ounce of evidence to support your claim. Did you find a bullet in that tire? Anything to indicate it had been deliberately blown? Anything other than your suspicions?"

"I'm experienced enough to know it wasn't an accident, and I'll be damned if I'll accept that explanation. I'll make certain the bastard making the attempts knows I'm not one of the dumbasses willing to accept your bad-luck theory," he drawled with utter confidence. "I'm going to make sure he knows he's being hunted. And you, Ms. Boudreaux, are going to help me."

TWO

TRACKER CALLOWAY WAS CRAZY, ISABEAU DECIDED.

Certifiably. Unaccountably insane. But thankfully quiet through the rest of the ride, giving Isabeau a chance to think, to try to put everything into perspective.

He expected her to help him prove someone was trying to kill her and to figure out who it was?

He seemed so certain that the tire had been shot out, rather than an accidental blowout. Of course, the coincidence of location played quite a bit into the suspicion the tire had been deliberately sabotaged, she told herself. At the juncture of the curve that was most dangerous, the cliff the steepest.

New tires.

She remembered Angel mentioning last week that Duke had taken the truck in for new tires, so they couldn't have been worn at all. That pretty much ruled out a blowout. If anything had been in the road—glass, nails, or the like—she trusted Rowdy would have noticed it. If not him, then Angel's stepfather, Natches Mackay, sure as hell would have seen it.

And they would have told Tracker.

But someone shooting out the tire simply made no sense. That meant someone was watching her, would have known she was going to the Mackays' lake house, and was lying in wait for Angel's truck.

It meant someone was tired of trying to make her death look like an accident rather than murder.

Her brother and their friends Saul and Seth August had suspected for years that the accidents were more sinister than law enforcement and private investigators were reporting. There was simply no proof, or so Burke had been told time and time again. Even Seth and Saul hadn't been able to find anything, and they were Navy SEALs.

Tracker and Isabeau finally reached the top of the mountain and started down the other side as Isabeau gave up trying to figure out if the investigators were right, or if Burke and Tracker were. She allowed herself to relax marginally, considering Mr. Asshole had kept quiet. He gave *rude* a whole new meaning.

But could she blame him? Angel had been raised as his baby sister. He'd looked after her for years under extremely rough and dangerous circumstances, according to Angel.

Isabeau knew from Burke's attitude after each "accident" she'd had that strong men with baby sisters tended to become pure pricks when said sisters faced any danger at all.

She remembered her first month at the ranch after returning from the school for the blind. While sitting by the pool at the back of the ranch house one day, the cage door that kept her uncle's guard dogs confined had somehow become unlocked. One of the dogs had attacked her before Burke's father could get to her, and vicious teeth had ripped into her leg.

Burke had gone insane. He'd loaded the dogs up and driven away, and refused to say what had happened to them when he returned. But when his uncle, Bill, had arrived, he and Burke had fought brutally. It had ended with Bill being barred from the ranch as long as she was in residence. And he was never to bring another of his dogs.

Burke had been a pure ass in the weeks before Bill had arrived though. His temper had raged so close to the surface that Isabeau had actually offered to return to the school in the hopes that it would still some of that anger.

He'd changed after their mother's death. Became harder, darker. He was no longer the playful, laughing young man that visited in the summers and during vacations.

"We're almost at the lake house," Tracker said, his tone blunt. "When we get there, I'll take you to your room. We need to discuss how we're going to save that pretty ass of yours."

It was all she could do to keep from rolling her eyes. Only the knowledge that it would likely piss him off more had her restraining the urge. The man couldn't have sounded more arrogant and chauvinistic if he'd tried.

"You could have talked on the way here," she pointed out, wondering why he even felt the need to talk. It was obvious he didn't want her there.

"Sorry, princess, I felt it best to keep my attention on driving just in case your admirer decided to shoot out another tire." His tone was a little too mocking and far too close to a sneer.

"My name is Isabeau, or Ms. Boudreaux," she informed him, keeping her tone cold now. "Princess is not acceptable, Mr. Calloway."

A distinctly male grunt met her statement.

"As I was saying"—the mockery thickened—"I felt it best to pay attention rather than arguing with you."

Arguing with her?

She shot a glare at his profile, certain he was laughing at her.

"You must be in the mood for said argument now," she responded, keeping her voice cool. "Unfortunately for you, I'm not. Now, nor when we get to the lake house."

Perhaps the best option would be to go ahead and call Burke. He'd make certain someone picked her up and escorted her quickly back to the ranch house. He'd send someone after her belongings once she was safely locked down.

Years of painstakingly hard work would be shot down the drain. Her determination to return home and teach wasn't worth anyone's life though. And if Tracker was right, then someone had just raised the stakes in whatever game they'd been playing with her for the past nine years.

Wasn't it enough that she had to live with the knowledge that her father had attempted to kill her after killing her mother? That she'd been blinded, her memories of that entire week lost?

"You're going to run again, aren't you?" The certainty in his tone was a little offensive. "Just like you've always done before. You'll call big brother and he'll whisk in and pull you out, give you six months to a year to convince yourself it's just bad luck, then try again." Derision filled his tone now. "What are you going to do when someone else ends up dead, Ms. Boudreaux? As my sister nearly ended up dead?"

He had no idea what he was talking about, she thought painfully. There would be no other chances. Burke had already warned her of that. Proof or no proof of intent, the next incident that occurred would be the last because he'd pull her back to the ranch, where she'd stay.

She rubbed at her temple, her fingers straying once again to the scar just inside her hairline.

"No, Mr. Calloway, regardless of what you think, I'd never intentionally allow someone else to be harmed because of me. Especially a friend." The very thought of what had nearly happened to Angel was terrifying.

Tracker heard the pain she tried to hide, and just as in her expression, she failed. The fact that the accident and the danger it placed Angel in frightened her had stilled some of the anger he'd felt toward her. Hell, she'd had no damned idea the accidents she'd been in had been deliberate rather than just bad luck.

It explained why the Mackays kept such a close eye on her, but damned if it didn't make him want to shake Angel. Every member of that family suspected Isabeau Boudreaux had a big red bull's-eye painted on her back, and still, they'd given in when Angel had insisted on picking her up.

Their arguments had been the same as Isabeau's reason for believing they were no more than accidents. No proof. No one else had ever been at risk, just Isabeau herself. And there had been no incidents in the two years she'd been in Somerset. As though she had finally traveled far enough away to find some peace, or a measure of safety.

But they knew better now.

The fact that Angel's tire had been shot out signaled the killer was getting more desperate. He hadn't taken a shot at Isabeau's head, but to do that would risk an investigation he obviously couldn't afford.

Had Angel's truck actually gone over that cliff, then it may have been impossible to prove it wasn't an accident.

One thing was for certain—neither of them had been meant to survive that drive.

Whoever wanted Isabeau dead must have had no idea who Angel was, or what a pain in the ass the Mackay family could be when a friend was targeted. They hadn't done their homework, or the moment they hit on Angel's history, they would have found another way to strike.

Because if the Mackays were known for their tenacity where an enemy was concerned, then Tracker and Chance were the definition of brutal. And where their sister was concerned, they were worse.

Isabeau Boudreaux said she was finished running, but he doubted it. She'd simply decided on the safest course of action, he was guessing.

"Hiding won't work," he told her as he turned along the final bend in the road that led to the narrow valley and the house the Mackays had built as a retreat. "Someone's determined to kill you, Isabeau. It won't matter where you go or how protected you think you are. They'll get to you. The only way to stop it is to stand your ground with someone experienced enough to protect you and figure out what's going on."

He knew what he was doing. He'd learned the hard way what monsters humans could be and the best way to poke at their fragile little egos to draw them out. He'd been honed in the fires created by their brutality, flayed by their treachery, destroyed by their games until he'd finally just stopped caring about life or death.

It wasn't life or death that drove such men. Those who tortured defenseless young women did it for the sense of power it gave them. That high that came from seeing the fear, the desperation. But the son of a bitch chasing Isabeau had obviously tired of the game and the stand luck itself had taken with her.

"And you think that person is you," she stated, shaking her head. "How well do you think Angel will like me if something happens to you? About the same as you, just knowing someone attempted to hurt her because of me?"

He had to chuckle at her argument. She simply had no clue who she was dealing with.

"Angel's a pure badass when she needs to be," he told her. "That woman's a mean-assed gutter fighter and hell with that knife she carries. But she's a woman, a daughter, a wife, and soon to be a mother, and that makes her vulnerable. I, on the other hand, don't have those handicaps. And I know how monsters work, how they think. Sometimes, that's all it takes."

By the end of the day Chance would have the full report Tracker had ordered on Isabeau Boudreaux as well as her family and her parents' deaths. He'd have more than the official reports though. Every near-fatal incident, each time she stubbed her toe would be evaluated, placed in context, and siphoned through his parents' experienced eyes.

He may not care for J. T. and Mara Calloway's parenting abilities, but they had an eye for piecing together a profile that was unsurpassed.

It was something he and Chance could do, if given the time, but time was something that might be limited at the moment. He wanted his parents' opinions, then he and Chance could go over that information to see if there was anything they could add in the coming days.

Until then, he had to gain her cooperation.

She began shaking her head, and he could see her refusal in her expression.

He let a smile curve his lips, one he was glad she couldn't see.

"Just think about it for a minute," he suggested. "We're coming up on the lake house. A two-story dream house painted white and red with a wraparound porch. Sits away from the lake a bit. In the back there's a covered picnic area with a cooking and barbecue station under a shaded pavilion, a gazebo for the band, and a huge open firepit surrounded by a tiled patio. Gorgeous place."

He glanced at her face as he tried to describe the setting and watched her features soften. He didn't want to think about how it made him feel, how his chest tightened with unwarranted emotion at her vulnerable expression.

"It sounds beautiful," she sighed.

"All the trees and the mountain rising around it, it looks peaceful as hell." He hadn't noticed that before.

It wasn't his first time at the lake house, but until now, he'd never really paid attention to the picture-perfect setting. He'd assessed it for damage control instead. It was a security nightmare, there was no doubt, but it was quiet.

"Here we are." He drew to a stop in the wide graveled parking area just as the vehicles that had followed came in behind him. Turning, he watched as she stared out the passenger door window as though she could actually see what he'd described.

"I'm sorry I endangered Angel," she said softly, turning to him slowly. "I never thought there was any danger in her being around me."

Hell.

Vulnerable. Defenseless, and she looked so damned innocent he should kick himself for the hard-on tormenting the hell out of him.

"Like I said, we're going to talk, but I'll let you get settled in first. Don't call your brother yet. Let's discuss options first," he suggested firmly.

She didn't agree or disagree, didn't nod or shake her head. She turned from him and felt for the door handle just as it swung open.

"I see he survived despite his bad attitude." Angel laughed as Isabeau stepped from the truck. "Come on, hon, I'll take you to your room and let you get settled in."

Tracker watched as his sister walked with Isabeau, giving her verbal directions when they came to the steps leading to the yard, and again at the steps going up to the house. He'd meant to watch her navigate her way, but damn if he didn't keep getting distracted by that cute little ass as she walked.

She moved gracefully, far more gracefully than he would have expected. Her shoulders and back straight, her steps slow but steady, and showing little hesitation.

If he didn't know better, he'd swear she had at least partial sight. It had something to do with the way she looked at him when he spoke, the way she kept looking at Duke and Rowdy earlier. She didn't act like someone with full vision impairment. It was just that little bit off. . . .

WHEN ANGEL AND HER MOTHER, CHAYA, FINALLY LEFT Isabeau alone in her room, she went to the shower, hoping to wash away some of the tension she could feel building inside her.

Nothing made sense at this point. But nothing had made sense since the summer she turned fifteen, she admitted. When she'd awakened, unable to see, to make sense of what had happened, she'd cried for her father.

Whenever she was sick, or hurt, it was her father who made it better. She was Daddy's girl, her mother would say, smiling at them both softly. Her mother loved her too, but her father had always been so strong, so perfect in her eyes.

When the police had arrived at the hospital and told her that her father had killed her mother, tried to kill her, then killed himself, she'd gone into hysterics.

They had to be lying to her.

Yet they hadn't been. She was blind, in a hospital, and the brother she loved was sobbing as he held her in his arms. And her parents were gone forever. Just because their mother hadn't had custody of Burke didn't mean he hadn't visited often, or that he hadn't adored his mother.

Stepping from the shower, she dried slowly, her thoughts lost in those years, in the pain, the loneliness and realization that her life had been changed in ways she could have never been prepared for.

Possibly, it was appearing definitely, deliberately changed.

Burke had always suspected her father and their mother had been murdered and that Isabeau had seen who had murdered them. And as bad as she had wanted to deny it, Isabeau was beginning to believe it as well.

And that thought was terrifying.

THREE

evenr.

Once the barbecue ended, party snacks were set out under the pavilion on a long table and a band set up in the gazebo at the far end of the clearing.

Isabeau sat in one of the comfortable padded chairs placed back from the warmth of a bonfire that burned between the house and the gazebo and listened to the music as it drifted through the conversation and laughter spilling around her.

She could hear couples coming together, the flirtatious banter and occasional sexual innuendo, and couldn't help but feel a bit of envy.

When she'd moved back to Kentucky, she'd promised herself she would be open to a relationship, to allowing a man into her life and her bed, but it hadn't happened yet. It wasn't that she hadn't had several chances to choose a lover—she had. It just hadn't felt right. And she was beginning to wonder if it ever would.

She didn't want to be treated like an invalid or a child. And that was how men tended to react to her lack of sight. They'd grip her arm, lead her like a stubborn puppy. She hated it. She walked quite well on her own if she did say so herself.

She was aware of someone sitting heavily in the chair next to hers. There was no particular scent of cologne or perfume coming from them, as there was from most of the other partygoers. It was more a scent that blended with the night. A distinctly familiar earthiness, clean strength and desert heat.

"Mr. Calloway," she murmured, casting him a knowing look. "I wondered if you were out and about tonight."

There was a moment of silence.

"What gave me away?" he asked, his tone curious.

She couldn't stop the smile that tugged at her lips. "You have a very unique scent. It reminds me of the desert after a rare, light rainfall."

She watched him as she spoke, saw the way he sat, still, silent, merely staring at her.

"Interesting," he finally murmured. "I'll have to see what I can do to fix that."

She shrugged, not commenting on that one as she turned her head and looked in the direction the music was coming from. She could see shadows mixing, gyrating, dancers moving to the tempo of sound and song as they relished the night and the music.

She didn't bother telling him that there was no way to "fix" his scent. It would always be a part of him no matter what other scent he may apply.

"The Mackays throw a hell of a party," she said, recognizing the talent in the local band playing, as well as the entire setup in the huge backyard.

"The house is actually used pretty often by family and friends," he told her. "The reunion weekend is particularly looked forward to, according to Angel."

"Everyone who's mentioned it bemoans the days when it had an open invitation," she agreed. "It became much smaller as the girls got older, as I understand it."

After Natches Mackay's daughter had nearly been kidnapped in the parking lot of the marina when she'd been a tender fifteen, the Mackays had begun drawing in closer to family and close friends only.

How sad that was, Isabeau had thought at the time, that the monsters of the world existed to destroy lives in such a way.

"You get older, you learn lessons," he murmured.

And sadly, that was the truth.

"I've heard your name mentioned several times tonight." She shot him a laughter-filled look. "Many of the women are admiring your manly form. 'Sexy' was one description. 'Like a marble sculpture' was another." A laugh escaped her. "'All hard muscle and prominent bones.'"

"Jesus," he muttered, and she could hear the confused irritation in his tone. "Scarred, scruffy, and most likely in need of a shower is more like it."

"Well, it's obviously a look they find 'dangerous and attractive,' as one enamored female sighed." Yes, someone had actually described him in such a way. And she had no doubt it was true.

"Would you like to dance?" he asked her then. "It can't be very entertaining sitting here alone listening to the inebriated gossip."

She stared at the fire for long moments after he voiced the question.

"Oh, it's entertaining," she finally forced herself to say. "You hear all sorts of things if you bother to listen."

Dance with him? The music was really too fast-paced, too enthusiastic, and she knew more than a few of the partygoers were in the designated dancing area. Bumping into other people and making the dance floor hazardous wasn't her thing.

"I'm sure you do." His voice sounded darker now, more intent. "But I just tipped the band rather well to ensure they played something nice and slow so I could have this dance. Are you really going to turn me down?"

Her head moved quickly toward him in surprise. "You did what?"

The lights strung around the area and the firelight hit just right to allow her an impression of his height, even as he sat next to her, and the width of his shoulders.

She'd heard enough of the women talking to know he was extremely well-built. "Without a hint of fat," one interested female had cooed. "All muscle," another had sighed.

"You heard me," he grunted. "Now, do I get this dance or not?"

Evidently, he was used to a quick response, she thought, wishing she could see more than the shadow of him. She wanted to see the intense blue eyes, the shaggy black hair, even the scar she'd heard one woman describe as piratical.

She tucked a strand of hair that fell over her cheek behind her ear, aware that he was watching her closely.

He'd bribed the band? No one had ever done that, even knowing how much she enjoyed dancing.

"Well, since you went to so much trouble." She tried to smile but had a feeling her nervousness likely showed in the attempt.

He moved, rising to his feet to stand in front of her. Licking her lips nervously, Isabeau rose, a little surprised when he took her hand and placed it in his bent arm.

She was always nervous when allowing another person to act as a guide, especially through crowds, but as she followed his movements, she realized how naturally he seemed to lead her. She could easily detect the shift of his body, but he didn't keep her close enough to make it obvious that he was guiding her. It was a very smooth, graceful ability that he possessed. A natural leader, she thought, as the music became softer and the band moved into a slower number.

Pulling her into his arms, Tracker held her close, one hand clasping hers as she rested the other on his hard chest, his other arm circling her lower back.

The school for the blind that Isabeau had attended had taught a wonderful dance course that included a variety of dances that allowed them to follow their sighted partner's lead. Isabeau required a partner who knew how to lead though. And this man did exactly that, with such confidence he was easy to follow.

Over the years, she'd learned that not all men, even those described as excellent dancers, knew how to lead when they had a blind woman in their arms. They depended upon their partner's ability to see, to adapt as they moved.

To a point, she could do so, but she'd found a lot of her dance partners would move too quickly, or not signal a change with their bodies in time for her to follow them without tripping on their feet or her own.

"You're graceful," he murmured approvingly, the hand at her back pressing her closer as his cheek rested against her head.

"You're a good lead," she answered back, knowing it wasn't so much her grace as his ability that made the move appear so seamless.

The slight shift of his body betrayed his surprise at her response. It wasn't overt, and Isabeau doubted other women would have noticed it. Even those who were visually impaired.

He danced with an innate male sensuality that she couldn't help but respond to. And that, she guessed, had more to do with the man than with anything else. His confidence in himself would have to be irritating to others, at times fraught with friction.

Isabeau would just about bet he was a man who automatically took charge in any given situation, no matter those who may disagree with him.

She'd only been around one other man, besides her brother, who had that ability. And never had she danced with one who held her so close that she was fully aware of the fact that he was aroused. And he wanted her aware of that arousal. Otherwise, it wouldn't be there for her to feel.

A part of her warned her that there was more here than any overriding passion he may feel. Tracker Calloway, from what she'd heard, wasn't a man who would give in to any surface attraction that he may feel for a blind woman. He was intensely active, dangerous, and he lived in a world she couldn't imagine.

He wasn't the only man she knew who lived a dangerous life, and not the only one present at the gathering who knew what danger was. But he was the only one who had asked her to dance.

Who had made certain she was comfortable entering the dance area in his arms.

She had friends from Texas who were present, who knew how much she enjoyed dancing, who hadn't made that move, but she understood their reasons and even agreed with them. This man didn't know her, and she doubted he knew more than his sister, Angel, had told him. And even Angel didn't know much beyond what she'd learned of Isabeau in the past two years.

So it wouldn't take a genius to know that there was more behind the dance besides attraction. He'd pretty much laid his plan out. He would catch the person who endangered Angel's life, and since it was Isabeau the shooter was after, then Tracker would have no problem using her to catch whoever was behind it. And the fact that he was allowing her to feel that very impressive hard-on he was sporting behind the denim he wore told her a lot. He may be using her, but he also desired her. And for some reason, that made a difference to her.

She was a woman, a woman who craved touch when she lay alone in her bed, who craved a body that hers could respond to. That last thought was always the one that held the most sway. Because there were so few times that she responded to a man as she was to this one.

That didn't mean he'd end up in her bed. It simply meant that she wanted to enjoy this as much as possible. This silence seemed natural, as though—for this moment at least—they knew everything they needed to know about each other. And anything else needed could be found in how well their bodies moved against each other and the warmth flowing between them.

She hadn't known how badly she needed this, Isabeau thought. To move against a man, knowing he desired her, knowing that the possibility for more was there.

As they danced, his fingers moved against her back—small, caressing strokes of his fingers that had her heart racing, her blood heating.

It was like nothing she'd felt with any other man, even the one she'd believed she could love if things had been different.

And it was always if things were different, she realized painfully. If she wasn't blind. If she wasn't such a good friend. If she wasn't a bad-luck charm. . . .

"Hey, Tracker, can a friend cut in?" A familiar voice invaded the cocoon of warmth Isabeau had felt Tracker weaving around her and, surprisingly, sent regret spinning through her.

Seth August.

He and his twin, Saul, were friends of hers and Burke's. At one time, she'd hoped Seth would be more. Instead, he'd become her reminder that she'd always be a weakness to a strong man.

"We're friends?" Tracker seemed to challenge the statement.

He knew the other man though. Isabeau could hear that in his voice.

"Well, even if you and I aren't, Isabeau and I are," he was assured. "Saul and I have to leave soon, and I'd like to say hi and share a dance with her before I go."

Tracker seemed to hesitate before he spoke. "You owe me," he growled at her ear before stepping back and releasing her as the next slow beat began. "And I always collect."

As he released her, Seth's arms went around her, similar to Tracker's hold. But so very different.

Tracker was a stranger, yet there had been an intimacy in the way he held her that wasn't there with Seth.

He pulled her against him, one hand holding hers close to him as she placed her other hand at his chest, his arm going around her waist, but he didn't hold her close enough for her to know if he was aroused or not.

Though she doubted he was. Seth watched his emotions far too closely, as well as his physical responses. As her brother had said, he wouldn't let a woman into his life until his need for her overrode his caution.

And she'd figured out she wasn't that woman a long time ago.

A sense of sadness, of regret filled her as they began moving to the music. There had been a time when she'd dreamed of this man, when she'd lived for his visits and his laughter, the warmth of his hugs. Always hoping there would be more. Hoping against a knowledge that assured her it would never happen.

"You look very pretty tonight, Isabeau." The smooth compliment was sincere, despite the guarded tone of his voice. "That skirt's a little short though."

She almost laughed at the hint of accusation. Yes, the skirt was a little short, a little flirty. The layered chiffon was cut a bit unevenly and fell about halfway to her knees, complementing the lightly tanned tone of her legs, Annie had told her.

The Mackay cousins Annie, Bliss, and Laken had loved the skirt and white sleeveless blouse they'd suggested she wear with it. Tiny purple buttons held the blouse together, and thin straps secured the bodice to her shoulders.

The outfit made her feel feminine.

"The skirt's perfectly fine. What are you doing here?" She stared up at him, smiling anyway because she cared for him, because he'd always mean more to her than he'd ever know.

"The Mackays are cousins," he told her. "We come to the reunions every year. I was wondering what you were doing here. And with him? Tracker Calloway's not an easy man to know, sweetheart."

She shook her head at his warning, knowing how protective he was sometimes. He was a friend, not just to her but to her brother.

"I'm aware of who he is, and I always know what I'm doing, Seth. You should know that." The reminder wasn't lost on either of them.

As he led her through the dance, she was aware he was guiding her slowly to the edge of the dance area, where he could escort her back to where she'd been sitting.

It would seem the night was ending. For her anyway. Because she knew him and Saul. They would hover like protective fathers until she simply retreated from the party before becoming angry with them.

Staying home alone was often more fun than a party where the twins or her brother was in attendance with her.

"That's what scares me, Isabeau," he sighed. "Look, I like Tracker, I do. But he's the type of man who breaks hearts. He likes his one-night stands and hates being reminded of them. He and I would disagree if he treated you like that."

As though his disagreement was all that mattered. As though he had any right to disagree if that was what she chose.

"And if I wanted the one-night stand with no reminders?" she asked him, refusing to allow the anger she could feel lighting inside her go free.

She couldn't get angry with Seth, simply because she knew how much he did worry about her.

"That's not you, honey," he sighed. "Don't try to pretend it is."

The admonishment was gently said. Seth wasn't kind to many people, but she was one of the few, and she knew it.

A sudden thought slid past the regret, and she frowned up at him.

"Were you here earlier?" she asked, suspicion gathering inside her.

"You mean when that call came in from Angel that her tire had blown out on that hairpin?" His tone hardened. "What do you think?"

Isabeau grimaced.

Dammit, she hadn't needed him to know about that.

"Did you call Burke? You know, the three of you are going to drive me insane." It seemed she didn't have to do more than stub her toe and one of them would be hovering over her like an avenging angel, searching for some crazy reason that she'd hurt herself.

"I wouldn't call your brother over someone's damned blowout," he grunted. "Stop being so paranoid. The song's ending. Are you ready to sit down now?"

As he spoke, the slower tunes eased away, and before she could speak, a rowdier song began.

"It would seem so." Why did she have a feeling that if she'd remained in Tracker's arms, the music wouldn't have changed until he was ready?

"It's getting late; I can walk to your room with you," he told her, leading her back to the bonfire.

In other words, he was going to feel as though he had to remain at her side, no matter what. Yeah, she needed that. The feeling of being someone's deadweight was exactly what she wanted.

"Just get me to the porch," she told him, resigned to the fact that the night was over. "I'd rather go the rest of the way myself."

He didn't pause but continued leading her toward the dark hulk of the large two-story house. She'd learned over the years that fighting Seth and Saul, or her brother, in these situations was useless. They wouldn't physically force her away from the party—they'd simply hover over her, monopolize her attention, until she'd leave just to get away from them.

She knew why they did it, which made it harder to fight. They worried. Seth, Saul, and her brother. Their suspicions concerning her parents' deaths and the attempts on her life made them incredibly overprotective. Which made her incredibly determined to get as far from the smothering atmosphere as possible.

The twins had visited several times since she'd moved to Pulaski County and the picturesque little town of Somerset. She'd known they were related to the Mackays, but she hadn't expected them to be at the reunion.

"Are you staying the full weekend?" he asked as they neared the path lights built into the steps of the cabin.

The illumination allowed Isabeau to walk more confidently alongside Seth. Sometimes he wasn't as aware of what was directly in front of him as he was what may be hidden around him, her brother had once said. And she'd found that to be true on occasion.

Whenever she walked with Seth or Saul, she was more prone to use her cane. There were few people she walked beside who she didn't need her cane with. One of those rare cases had been Tracker. Burke's father, Mac, was easy to follow as well.

"Actually, if you and Saul would take me home in the morning, I may as well return. Parties are rather boring with the two of you around," she told him.

He tightened beside her. "That's kind of harsh. We care about you."

"Sometimes too much." She sighed. "I'll make it easy for you and return to the house. That way you won't feel as though you have to babysit."

It would ensure no one was hurt on the return too. She knew the twins—they'd make certain no one had a chance to strike while she was with them.

"Here are the steps," he told her, pausing at the bottom. "I'll watch you in, just to be sure. Be ready by noon and we'll head to Somerset then."

She'd bitten her tongue for years over their protective habits, and she was tired of it. She'd go home, just because she wanted to be certain no one was hurt taking her back. But she wanted ground rules from here on out. Whether she returned to the ranch or not, it was time to put a stop to this.

"The next time you drag me away from someone whose company I'm enjoying, or pressure me away from an event, Seth, then you and I are going to have words. That goes for Saul as well. I've had enough of it."

A tense silence met her words for long seconds.

"We worry, Isabeau," he said softly. "You have your opinion of why, and we have ours. Until then, you don't have a choice but to deal with us."

Holding the railing, she took the first step and then stopped again.

"As long as you're here?" she mocked the comment. "You'll probably be gone come Monday. Burke's in Texas, and I'll be here in Kentucky all by my sweet self, just as I always am. What will you do then? Because I doubt that if Tracker's interested, you'll have much success in warning him away."

"What I always do," he said, his voice low. "I'll pray. But I won't watch a man like that take advantage of you while I'm around."

She turned to him, realizing just how many years she'd put up with this.

"The next time it happens, you'll have a fight from me. This is your fair warning. You're not my husband, or my lover, and I'll be damned if you're going to keep acting like one. You're my friend, that's all. Please respect that boundary, since you're the one who put it in place."

He'd done it gently, but he'd made his point clear. They were friends. Despite the undercurrents of emotion she'd once felt from him, he'd informed her they'd never be more, and she'd had no choice but to accept it.

"I catch him around you again, then I'll discuss it with him personally." It was a threat that would have worked in the past.

Now she just shook her head, restraining a laugh at the thought. "No, you won't. Because you know he'll not be threatened away from me. I'm the only one who could make that stick with that particular man. And we both know it."

"Then make it stick." The lower, deeper tone of his voice was a warning.

"That's not your call, Seth," she informed him coolly. "It's mine. It's my bed he'll be sharing if I make that decision, not yours. Just because you didn't want me doesn't mean no one else can have me."

She doubted there was anything or anyone on the face of the earth that Tracker Calloway feared. Respected, perhaps, knew he couldn't conquer, maybe. But fear was another story.

"You think I didn't want you, Izzy?" The gentle, softened tone didn't have the power to choke her with regret as it would have years ago. "No man in his right mind could look at you and not want you."

"But I'm Burke's sister, and a friend." She reminded him of his excuse. "No, Seth, I'm blind and unable to participate in the lifestyle you prefer while home. I hate ball games, you can't trust me to navi-gate the parties you attend, and you'd worry incessantly while on duty." She ticked off the excuses he'd given to Burke once when he thought she wasn't home.

The small silence that followed her words attested to the fact that he was well aware she was repeating what she overheard.

"I worry anyway," he snapped, though she thought the undercurrent to his tone may have been regret.

"Too bad," she bit out, then sighed wearily. "We're friends, Seth. But friends have boundaries, and you're seriously overreaching that boundary now. Who I sleep with and why is just none of your business."

"When it's a man like Tracker Calloway, you can bet I'll make it my business," he argued.

And he would stand there and argue with her all night if he felt it would do any good.

Tonight, she just wasn't in the mood for it.

"Good night, Seth." For the first time in years, she didn't hug him, didn't lift her face for his kiss on her cheek.

As she moved up the steps, she wondered if there was a single ef-fective argument that would convince the August brothers to stop hovering over her. She hadn't found one yet. Maybe once she reached her room, she could enjoy the party from afar.

The French doors that opened onto the wraparound porch would allow her to slip from her room and sit on the porch to at least listen to the music that filled the night.

As long as neither of the August twins was watching for it.

Damn. She'd wanted to at least sit amid the party this one night, hear the laughter and the gossip, feel the air of fun and friendships. Maybe have a few beers.

She'd never imagined the twins would have reason to interfere this weekend. She couldn't have foreseen Tracker, no matter how good her imagination. But she knew the twins. It was like having her brother in attendance.

Grimacing at the thought, she entered her bedroom, closed and locked the door behind her, then froze in place. One hand on the doorknob, she waited as she literally felt the presence in the room and took in the scent of a desert night touched by rain.

The feel of eyes watching her too intently, that sense of waiting, of confidence. He'd known she'd be alone. That no one would be with her.

This time, there would be no one there to stop him.

If he did anything to warrant being stopped, she thought wearily.

Attraction wasn't the only reason Tracker was interested in her. He wanted whoever caused the near-fatal wreck that afternoon more than he could ever desire a woman, she reminded herself.

And as bad as she wanted to know who that person was herself, she wasn't certain chancing a broken heart was the way to find them. But then again, she could live through a broken heart. . . .

FOUR

SHE STOOD IN FRONT OF THE DOOR LIKE A FRIGHTENED little doe, uncertain if she scented him or something else. She stared right at him, though he didn't see recognition in her gaze; all he saw was a distant, unfocused look.

"What are you doing in my room, Tracker?"

He didn't move from the chair he sat in, just continued to watch her, wondering how in the hell she knew it was him. There was no way she could smell him that far away.

He could see her clearly in the low light of the lamp next to her bed, and it still confused him why it was on. It had illuminated the room with a low, diffused glow when he'd slipped into it, though, thankfully, the heavy curtains on the French doors were closed.

He could see the light flush that mounted her cheeks, the way her breasts lifted and fell against the summer top she wore, the way the material revealed the upper mounds. The fragile straps that held the shirt over her breasts could snap easily, he thought. The lace bra beneath might take a second or two longer to dispose of. That flirty little skirt would just slide out of the way.

"The least you could do is speak," she told him, and his lips lifted at one corner at the awareness that she might not be as confident as he'd thought that it was him watching her.

"I was enjoying the view," he told her, still watching her eyes, becoming more suspicious by the moment that her vision might be a bit better than she let on.

She couldn't see enough to not need help; he'd studied her too closely, analyzed each move as he watched her throughout the day and that evening. But she wasn't as blind as everyone believed either.

"Which doesn't answer my question." One hand gripped the door-knob, the other her cane. Both objects were held tightly enough that her knuckles were turning white.

She wasn't staring into his eyes, but it was close. Too damned close.

And she was angry. Hurt, angry, disappointed. Seth August had somehow managed to destroy the gentle pleasure that had filled her expression that evening.

Bastard.

"Why am I here?" he asked, verifying the question. He still watched her, still keeping track of where her gaze centered on him.

"That's what I asked you." She relaxed, but only marginally.

She was certain it was him, but she wasn't so sure of why he was there, or what he wanted.

"Because Seth August broke into my dance and rushed you away from the party like some teenager," he said, still uncertain why he was so damned irritated when he'd fully expected August to do exactly what he had done. "Does he do that often?"

She dropped her gaze from him, her eyes directed at the floor as she folded the cane. Once she'd finished, she placed it on the table next to the door, though her gaze didn't return to him.

At least, not until he rose to his feet. Lifting her head, she watched the movement. Not his eyes, but the movement.

Hadn't anyone paid enough attention to this woman to realize she was so much more than she let others see? Even August. As the other man had held her, Tracker had seen her smile, the way it transformed her face from merely pretty to beautiful. But in it, he'd also seen regret and acceptance.

Whatever she felt for the SEAL, it was something she'd left behind her, and that was a damned good thing.

"Him, Saul, my brother." She gave a little roll of her eyes. "They're very protective." She sighed heavily. "Seth says you're a heartbreaker and a one-night stand. He and his brother, and mine, like to believe I'm a virgin with only the purest thoughts where men are involved."

Oh, Seth August might let her believe that, but Tracker had seen something far different in the other man's expression. And it was nothing pure or innocent.

"Are you?" he asked, actually curious now. "A virgin, that is?"

Her brow arched, a mysterious little grin tugging at her lips.

"I don't consider that any of your business," she stated, crossing her arms over her breasts as she cocked one hip in subconscious feminine challenge.

"I intend to end up in bed with you, Isabeau," he informed her, a bit surprised that he was letting her know what he intended. "So I guess I should know."

Her lips pursed, giving her a thoughtful look. Though he doubted it was a thoughtful gesture. He was betting Isabeau was a bit more impulsive than she let others believe.

"So smooth." She cast him a look of exaggerated disappointment and amusement. "But thanks for the warning." She moved away from the door. "You can leave now."

He couldn't help but chuckle. She had a very expressive face, and he rather doubted anyone had warned her of that. Her inability to see hampered her ability to understand expression, he guessed. And her brother and his family had evidently not instructed her on it.

He'd have to rectify that, but not tonight. Tonight, he had other plans.

"It wasn't a warning, Isabeau," he assured her. "That was a promise. A statement of intent. And I don't think you're completely against the idea."

Those hard little nipples pressing against her top sure weren't against the idea.

"I think I don't really know you well enough to consider it," she said. "But I definitely know I'm not into one-night stands. Sorry, Tracker, you picked the wrong girl this time."

She moved from the door to the foot of the bed farthest away from him, taking her out of his path if he were to consider leaving, he thought.

"The thing about one-night stands," he told her softly as he walked to her. "Is that they rarely last for a single night." He wasn't surprised at this point that she tracked his progress. "They can last for a weekend, a week, sometimes several weeks."

He stopped in front of her as she lifted her head, her expression reflecting far more vulnerability than he was comfortable seeing. Even as he realized that, his hand rose, his fingers brushing back a heavy ribbon of hair that had fallen over her cheek.

Gently, he tucked it behind her ear before he slid his hand into her hair, his fingers clenching around the strands before he tugged her head forcibly.

Her breath caught, her eyes dilating as the flush mounting her face deepened.

"I would never hurt you," he promised her as he caught the flicker of uncertainty in her expression. "But I'm not a wine-and-roses lover, baby. I'll ride you until you're covered in your sweat and mine, your body slick and hot from so many orgasms you're certain you can't come again. Only to realize you can. Again. And again." He nipped her lower lip, feeling her uneven breaths against his. "There won't be an inch of your body that doesn't know my touch, and"—he slid his lips to her ear—"my bite."

He nipped her ear, satisfaction rolling through him as he heard the small, shocked moan that fell from her lips.

Her hands jerked to his hips, fingers clenching in the material of his shirt, tugging at it as his lips moved to hers and he kissed her. He didn't make allowances for any innocence she may or may not have possessed. He kissed her with all the lust that had been building since he'd watched another man hold her through a dance meant for him.

As he held her head in place with his fingers in her hair, he moved the other to her curvy little ass, gripped it, and jerked her closer to him. He tested the toned curve, her fingers clenching on him as he explored her lips, her adventurous little tongue with his own.

She kissed like a woman discovering a new treat. One she found herself liking. One she wanted more of. And Tracker had to admit, he had never felt anything quite like this in a woman's response to him.

It was unique enough to want to explore further, and unique enough to make him extremely wary.

That didn't mean he was finished with her yet. When he left her room, she was going to remember him—he was going to make certain of it. And if Seth August made the mistake of attempting to frighten her away from him again, he'd find his way blocked by the pleasure Tracker gave her.

He knew the other man hadn't had her, even though he desired her. If Seth August had possessed her, Tracker had a feeling the other man would be a hell of a lot more forceful about ensuring her safety.

Pulling back, he released her hair before cupping the side of her neck and sliding his hand around until he gripped her neck beneath her chin, his hold firm, confident.

Lowering his head, he let his lips brush against hers as she lifted one hand to grip his wrist, uncertainty showing on her face amid the peaking sensuality. She was learning there was much more to arousal than she'd imagined. Something he'd guessed she hadn't known.

"This isn't a one-night stand, Isabeau," he assured her, his voice soft as his lips caressed hers. "It's a seduction, baby."

Her lashes lifted, her gaze drowsy with heightened arousal and confusion.

"And if you succeed?" she whispered, her voice shaking, her body trembling with pleasure, a hint of wariness, and a need for more.

And it was that need for more that he craved. The question she asked, not so much.

"A bridge we cross when we get there," he told her, though for some reason, lying to her didn't sit well with him. "But don't fall in love with me, Isabeau. That would be the most disastrous thing you could do. For both of us. But feel free to enjoy me, baby. I definitely intend to enjoy you."

His fingers tightened marginally at her neck as he let himself sink into the pleasure of her kiss once again.

It was like a particularly dangerous drug, he decided, even as he gave in to it. Her kiss, filled with hunger and need, with a hint of innocence and such heat he was tempted to take more and more of her.

And it was too damned soon.

She was too damned dangerous.

He pulled away, surprising himself at how quickly he jerked from her. As she swayed, reaching for him unsteadily, he gripped her arms, just long enough for her to get her bearings. Once she held the footboard of the bed, he released her and stepped back.

"The next time August gets between us, he'll regret it," he warned her. "Until this is decided, it stays between us."

She blinked back at him, licked her lips, and took a deep breath.

"I'll tell you what I told him," she stated, her breathing still harsh. "My decisions don't rest with either of you but with me alone. That's something neither of you should forget."

Damn her. She was right. As much as he hated it, as much as he wanted to fight it, he knew she was right. Except for one thing . . .

"Wrong," he growled, knowing how harsh his voice sounded as he gripped her chin and stared into her eyes, making damned certain if she could see anything of his expression, she saw his raw determination. "I'm telling you, promising you. He steps between us again, and neither of you will like the results, Isabeau. Especially him."

Because he'd ensure there was hell to pay.

Releasing her, he stalked from the room, using the French doors just because he suspected one of the August twins was watching them. And he dared either of them to face him about it.

And that could be a problem, because Tracker had never wanted a woman bad enough to fight for her. Not even the one he had nearly died because of.

SWEET HEAVEN.

This was so bad.

This was probably one of the biggest mistakes of her life.

Maybe.

Isabeau drew a deep breath as the doors snapped closed behind him, the sound indicating Tracker's irritation.

He was nothing like the man Angel had described.

Well, not so much like him maybe.

He was definitely as arrogant and certain of himself as his sister had described. But she hadn't mentioned he could be charming. Or possessive.

Isabeau shook her head. Everything she'd heard about Tracker said he wasn't in the least possessive.

Those few, brief moments when she'd glimpsed the blue of his eyes, surrounded by heavy black lashes, intent, and gleaming with some emotion, she couldn't have seen possession. But his words said otherwise.

She swallowed tightly. She'd seen his eyes. Not his face, just his eyes, his expression blurred, but the intense blue of his eyes had been incredibly clear. Dark.

And he meant to seduce her.

Inhaling shakily, she lifted her hand to her throat, remembering the feel of his fingers gripping it, the sensuality that had washed over her rather than fear. She should have been terrified of him. She should have fought the grip; though it hadn't restricted her breathing, it had reminded her on a very visceral level that he could stop her breathing if he wanted to.

That wasn't what he wanted though; she knew that instinctively. He hadn't lied when he said he wouldn't hurt her. He had no intention of hurting her, but that didn't mean she wouldn't end up that way.

She wasn't prepared for him, and she knew it. Her limited experience with men, with her own sexuality, and her need for touch, would work against her. And Tracker's experience, his ability to reach into those parts of her, would ruin her for any other man's touch.

She'd almost made that mistake once. She had almost let herself believe that Seth's friendship was so much more, and she'd come close to destroying a friendship she depended on. Realizing that and pulling herself back from that edge hadn't been easy. It had hurt. For years it had hurt, and in some ways, it still did.

And she still felt the sharp bite of regret that it affected her view of their friendship now. The knowledge of what she'd done still followed her, as did the remnants of the emotions she'd allowed herself to feel.

She hadn't loved him, but only because she'd pulled back in time.

What Seth had been a part of building inside her still remained though. He, along with Saul and Burke, had taught her how to deal with strong, far-too-confident men. Not sexually, but in real-world applications. She'd just have to bend those applications to apply to Tracker Calloway.

He had the edge on her, and she knew it, but she wasn't such an easy pushover that she'd sit back and willingly allow him to just use her. He may make it into her bed, but he'd have to get past more than just her need for touch.

He'd ambushed her that evening.

She'd make certain that didn't happen again.

"YOU'RE PLAYING WITH THE WRONG WOMAN, CALLOWAY. Seth will make a very bad enemy."

Tracker wasn't surprised when Saul stepped from the shadows at the edge of the lake, cast by the multitude of houseboats parked within easy reach of the shore.

He was tall, with black hair and green eyes closely resembling the Mackays. He was a dangerous man; Tracker knew that. But so was Tracker, and he was damned confident in his own abilities.

"Seth knows where to find me, then." Tracker shrugged, still thrown off-balance by his response to Isabeau and trying to make sense of it.

He didn't need to deal with an August right now. Not Seth, or his irritating brother.

"Isabeau is no match for you, man." Saul sighed, leaning against the tree next to him as he crossed his arms over his chest. "You'll break her. Is that what you really want to do? Because she damned sure doesn't deserve it. If any woman deserves a man who loves her, then it's Isabeau."

Son of a bitch, he just didn't need this.

And if the twins had been the friends they claimed to be, then they would have done what it took to catch the bastard who kept shadowing Isabeau with his attempts to kill her and make it look like an accident. And it was evident he didn't fucking care who he took out with her.

Tracker didn't have the full background report on her, and he knew Angel was waiting on the one the Mackays had coming in as well. By daybreak, he should know everything he needed though.

"What I really want is the two of you out of my fucking business," he growled. "And that includes where Isabeau is concerned. That's your only warning, August. You and your brother. Don't try to step between us again."

"There's more to it, Tracker. . . ."

"Fuck you," Tracker grunted, wondering how in the hell the twin had managed to resist Isabeau. "I don't care what there is to it. Seth walked away. All of you walk away instead of hanging around long enough to find out who the fuck is trying to murder her, don't you?" That enraged him and sent fury twisting through him. "Seth doesn't fucking deserve the woman for that alone. But I'll make damned sure I don't make the same mistake. Count on it."

With that he turned away from the other man and stepped into the shallow water, taking the half dozen steps to the deck of the houseboat Angel and Duke had loaned him and Chance for the weekend.

The water-resistant leather boots he owned kept his feet dry. Stepping onto the deck, he didn't bother checking back to see if Saul still stood in place. He didn't really give a damn where the bastard had gone.

He was pissed off, horny, and still uncertain what effect Isabeau was having on him. One thing he knew for damned sure—if he wasn't careful, real damned careful, Isabeau Boudreaux could become an addiction.

And that, he couldn't—wouldn't—allow.

FIVE

DUKE MACKAY STARED AT HIS FAMILY, WIFE, TRACKER, and Chance, who had gathered in the living room/kitchen area of the houseboat loaned to Tracker. Each of them held a copy of the background report Duke had put together through the night.

"Six attempts in ten years," Duke stated as he sat at the counter facing them. "Assuming her parents were both murdered, then the bullet that bounced off her skull was the first attempt. At sixteen, she was mauled by two rottweilers belonging to her brother's uncle. He kept them in a secure area, locked behind a ten-foot chain-link fence. Somehow, the gate was unlocked and left open while Isabeau was on the patio next to the pool. Eighteen, an attempted hit-and-run on a Saturday evening after dining with family in Beaumont. Twenty, while out with her roommates—two young women training for law enforcement—an attempted abduction. At twenty-two, while living in Houston and teaching at a private school, a gas explosion in the apartment next to hers. She'd just left to visit with a friend downstairs. She's twenty-five now, and we're certain Angel's blowout was caused by a bullet or another projectile of equal power. We haven't found evidence of what, but we did find what the August twins suspect to be a sniper nest."

"Whoever it is must be a damned amateur," Natches grunted. "Six attempts and six failures."

"Or six unplanned attempts," Tracker interjected. "Other than the first, the night her parents were killed, each one seems to be planned hastily. And she's been lucky. Incredibly lucky."

"According to her, she's a bad-luck charm," Angel replied. "She calls them near-fatal events, but she's scared. She asked Seth and Saul to take her home this afternoon rather than waiting until Sunday, when everyone usually leaves."

Oh, he so didn't think so. He'd be discussing that with her as soon as he was finished here.

"She's beginning to suspect, then," Angel's stepfather, Natches, said. "And she won't want anyone else hurt, so I believe she'll call her brother and be gone before the new school year begins."

"She'll be easy to pick off," Chance guessed. "She'll find a way to separate herself from her family. Perhaps live alone to alleviate danger to those she loves and just wait to die rather than allowing anyone to risk themselves."

"She'll sacrifice herself," Angel said softly, her expression somber as she sat at the table with her mother, stepfather, and one of Natches cousins, Rowdy Mackay.

"She's not going anywhere." Tracker made the decision aloud, his gaze meeting the surprise in his sister's expression.

"What makes you think that?" Duke asked curiously.

Sitting forward in his chair, Tracker lifted a brow mockingly as he braced his elbows on his knees and stared back at the other man.

"Because I intend to keep her in Somerset," he informed the other man. "No matter what it takes. That's the only way to figure out what's going on. Her brother jerks her to a new location every time she has one of her so-called near-fatal events. This time, she's staying put. Right here where it began. She's not going to be safe until the threat is neutralized, Duke, and you know it."

"You're going to seduce her into staying," Duke guessed, his expression flashing with disapproval. "Hell, Tracker."

Telling the other man the conflicts he had with it himself wouldn't do any good. And it was none of their business that he was enraged over the fact that no one else had taken the required steps to ensure her safety.

Silence filled the room for long moments as all eyes turned on him, the expressions ranging from questioning to angry. But it was plain as the noses on their faces that no one agreed.

"You'll break her heart," Angel said, remorse heavy in her voice. "Whether she knows why you're convincing her to stay or not."

His lips curled mockingly. "You can't break a heart that another holds," he told her. "But seduction . . . that's another story."

Was that jealousy biting at him? Whatever it was, it was enough to send anger attempting to burn inside him. Neither her brother nor her friends had taken the attempts on her life seriously enough, and because of it, her would-be killer was stepping up his game. If no one else wanted to save that pretty little ass, then he would.

He knew how to do it.

Angel shook her head. "She's not in love with anyone. . . ."

He would have laughed at that, but the sound wouldn't have come across as amused.

"Seth August." He watched her face as he spoke, saw the instant knowledge flash in her gaze before she tried to reject it.

"She would have told me, Tracker."

"She didn't have to tell me." He shrugged. "But the Augusts will try to stand in my way, and that I won't have. If we don't stop this here and now, then you'll be attending Isabeau's funeral in the very near future. I don't think any of you want that."

He wasn't going to allow it. Besides the fact that his sister had been endangered, the thought of Isabeau, all that life in those pretty violet eyes stolen away, was something he refused to allow.

"I don't like it." Natches sighed, sitting back in his chair and watching Tracker from narrowed green eyes.

Hell, like Tracker cared what Natches Mackay liked. That asshole was so close to an ass whipping from Tracker that it wasn't even funny.

"Let him see if he can pull it off." It was Rowdy who spoke in favor of it when Tracker had expected him to argue the loudest. "You have three weeks to show progress, and you won't lie to her, Tracker. You'll let her know why you're interested in sleeping with her."

Tracker frowned back at the older man. Rowdy's graying black hair didn't detract in the least from the fact that he stayed in damned good shape.

"One has nothing to do with the other, Rowdy," he sneered back. "I want to sleep with her because she makes me fucking hard. Whoever's stalking her got my attention. They endangered my sister and her child. Not to mention an innocent woman with no hope of protecting herself."

"Three weeks isn't a one-night stand." Rowdy rose to his feet, his green eyes flint-hard. "And Isabeau isn't one of the war groupies you usually amuse yourself with either. Don't lie to her. Or you'll deal with me."

"And me . . ."

"Me . . ."

"And me . . ."

The echoes continued until only Angel and Chance were left.

"She's my friend, Tracker." Remorse lay heavy in Angel's expression. "You're my brother. If you're going to risk my friendship with her, then I agree with the others. You have to be honest with her."

He turned and glowered at Chance. "Well? Your nuts knotting over her too?"

It pissed him off that they believed he would actually lie to her.

Chance shook his head as amusement quirked his lips. "I'd hate to see her hurt, but I'd hate like hell to see her dead. Those fuckin' August boys haven't looked out for her, so that leaves us. I'll do what I've always done, watch your back. And hers."

Well, at least someone was in his fucking corner here.

Rising to his feet, he stared around the room, disgusted with each and every one of them.

"I'll tell you the same thing I told those Augusts. However I go about this, whether you like it or not, don't get between me and that woman, or you'll regret it."

"Or what?" Natches's grin was pure challenge as amusement danced in his emerald gaze.

Tracker shook his head. There were days that he could almost like the other man.

"I don't deal in threats, Natches, you know that. This is a promise. Get between me and Isabeau, and all of you will regret it." And that was a promise he'd keep, no matter his sister's objections.

With that, he left the houseboat, despite the fact that he should have thrown them out instead.

AS THE DOOR SLID SHUT LOUDLY BEHIND HIM, CHANCE rose to his feet and faced them as well. He knew what they saw. He could have been Natches Mackay's son, he looked so much like the bastard, and they both knew it. But he wasn't. He was the bastard half brother none of them had acknowledged.

"What?" Natches snapped, glaring at him. Daring him.

"Ask Angel," he stated, his voice low as he gave his sister a long, knowing look before meeting Natches's gaze again. "Do as he asked, rather politely for Tracker, and that girl might live. Fuck with him, distract him, and anything happens to either of them, and I'll finish whatever fight he walks away from. That's not a threat. It's a promise."

Chance didn't bother to close the door loudly when he left. He closed it as he normally would, quietly, and joined Tracker within the mists that slid sinuously from the lake to the house and the clearing.

"Those twins took up position in sight of the French doors. They're expecting you to sneak in that way. I didn't see anything in the hall to give them a view of the hall door, but I couldn't exactly check for electronics either," Chance said, his voice low, soft, to ensure it carried no farther than the two of them.

The twins knew Tracker would find out she was leaving, and they knew he'd make it his business to change her mind.

They were up to something—there was no doubt of that. He'd seen the way they looked at Isabeau. They cared about her. Seth cared too damned much for her, though Tracker had a feeling the other man would never act on it. They would never leave her undefended though. Not in a million fucking years would they allow it. But neither would they do what was necessary to protect her. A mistake he wasn't going to make, and he knew that decision would piss off both twins.

"I'll end up hurting one of those boys," Tracker sighed as he stared around the area, his eyes narrowed against the mists. Crossing his arms over his chest, he glanced at Chance. "I won't enjoy that."

"Is she worth it?" Chance asked him, his tone curious.

He knew Tracker bit his tongue and stayed his fist often where the Mackays were concerned, for Angel's sake.

Tracker was silent for so long, Chance began to wonder if he'd even get an answer.

"Doesn't matter if she is or not," he finally breathed out heavily. "She's innocent. And she's Angel friend. Angel will get involved if we don't."

Chance didn't point out that this was the first time in eleven years that Tracker had refused to give him a yes or a no to that particular question.

And that was very interesting indeed.

"Shall we see how close they're watching her, then?" Tracker suggested, then headed for the front door of the house.

As he always did, Chance moved into position to see what could be coming, what or who could be watching. And why. As he'd told Tracker, he had his back and he'd make sure it was protected.

Because once, it hadn't been, and Tracker had nearly paid with his life.

Chance had sworn that would never happen again.

SIX

ISABEAU THOUGHT SHE WAS GOING TO LEAVE. SOMEHOW it only added insult to injury that she'd asked the Wonder Twins to take her home rather than him and Chance. That woman had set her heart on Seth August at some point in the past, unaware that she'd given it in vain. And somehow, for some reason, that just fucking pissed him off worse.

What was next? Her brother showing up in the middle of the night and spiriting her away as usual? Before anyone so much as suspected her intent, she'd be packed up and back in Texas, hiding, no doubt frightened and trying to deny the truth once again.

Someone was trying to kill her, and each attempt had been made in such a fashion that not so much as a whisper of a suspect could be found.

He didn't bother to attempt to sneak into the house; he went straight up the steps, strode across the porch, and entered the un-locked front door as though he owned the place. If Seth and Saul were watching, then they'd understand loud and clear that they weren't even a consideration as far as he was concerned.

Striding through the silent predawn house, he moved to her bedroom door, quickly picked the lock, then stepped inside the room.

The low light was still on beside her bed, the soft glow bathing the sleeping woman in a luminescent sheen. Champagne-blond waves of hair tumbled around her sleeping face, soft pink lips slightly parted as she lay on her side, curled beneath the sheet as though chilled.

If he didn't have every intention of waking her, then he'd pull the quilt at the foot of the bed over her fragile body. Or crawl into that big bed with her and warm her with his own body. The hard-on tormenting the hell out of him thought that was a great idea.

As he considered the possibility, her eyes suddenly flashed open, filled with drowsiness as they connected with his. She blinked, uncertain, confused, before those incredible violet eyes lost their laser focus and she was simply staring in his direction.

"Tracker?" She sat up slowly, the sheet sliding away from the thin, silky-looking white sleep shirt she wore.

One strap fell over a delicate shoulder, and he swore he could see the shadow of pretty pink nipples beneath the material.

"Morning, princess," he murmured, moving to the side of the bed. "Sleep good?"

He toed his short boots from his feet.

"I . . . I guess." She pushed her fingers through her hair. "Why are you here?"

"For this." Before she could do more than gasp, he pushed the sheet quickly from her, noticing the shortie shorts she wore, the slender legs, curvy thighs, just before he came over her and pushed her to her back once again.

In the back of his mind, he knew she should be screaming, scared.

She'd fight him, struggle, cry out, and bring those damned twins running to the rescue.

At least, that was how he'd assumed she'd handle his actions.

Instead, she stilled, lying beneath him as he straddled her body and secured her arms over her head.

Like a tempting little sacrifice.

But he could see the defiance in her eyes, the flush of pending anger on her cheeks. She wasn't submitting, she was just biding her time and letting him know, albeit silently, that she wasn't scared of him.

He didn't know anyone who wasn't at least wary of him, and those were full-grown, fighting-age men. Women were always scared of him, drawn to him, like a moth to a flame, but always riding that edge of fear.

"You and I are going to have to discuss your actions at some point, Tracker." She would have sounded fierce if it weren't for the sleepiness that still lingered in her voice. "You're beginning to act as though you have rights you simply haven't been given."

"I heard an interesting little rumor a few minutes ago," he drawled, lowering his head until his lips were brushing against hers, his gaze narrowed on her eyes. "And I have to admit, it left me a tad bit overset, princess. My delicate feelings might not recover."

The mockery, the sneer in his tone must have been missed because, rather than trepidation, her expression flickered with amusement.

"Overset, were you?" Her lips were plump, tantalizing as she spoke against the curve of his. "Delicate feelings that may not recover? My, Tracker, I have to admit, I didn't see you as the type to hang your feelings on your sleeve like a pretty little Christmas ornament."

She was pushing.

"Oh, you might be surprised." He dropped his voice to a warning growl. "Be good now and tell me why you think you're leaving with Irk and Jerk August later today."

Her eyes widened, and the soft, fun-filled laugh that escaped her lips was damned charming. "Irk and Jerk? Tracker, they hear you call them that and they'll kill you."

"I doubt it," he snorted, then nipped her lips just sharp enough to still the laughter and cause her eyes to darken as her breathing began to escalate. "Now pay attention, baby, I'd hate to have to spank you over that sharp little tongue of yours."

A flush rushed over her cheeks, her eyes turning drowsy, lips parting to drag in air.

"Should I call you daddy, then?" she whispered, her tone just slightly sarcastic, and he was surprised at the interest he saw in her expression. Not to mention the interest that surged through his senses.

Damn her. She was pushing a boundary he wasn't certain she was brave enough to cross, despite her bravado.

Anchoring her wrists with one hand, he moved the other until his fingers curled around her neck, holding her in place, watching the pure feminine heat as it seemed to race through her.

She had no idea what she was allowing, what she was asking for. His dominant tendencies, driving sexuality, and dark hungers were rarely given such a sweet innocent to snack on.

She was teasing, playing, and he was getting ready to show her the animal she was playing with.

"Oh, baby, just let me show you what Daddy can do. . . ."

Something intense and sharp with pleasure detonated low in Isabeau's stomach at the dark, sexual tone that whispered over her senses a second before one hand slid to the back of her head, his fingers clenching in her hair and dragging her head farther back against the pillows.

As a gasp left her, his lips covered hers, his tongue taking instant ownership, stroking, licking, possessing her in ways other kisses had never thought to. Pleasure slammed through her, racing through her bloodstream, holding her suspended amid the exquisite sensations. The hard, carnal kiss; the pressure his fingers exerted on her scalp and the feel of his body lowering over hers; hard, muscular thighs pushing between her softer, weaker ones.

She could sense her femininity in ways she had never thought possible. He controlled the kiss, his lips moving over hers as his tongue licked over them, slid inside, stroked over hers, and built a heated, overriding pleasure.

Pleasure or addiction? she wondered hazily. Because she had never known a kiss like this. Never known such a need to be closer, to take as much of this man as he was willing to give her.

Her hands burrowed into his hair, clenching into the strands as his lips slid from hers to her neck, his teeth raking over the sensitive flesh and dragging a startled moan from her. Tilting her head to the side, she begged for more, her body arching to his as she used the hold she had on his hair to pull his lips back.

"Oh God!" The words whispered from her lips as he caressed the line of her neck with alternating rough, then gentle kisses. The short scruff of his beard and mustache raked her flesh, barely there, trimmed close, but destructive on her senses.

Her hips arched into his, the thick wedge of his erection grinding into the vee of her thighs, caressing her swollen clit, drawing a heat and moisture from her that quickly dampened the silk of her panties.

She'd been kissed before, touched, but never like this. His hand gripped her hair, the other her hip, simply holding her, allowing her to move, to arch to him, as he used his lips and tongue to drive her insane with those hard, deep kisses and caresses to her neck.

He alternated between little nips, the rake of his teeth, and a suckling caress at her neck as he thrust against the steadily heating flesh of her pussy. The quick little strokes against her clit were making her as crazy as the hungry kisses and firm caresses along her neck.

"You wanna be Daddy's girl, sweetheart?" he crooned against her ear as she fought to catch her breath, to make sense of the incredibly heated pleasure building inside her.

"Yes." Whatever he wanted, if he'd just make it continue.

HIS LIPS COVERED HERS AS HE RELEASED HER HIP TO slide his hand inside the sleep shorts and silk panties she wore beneath.

His fingers rasped against her clit, the sensation causing her to jerk, to cry out from the incredible pleasure. Parting the bare flesh, he went lower, found the slick moisture spilling from her, and pressed slowly inside.

Isabeau lost her breath, her senses. The orgasm that rushed over her had her shuddering violently, a cry tearing from her as ecstasy washed over her like a wave of pure, fiery sensation.

Tracker stilled, two fingers barely penetrating the lush, snug flesh of Isabeau's pussy as he felt her orgasm begin rippling through her flesh. Silky heat spilled against his fingertips as her knees gripped his thighs and her hips jerked against the penetration.

Son of a bitch.

It was all he could do to keep control, to resist the need to strip her pajama bottoms and panties from her and thrust the throbbing length of his cock as deep inside her as possible.

Never had he held a woman so responsive, so fucking attuned to every touch, every caress. It made him wonder how far he could push her, how much pleasure he could give her before he lost his own control.

She was dangerous. She could become addictive.

If he allowed it.

He knew better than to allow it.

Holding himself still against her, he eased her through the shudders, his fingers sliding from the tight flesh to slowly pull back as her hips stilled and her body calmed beneath him.

Just enough to make her ache for more, to make her wonder how much better it could get. Not that he'd expected the response he'd gotten, but he knew she'd want more. Because, by God, so would he.

"There, baby," he crooned against her neck as her breathing still came hard and heavy.

As the words left his lips, a low, warning knock sounded at the door, and his head came up, anger beginning to burn inside him.

Chance's warning that the Augusts were heading for the house. Those bastards were going to get on his wrong side real damned fast.

"Tracker . . ." Her hands fell from his hair but gripped his arms, clenching as he lifted to move from her.

"You're about to have company, baby girl," he whispered. "That was Chance's warning that Irk and Jerk are on their way."

She didn't laugh at the nicknames that time; she didn't even smile.

"I don't want anyone hurt because of me," she whispered, and he saw the fear that filled her gaze.

"Leave me, and I know a set of twins that may well get more than hurt," he snorted, forcing himself from the sweet heat of her lying beneath him and rising to stand by the bed. "And that ache you're going to feel here soon will get a hell of a lot worse before I ease it next time. Think about that. Me and the Mackays will make sure everyone stays safe, but you're not leaving. Period."

He had a feeling that trying to make Isabeau do something wasn't the wisest move, but damned if he was pulling back now. He wasn't begging her to stay, but there would be hell to pay if she left.

"I'll see you this evening," he told her. "At dinner. Don't make me go looking for you."

With that, he turned and quickly left the room before she could object or argue with him. He had a feeling that arguing with her was the worst thing a man could do. She was a stubborn little thing. If she hadn't been, she wouldn't have fought so hard to get away from her brother and return to the place she called home.

Why her brother allowed it, Tracker intended to find out when all this was over. If Burke Weston had been foolhardy enough to allow his baby sister to move states away, without protection of any sort, then Tracker just might end up killing him.

And he'd get away with it too.

He'd learned how to play with monsters years ago, and he'd learned how to destroy them. Once a man survived his own destruction at the hands of such beings, he learned some damned hard lessons.

Lessons he swore he wouldn't forget.

Even for one sweet, seemingly innocent vision-impaired princess. Especially not for her.

"WHAT DO YOU MEAN YOU'RE NOT LEAVING?" SETH sounded angry, but Isabeau had known he would.

He wanted her away from the lake house and back home for some reason. She had a feeling she knew what that reason was too.

"Exactly what I said," she told him firmly. "Natches, Dawg, and Rowdy promised everyone would be safe while I was here. I've looked forward to this weekend for over a month."

And it was the truth. Natches and his cousins had been waiting for her when she'd left her room for breakfast. This was their property, their mountain, and they assured her no one could get to her with the number of Mackays, friends, and kin who were gathered there for the weekend. When it was time for her to leave, Tracker and Chance would accompany her and make certain she got there safely.

Then she could decide what to do. Call her brother or allow Angel's brothers to protect her and draw whoever wanted to hurt her from the shadows.

"Isabeau, this isn't going to work," Seth stated, sounding as though he was talking between clenched teeth. "Honey, you're staying here because of Calloway, and I know it. He's only going to hurt you. Let us take you home."

Of course he was going to hurt her; she wasn't fool enough to think Tracker was the settling-down kind, especially with a blind woman. A woman who couldn't share his life, or the danger he sought on a regular basis.

Just as she knew that she wasn't a woman who could sleep with a man without caring for him. And Tracker had started her downfall when he'd paid the band to play something slow so she could dance. Something even friends had never thought to do.

"I'm more than capable of deciding for myself who to be interested in and who not to be," she informed him. "It's my life, Seth. It's my decision. At least for now."

Silence filled the large living room they stood in, but she could feel the tension in the air. She'd rarely told Seth no, and never over anything important and where her safety was concerned. But then, he'd never involved himself in her life at any other time, had he?

He stayed carefully in the periphery of her life, and she was thankful for that. She'd never had to fight to draw away from the feelings she'd once begun having for him. That didn't stop the regret over the years though, or the what-ifs. It hadn't stopped her from lying in her lonely bed and aching for touch, his touch. Because she knew him. Because she trusted him. And because she cared for him.

It wasn't easy to meet men who drew her attention as well as her desire. Being blind didn't make her pickier, it made her more aware of certain things where meeting men was concerned.

Those who pulled at her arm when walking with her, as though forcing her to follow them, rather than simply providing guidance when needed. She rarely found guidance, even with Seth. A man who paid a band so she could dance, who described the area where she'd be staying for the weekend, who gave her pleasure, who wanted to include her in her own protection rather than hiding her, she'd only found that with Tracker.

"And if I call Burke?" he asked her just as she'd had her fill of the silence. "You know what he'll do, Isabeau. He'll take you back to the ranch...."

"Burke can't force me to go anywhere," she snapped, hearing the threat, the blackmail. "Don't presume to think any of you can force me back or force me into a decision I don't agree with."

"You're staying because that bastard keeps sneaking into your bedroom and convincing you he's doing it for you," Seth argued, anger showing in his voice. "He's fucking pissed because someone nearly killed his sister. You're a means to an end, nothing more, little girl, and you're too fucking—"

He broke off, but she knew what he'd meant to say.

"Too blind to see it?" she asked him, pushing back her own anger, the hurt she felt. "Too stupid to realize a man like Tracker Calloway would only want to use me? That he couldn't seriously want me for any other reason?"

"That's not what he said, sis." Saul spoke up, his voice gentle, but then, Saul was always the easier of the two.

"That's what he meant," she informed him, hiding her hurt feelings and sense of betrayal.

That was the reason Seth had rebuffed her so long ago. She was blind, unable to do more than keep his bed warm when he was home, when he needed a woman who could party, who could move in his world with him.

"That's what you want to think," Seth growled back at her.

Isabeau had to laugh at that. "I know you, Seth. If it wasn't the truth, you would have denied it immediately." She shook her head at her own ignorance. "Why don't the two of you just do whatever you do when I'm not around, and let me worry about Tracker Calloway, what he wants from me, and why? We'll get along better that way."

She was tired of wondering if it was bad luck haunting her, some kind of messed-up karma, or someone who really wanted to hurt her. Those questions had bothered her for far too long. Tracker was offering to make it stop. She may be left with a broken heart, but he hadn't lied to her. He wasn't pretending to care for her or giving her excuses why he couldn't love her.

He was straightforward and determined, and he was offering her more than a hollow illusion while he did it. He wanted her, and he was willing to do something about it. What was more, her body was more than willing to accept it.

He could do what so many men hadn't. He could make her forget the world around her—and Seth August—with just a kiss.

"I'll kill him, Isabeau," Seth snarled as she felt him grab her shoulders as though to shake some sense into her. "Do you hear me? When I have to watch you grieve over him because you loved him and he walked away, after knowing he used you like he's used every other woman he's ever slept with, I'll kill him."

Distrust like that, that focused and all-consuming, could only be caused by an immeasurable amount of pain, Isabeau thought.

"Just because you weren't man enough to step forward when she wanted you is no reason to threaten another man, August. Take your hands off her." Chance's voice was deep, rough with ire as Seth suddenly let her go, stepping back then stomping to the other side of the room.

"He'd never hurt her." Saul to the rescue, as usual. "And this isn't your fight. It's between Seth and Isabeau."

Saul always played referee for his more temperamental brother. Once, Isabeau had found it amusing. Now, it wasn't amusing in the least.

"I don't need any of you to protect me from the other," Isabeau snapped. "It's my decision to stay. If Tracker changes his mind about taking me back once the weekend is over, then I'll walk. I don't need the rest of you fighting over it, threatening each other, or irritating the hell out of me."

She'd had enough.

"Isabeau, this is dangerous. Calloway is dangerous," Seth stated, and he sounded tortured, hurt.

They were friends, she reminded herself. That was a bridge she didn't want to burn, but it didn't give anyone the right to direct her life.

"Evidently, I'm the one who's dangerous to be around," she told him painfully, hating the truth of that statement. "He can't possibly be more so. If someone's trying to kill me, they're getting bolder. The next bullet will hit my head rather than someone's tire, Seth. I'd rather die than live day to day wondering when it's coming. Or wondering who I'll get killed with me. This is Tracker's life, according to him. And it would seem he's determined to figure it out, no matter the reason, no matter my wishes. So, your wishes or fears aren't part of the equation this time."

"I'm calling Burke." Fury filled his tone.

She wanted to roll her eyes at his favorite threat.

"Go ahead." She threw her arms out as her anger began to get the best of her. "I just got off the phone with him myself an hour ago. He's already aware of what I'm doing and I'm sure the two of you will have fun commiserating with each other. Now if you'll excuse me, this little argument is over as far as I'm concerned. Find someone else to harass."

Arguing with her brother, then with Seth, was damned tiring. And emotionally draining.

Turning, she extended her cane and made her way from the living room back to the hallway and out onto the porch, where bright sunlight pierced the mists and allowed more shape, a bit more detail to the shadows that filled her gaze.

The heaviness in her chest she wasn't certain what to do with. She'd stopped crying years ago, knowing that tears did nothing but upset her brother and his family. She'd hated that.

She wasn't going to cry now, even in secret. She didn't wear makeup, so it would be impossible to hide afterward if she did cry. Instead, it just lay inside her, becoming heavier by the day and reminding her that she was broken in too many ways. A burden on friends and family when that was the last thing she wanted to be.

It was the one thing she was determined not to be.

Yet she'd found there was no avoiding it either.

SEVEN

A MAN HAD TO SLEEP SOMETIME, TRACKER REFLECTED, but sometimes, that sleep came with a price. It seemed the price he was paying was acknowledging that in sleeping, he'd given Seth August the perfect opportunity to hurt Isabeau deep enough that even he could see the proof of it in her sober expression early that evening.

The very fact that the moisture wasn't welling her eyes, that the pain hadn't escaped, bothered him on a level he couldn't explain. The fact that he noticed the emotion at all should have bothered him, but he let that slide.

It was her eyes, he excused himself. That violet color was darker, deeper, and the smile she normally carried had dimmed.

The curve of her lips was restrained, the animation in her expression nearly absent. And he had a feeling it was damned hard to darken either her smile or her laughter. But both had been dimmed in her eyes that day, and that just pissed him the fuck off.

"Where's Irk and Jerk?" he muttered to Chance as they stood on the porch observing those who were currently gathering in the backyard with drinks and plates of predinner snacks.

Dinner wouldn't be served for another hour, then the side dishes, desserts, and sandwich makings put out for later in the evening.

"Pouting somewhere out of sight?" the other man grunted. "Seth's less than happy that Isabeau's daring to stay this weekend rather than letting him take her home. He threatened to call her brother on her. Saul's pissed off with Isabeau and Seth both, from what I understand."

Tracker lifted his brows in surprise, his gaze on Isabeau as she and Annie, Bliss, and Laken Mackay sat beneath the sheltered picnic area talking. Or rather the Mackay girls sat talking as Isabeau listened.

"She already called him," Chance told him, his expression thoughtful as he too watched the women. "I don't know what was said, but I get the feeling Isabeau believes Burke Weston will stay at home like a good little boy. I'm not sure about that. He's not exactly good-boy material."

No, he agreed with Chance, that simply wasn't in Burke Weston's repertoire.

"Do you expect him to show up?" Tracker asked.

If he knew Chance, the other man had already pulled as much information as possible on Weston, shot it to J. T. and Mara Calloway, and come up with an answer to that question.

"My opinion, Seth and Saul August have already mentioned your name to him. They'd be a fool not to. So far, he's still in Texas though. If that changes, I'll know about it." That was Chance, protecting their back.

"So, if Burke Weston knows the big bad wolf is getting ready to bed his sister, why isn't he on his way?" Tracker mused. "No doubt the Jerk-Off Twins were properly descriptive when informing him of the type of man Isabeau's tangling with."

He would have been, if the positions were reversed.

On second thought, he wouldn't be so brick dumb as to not claim the woman he wanted, as it seemed Seth August had wanted Isabeau.

But evidently, he hadn't wanted her bad enough. Not even enough to ensure her safety before now.

And Tracker couldn't help but wonder why.

"He needs to be punched for that look in her eyes," he stated, wondering why he cared.

He'd seen worse pain in other eyes, he told himself, women he hadn't known, hadn't held as they found their pleasure.

He watched as she shook her head to something Annie said, her lips curving as though smiling, but the sadness remained in her eyes. And no one seemed to realize it, even the normally perceptive young women she sat with.

"J. T. and Mara called earlier," Chance told him. "Mara believes, based on the information I sent them, that each near-fatal episode was an attempt to kill her, just as you suspect. Each attempt was hurried, without planning. A desperate attempt to ensure it appeared an accident."

"We already knew that," he stated, leaning against a support post as he continued to watch her.

"Mara believes it's the same person that killed her family. And it's someone Isabeau must know. Did you already know that?" Chance asked, almost amused.

Tracker flicked him a knowing look.

He'd suspected as much. When going over the police reports, investigators notes, and the series of events, there were no other possibilities.

"I figured," Chance said heavily.

"Seth and Saul have been following her for years whenever they're back in the States," Tracker said softly. "Always from a distance, but nothing happens whenever they're around, until now. Because her would-be killer didn't know they were back."

"He doesn't know who Angel is either," Tracker told him. "Or who we are. He's more focused on the Augusts and the threat they pose than some Mackay wife he believes got lucky and avoided going over that cliff."

"It's kind of hard to identify or trace us," Chance pointed out. "J. T. and Mara made certain of that when we were just babies."

Yes, they had, and as technology had changed, they had ensured the team remained unidentifiable and untraceable.

"He doesn't consider anyone else a threat yet anyway," Tracker mused. "He's not considering other enemies. He doesn't believe anyone suspects she's in danger any longer, with the exception of her brother and the Jerk-Off Twins."

Chance grunted in amusement. "Irk and Jerk, huh?"

Tracker couldn't help but chuckle. "Damn good fighters, but those two have no idea the woman they've overlooked all these years."

He watched her, watched her eyes, when he knew no one else paid attention. She was definitely vision-impaired, for the most part, but there were times he knew she saw more than she let on.

He'd watched her track movement, so she at least saw shadows, perhaps hints of color. And she told no one. She allowed no one to know that her sight could be returning.

Were her memories returning as well?

Something had to have happened to cause the killer to up his game and take a chance and prove that she was a target.

Tracker thought she must have told someone or somehow given the wrong person cause to suspect that her memories, or vision, or both, were returning. And with their return, they could be identified in a murder everyone believed her father had committed. It was the only thing that made sense.

So, if Carmichael Boudreaux hadn't pulled the trigger, who had? And why?

"Tell Mara I need a list of suspects for the murder of her parents," he told Chance. "And we don't have a lot of time."

"She's already on it," his brother murmured. "She and J. T. also suspect that's where the problem stems from. There were inconsistencies in the crime scene that the investigators made note of before the murder/suicide ruling was made."

Tracker nodded slowly, watching as Isabeau glanced toward the house, her gaze pausing where he and Chance stood before moving away again.

Yeah, her vision was at the very least changing. And he would bet money someone else suspected it as well.

"I want updates and copies of everything they pulled in," he told Chance as he straightened from the porch post he'd been leaning against. "He's going to strike again soon, and we have to be ready. We need to know who to be watching for if we have a chance of saving her ass."

And it was a damned cute ass. One he had no intention of allowing some bastard to kill.

"There's something else." The hesitancy in Chance's tone was unfamiliar. That made it concerning.

"What else?" Tracker growled.

"Notice that light covering she's wearing over her top?" He nodded out at Isabeau.

She wore a short-sleeved, dark blue sheer-looking open shirt of some sort over her normal sleeveless top.

"Yeah?" He knew he wasn't going to like this.

"Seth August put his hands on her. Grabbed her shoulders when she refused to leave with him and Saul. I think she has some faint bruising."

Son of a bitch.

He would have been shocked, but people had ceased to truly shock him years ago. The fact that the bastard had dared to put his hands on her because of her desire to stay at the lake house sent anger surging through him though.

She trusted the Augusts, was half in love with Seth, and he'd dared to bruise her?

Oh, he'd pay for that one. And he'd pay hard for it.

As Tracker headed to the pavilion, where the picnic tables were being laden with dinner plates, the thought that he could possibly be letting himself become too involved crossed his mind. He pushed it away immediately.

He never became too involved. He refused to allow it. And he wouldn't allow it this time.

Making a bastard August pay for putting his hands on Isabeau and bruising her delicate skin wasn't getting involved. For the moment, until she was safe, she belonged to him. And no man, nowhere, no way, bruised what belonged to him and got away with it.

ISABEAU COULD FEEL TRACKER'S EYES ON HER LIKE A ghostly heated stroke. A faint sensation that reminded her far too much of his touch, his kiss.

He was watching her.

Looking around, shifting through the shadows that moved against the sun-filled backdrop, she searched for him. And within seconds found him.

The shape of his shadow was just different, she thought, and as he stood on the porch of the house, the arrogance and sheer confidence he exuded seemed to make the dark shape of his body even more imposing.

She had to force her gaze from him, too terrified he'd realize that she was actually staring at him, rather than just staring blindly. She'd forgotten her sunglasses in her room, though truth be told, she hated wearing them. They darkened anything she might actually be able to see.

Her vision was becoming a bit clearer, the mists beginning to lighten further. She stayed in a constant state of hope now, always searching for hints of color, of detail. And she was too terrified to tell anyone. Even her doctor.

Why she was so frightened of anyone knowing, she couldn't fully explain. Perhaps it had something to do with the nightmares that were coming more often, that sense of panic she felt after waking.

Because she suspected when her sight finally returned, so would her memories. And why would she be so frightened of that unless her father had been the one to pull the trigger all those years ago?

She'd heard Burke and Mac discussing it more than once at the house. The patio was directly beneath her bedroom, and her sense of hearing was exceptional. She'd listened to them discuss her parents' deaths, her accidents, and their fear that they were connected.

"Would you like anything else to eat or drink, Isabeau?" Annie asked as Isabeau slid her plate back from her, her appetite suddenly gone. "There's dessert. The pies are to die for."

Isabeau shook her head. "I'm fine, Annie."

"Well, Tracker's heading this way." Amusement filled the young woman's voice. "He looks like a big wolf or something, the way he walks. All predator-like. I have to say, Angel has some hot brothers."

"Better not let your dad hear that." Bliss laughed from Isabeau's side. "He'll lock you up in your room until both of them are gone."

"Dad has nothing to worry about," Annie sighed. "They look good, but I'm not interested in either of them. Even more, there's not a chance they'd be interested in me."

There was a vein of sadness in the girl's voice, as though whoever she was interested in simply wasn't an option.

"Lots of guys are here you could be interested in," Bliss pointed out. "I think Uncle Rowdy's getting worried that you don't date."

"No, Mom's the one that worries," Annie stated. "Excuse me, speaking of Mom, she's waving me to her, and Tracker is almost here."

"Our cue to leave," Bliss stated, her voice bordering on laughter. "Later, Isabeau."

The two girls deserted her quickly, and Isabeau could have sworn she heard chuckles from nearby tables. It seemed everyone was now aware of Tracker's interest.

"Looks like you've been abandoned." Tracker slid into the chair Bliss had left, his voice low and amused.

"So it would seem." She almost wished they'd stayed. "They seem to believe the romance of the summer is beginning."

She injected just enough dry humor to save herself from being pathetic. Who could possibly care that she'd longed for romance, passion? For someone who wanted her, not because she was a means to an end but just because she was Isabeau Isadora Boudreaux.

"Perhaps it is." That low, rough-velvet, midnight rasp had her blood heating, her senses skewering.

"Hmm," she murmured, rather doubting it.

That voice was sexier than hell, the suggestive implications almost enough to make her want to drag him to the nearest bedroom. But she couldn't, wouldn't allow herself to believe in the impossible.

"There's a glass of lemonade three inches directly in front of your right hand," he stated rather than commenting on her lack of belief in the summer romance.

"Is it spiked?" She couldn't count the number of times she'd been offered the hard lemonade.

He snorted at the comment. "Too early for that. I like to wake up before I begin the seduction part of the summer romance."

Isabeau stared at his dim shape in astonishment. Outrage. She was sure the snorts of laughter to their side went past both.

"Smooth, Calloway." She sighed, picked up the drink, and brought it to her lips. "Real smooth."

She was beginning to wish it was spiked.

"Truth nonetheless," he murmured, amused, but she could hear something more. Intent. He wouldn't have approached her, no matter any sexual interest he felt, if she wasn't the only way to strike back at whoever had endangered his sister's life in their attempt to get to her. But there was sexual interest. He desired her.

He didn't hunger for her, ache for her, or need her, but for the moment, he wanted her. For whatever reason.

"I highly doubt you're not quite awake," she murmured, lowering the cool drink to the table. "You're likely awake and aware even when you're asleep."

"Possibly," he drawled, leaning closer, one hand stroking down her arm. "Does that mean I can start the seduction now?"

Isabeau couldn't help but roll her eyes. "Not the sort of entertainment the Mackays have in mind, I'm sure."

"Probably not," he agreed, his hand caressing up her arm to her shoulder, back again.

She couldn't feel the dark chiffon sleeves of the wrap moving, so she didn't protest. According to Annie, the bruising there was very, very faint, but Isabeau had a feeling that allowing Tracker to see them would be a very bad move.

Almost as bad a move as Seth made when he grabbed her. He knew better than anyone how easily she bruised.

"I'm glad you stayed," he told her, his cheek brushing against her hair. "I expected you to leave with Irk and Jerk."

"You have got to stop calling them that," she told him, fighting to hold back a laugh. "And you knew I'd stay." She sobered just as quickly. "I didn't have any other choice. Did I?"

He was silent for long moments. She finally felt him pull away from her, his hand brushing against her shoulder once again as he straightened in his chair.

"Not if you want to live," he finally said, his voice soft enough to ensure only she heard him. "And, sweetheart, I'd really like to make certain you live."

Her heart was racing, and Isabeau had a bad feeling it wouldn't be hard for a casual observer to tell she was becoming more aroused than she should be in public.

If she didn't know better, she'd believe there was emotion involved in that statement. That he was intent on doing more than finding a killer and fucking her in the bargain.

And yes, she knew he intended to join her in her bed. Soon. He wasn't a man who would wait for long either. And she had to admit, it would be impossible for her to deny him. It wouldn't matter where or when.

"I have to find Chance," he murmured a second before she felt his lips on hers, a quick, hot stroke of his tongue against her lips, and then he was gone.

She felt him, quick and silent as he left, the blur of his shadow retreating quickly.

To find Chance.

But he'd been standing with Chance on the porch before he'd come to the pavilion. Why would he need to find Chance again so soon?

"THEY'RE WAITING FOR YOU," CHANCE SAID AS TRACKER met him at the tree line where he stood. "Seth knew you'd be coming for him."

"Of course he did," Tracker sneered. "He touched her. Bruised her."

Moving ahead of his brother, he made the short climb to where the ground leveled to a small flat that overlooked the lake, with the twins standing at the center of it.

They were imposing figures, true. Over six feet, warriors primed for battle. But they weren't the only ones built and primed for battle. Unlike the Augusts, Tracker's skills had been honed by monsters, his body trained by them. Scarred by them.

As he neared, Seth watched him closely, green eyes narrowed, his body prepared for battle.

Amusement curled into Tracker for a moment, then it was pushed back, along with anger, the sense of personal affront he felt at the sight of Isabeau's bruises, and any sense of vengeance for them.

This wasn't vengeance. It would be a lesson.

Neither of her so-called friends had done what was needed to stop the bastard tormenting her. And Seth, he dared to place bruises on her body when it was obvious that Isabeau, at least at one time, had needed so much more from him.

Tracker stopped several feet from the twins, aware of Chance moving into position to defend his back should Saul move into place to attack.

"If you ask Isabeau, she'll tell you a strong wind bruises her," Seth breathed out heavily, hands going to his hips as he stared back at Tracker coolly. "I should have been more careful, because I do know. But I didn't harm her."

Tracker crossed his arms over his chest and allowed a small, amused sneer to curl at his lips.

"I'm going to punch you in the fucking face, August. Had you been a smart man, you would have done whatever it took to draw her stalker out in the past years. Instead, you've flitted around the world playing SEAL while she faced it alone," he reminded Seth.

"There's no proof," Saul stated calmly. "We've searched every corner possible looking for a suspect. There is nothing to be found. If there was, we would have found it by now."

Tracker saw the tightening of Seth's jaw, the slow tension that invaded his body and the narrowing of his eyes as Tracker held his gaze.

Seth knew Saul's words didn't mean shit to him. This had to be done; otherwise, Seth August would never respect his place in Isabeau's life. However long he was in it.

This wasn't the first time he and one of the twins had come to conflict. It had never come to blows, but this time, it would.

"You're not in love with her, Calloway," Seth breathed out, his tone knowing as he stared back at Tracker with a hint of anger. "You're using her."

"I'm doing what has to be done to save her. Which is more than those who supposedly love her have done," Tracker corrected him. "Perhaps you should have considered the option."

Seth got as far as opening his mouth to speak before Tracker's fist was in it.

The first August twin went flying before the second moved, but Tracker knew he was coming. He'd watched them fight countless times, knew how they worked, how in sync they were. But they were still two men, and no matter how well trained, they were fighting a man who didn't just know their moves but had been trained and honed in ways they had never imagined.

A back kick planted his foot firmly in Saul's chest, throwing him back, and in the next breath, Tracker used the foot he had firmly planted on the ground to propel himself forward and drive his head into Seth's diaphragm.

As soon as Seth went backward, Saul was there, but a fist to his jaw and a well-planted kick threw him away once again even as Tracker ducked, balanced, turned quickly, and managed to plant Seth's head into the closest tree trunk.

Just enough to addle the bastard. If he actually managed to seriously hurt him, then Isabeau would never forgive him.

That could be a bad thing. He really didn't want to piss her off too bad.

So, he took a blow to his face, punched back, and allowed two to his ribs.

He took another blow to his jaw, one to his kidney.

Seth tried to take Tracker's feet out from under him but failed. Saul managed a hard jab to Tracker's jaw, filling his mouth with blood.

Then Tracker smiled.

There it was. The pain.

Adrenaline began jacking his system, the pain feeding it as nothing else could. The dark core of his soul that he fought to keep controlled broke free. Memory and madness. A fury kept contained and only allowed free when he fought.

The pain was almost a high now, like having electrical energy shoved through his system.

The blows ensured Isabeau wouldn't be too damned pissed off at him. She'd be mad, but she'd get over it.

Now he gave his instincts free rein, just for a moment, he promised himself. Just enough to make sure these fucking twins knew he meant business.

He saw Saul's blow coming through one bloody eye, jerking his head back and to the side. As the fist flew past his face, Tracker let his fists do what he'd trained them to do.

Inflict pain. Make certain he survived and his enemy went down.

"Enough, dammit. . . . Goddamn, Tracker. . . ."

Hard hands were jerking him back, pulling him away from his enemy. "I said enough. . . ."

It was Chance. The voice of reason.

The only one capable of pulling him back from the pit.

Jerking away from Chance, he stared around. Saul was leaning against a tree holding his ribs; Seth was slowly pulling himself to his feet. Both men were bloody, breathing hard, and staring at him like the monster he was. Chance, as usual, stepped back, waiting, watching.

"Fuck," Seth groaned, swaying for a second before righting himself. "Where the fuck did you train?"

"In hell. Bruise Isabeau again and I'll send you there," Tracker snapped, pausing long enough to wipe blood from his eye and to realize they had company. If there weren't a dozen of the lake house guests plus the better part of the Mackay family standing around, then he'd be surprised. "What are these fuckers doing here?" He turned on Chance accusingly.

Bright green eyes widened in mocking surprise. "I'm supposed to stop them?"

He snorted at the question. Stopping a Mackay was like trying to wrangle lightning. It simply wasn't going to happen.

As Tracker glared at Chance, he caught sight of platinum hair and violet eyes staring at the scene in front of her in disbelief.

Isabeau.

His eyes narrowed on her.

And he was betting his very sizable bank account that she was seeing every incriminating detail.

Fuck!

EIGHT

HIS GAZE WAS A FIERY BLUE, SHAGGY BLACK HAIR MUSSED, his face bloody, pulled into brutal lines and reflecting a cold hard savagery that should have been terrifying. One eye was already swelling shut, his lip split.

His chest looked wider than she thought it was, the muscles of his arms pumped, his still fisted hands bruised, bloody, weapons.

It should not be arousing.

She shouldn't be aroused.

She shouldn't be so wet she felt as though she should change panties.

A second later, she told herself that she shouldn't be so thankful that the mists that normally obscured her gaze eased over it once again. Because the sight of him was simply destructive. Life changing. Heart changing.

Because she hadn't even looked at Seth.

Hadn't wanted to look at Seth.

She'd only had eyes for Tracker.

"Brace yourself." His hard voice was her only warning just before hard arms went around her, and she found herself swept from her feet.

"Tracker," she gasped, her hands gripping shoulders that felt like iron—hard, heated iron.

"You were not supposed to be there." The hard rasp of his voice sent a shiver racing up her spine and yet more moisture to her vagina.

Damn him.

"Why were you fighting them?" But she had a feeling she knew.

"Because they're pricks, and they asked for it." That growly sound to his voice was driving her insane.

It only took a few minutes until she felt his steps even out, indicating he'd reached the backyard once again, then he was striding across it quickly.

No doubt back to the house, she thought. Everyone seemed to think she should just be deposited back into her room and left to her own devices.

No one could have been more surprised though when instead of going up the steps to the porch, he moved beneath the pavilion before placing her on her feet, pushing her back to the wall. Then he pulled her head back for a kiss she had no chance of resisting. Even if she wanted to.

Resisting was the last thing on her mind though.

Her fingers speared into his mussed hair, clenching on the strands as she nipped at his retreating lips.

"Oh, bad girl," he rasped.

He nipped back, then pushed his tongue past her lips as the hand clenched in her hair moved to hold her jaw, his fingers placed to keep her from nipping at him again.

And it was the sexiest kiss she'd ever had in her life.

Lips rubbing, tongues licking as the hard, muscle-corded length of his body pressed her against the wood post behind her.

It was so damned good that when he pulled back, she found herself reaching for him again before she could stop herself, desperate for more.

"Dammit. I should just take you the fuck out of here now and find the nearest motel," he groaned a second before pulling back, one hand at her hip, bracing her. "This fuckin' pavilion is no place for this."

Isabeau was just trying to remember how to breathe without begging him to do just that.

"By time you got to the hotel, you'd be too sore to do anything but sleep," she murmured, her voice rougher than she liked.

"Something else we need to discuss," he muttered.

"Calloway, we have a no-fighting rule here." Natches's voice jerked her back to reality.

"Yeah, 'cause having a no-prick rule would pretty much ensure no one showed up," he snorted.

There were several chuckles and few agreements as Tracker placed her hand on his arm.

"Come on, let's get a seat. I'll get you a cold drink," he suggested as she began moving with him.

"I'd get a few ice compresses too if I were you," she murmured as he placed her hand on the back of a chair.

"Hmm, yeah, we'll discuss that," he whispered as she sat down. "Here come the Mackay hellions. You can talk to them while I go change shirts."

She didn't say anything, but she'd seen the blood on his shirt, just as she'd seen it on his face.

"Ask Annie to get me a lemonade," she suggested. "Go do whatever you need to do, Tracker. I'm good here."

She needed just a few minutes to breathe, to make sense of everything she was suddenly feeling. Those few brief moments of sight had been destructive to her senses.

All of them.

"Another tough, hot male bites the dust." A familiar voice laughed as Isabeau watched the shadow of a fellow teacher slide into the seat beside her.

"I don't think Tracker's the kind of man to bite the dust," Isabeau stated, grinning wryly as Mattie Watts gave her shoulder a little nudge.

Mattie laughed at the comment. "Well, he definitely seems intent on taking a nice little bite out of you. Damn, that kiss looked hot as hell."

Isabeau covered her face for a moment, shaking her head at the knowledge that everyone had likely seen the exchange.

"He's like a tornado," she sighed.

"Yeah, I can see your problem there." Good-natured and amused, Mattie at least kept her voice low. "Being swept off your feet by all that hard muscle and rough, manly good looks would definitely put a girl off her stride."

Her friend simply had no idea.

"Hey, Mattie." Saul's voice intruded, his tone a little too grim to suit Isabeau.

They were acting like little boys and had the nerve to use that serious, *We got problems* voice?

"Saul, that's a hell of a black eye." Mattie sounded very approving, then leaned closer to Isabeau and murmured, "I better go join my date. I think he's feeling very underdeveloped right now."

Most men would feel that way, Isabeau thought in resignation. Hell, she was starting to wonder if she shouldn't feel that way.

When Mattie moved from the table, Isabeau felt Saul slide into the vacated chair and turned a glare in his direction.

"What the hell were the three of you fighting over?"

"Fighting?" Saul asked, the sarcasm in his voice heavy. "We didn't fight much. We were too busy trying to stay alive."

The sight of Tracker—his face bloodied, muscles pumped, and a savage smile of triumph on his face—was forever branded into her brain.

"I asked why?" she questioned him again, looking directly into his face as she allowed her ire to show.

She had never seen either man, not clearly enough to distinguish their features. The fact that she hadn't taken the time to see them during those brief moments, to at least search for Seth, was incredibly disconcerting.

She'd wanted nothing more for years than to see his face, to see the handsome features women talked about. The deep green eyes, hard masculine features, muscular body. And what did she do the first time her sight had been clear while they were around? She'd been entranced by another man instead.

By Tracker.

"Saul, I'm running out of patience," she warned him, making certain her tone conveyed the fact that she wasn't waiting much longer.

"Hate it when you sound like that," he griped. "At least let me get my beer first."

She heard the tab pop, watched as his shadow moved further, his arm coming up to his face.

She waited. Gave him time to drink but didn't cease glaring at him.

"The bruises Seth put on your shoulders this morning when he grabbed you," Saul finally said softly. "I guess Tracker saw them when he was brushing that little wrap of yours back and forth. Chance no doubt told him about the argument."

No doubt.

Isabeau rubbed at the back of her neck, then her left temple. She could feel a headache building and had a feeling there would be no avoiding it.

"That's ridiculous," she hissed, her voice low, confused at why he'd even bother to lie to her. "Tracker Calloway isn't a man to be motivated by emotion, Saul."

A long silence followed her words, but she was used to that whenever talking to Saul or Seth. When it came to emotional problems, the two men didn't think too fast on their feet. Especially another's emotional issues.

"I didn't think he was," Saul agreed after a moment. "Maybe I'm wrong."

"No doubt you're wrong," she assured him. "Let me guess, Seth was being a complete prick and pushed Tracker too far?"

"Hmm, yeah, I can go with that one," he agreed.

"Seth pushed him into throwing the first punch, right?" She shook her head in disbelief.

Tracker had managed to get the best of the two strongest men she knew, but not because of any emotion. Male pride, ego, or whatever. But not because he cared about her.

Would he go to those lengths to preserve the illusion he was setting up of an emotional connection with her?

And why the hell was he even going that route? Surely to God he didn't believe any perceived emotion toward her would push a would-be killer to act, did he?

Another question she was going to have to ask him when he returned.

And she had no doubt he would return.

"I think Tracker voluntarily threw that first punch actually." The twin sighed. "And don't ask me why he'd do it; I can't read his mind. He's acting very un-Tracker-like though. And that bothers the hell outta me."

The ache at her temple was going to get worse fast.

"You know, Saul, I'm rarely invited to parties, especially summer lake parties. If there's music, I rarely get to dance. Especially if you and Seth are around." She'd had enough. "Even at the ranch, the parties are strictly off-limits."

"Isabeau." His voice was soft, low as she pulled the folding cane from her back pocket and extended it to its full length. "Honey . . ."

"I might get hurt. It's too rowdy. The partygoers are getting too drunk," she continued, trying to keep her voice down. "Always an excuse. And it's always total bullshit."

"That's not true, Isabeau," he argued, his voice equally soft, but she knew they were drawing attention.

"You and Saul should have stayed in Texas, or wherever the hell you go when you disappear, and let me be. Because you're just like Burke. Your only answer to whatever the hell has been going on is to stash me at the ranch, where the rest of you can go about your lives without worrying about the stupid little blind bitch, who either has a hell of a streak of bad luck or a killer dumber than she is gunning for her." She rose to her feet, her head throbbing now. "Let me just fix that for you."

"Goddammit, Isabeau." He came to his feet, blocking her path as shock filled his voice.

The silence that suddenly surrounded her assured her that despite her attempt to keep from being overheard, there were far too many ears too close to them.

"Get out of my way. Dealing with you, your brother, and whatever your preconceived notions of others may be is giving me a headache." As she moved to step around him, his fingers curled over her lower arm. The grip, though gentle, was a warning.

And she'd had enough.

She'd really had enough.

Jerking her arm back, she tried again to step around him.

"We need to talk about this," he growled, blocking her once again.

"Saul." It was Natches's voice that had him stopping, tensing. "That no-fighting rule includes not instigating the conflict as well." The deep, measured voice was filled with ice rather than the warm humor she'd always heard in it before now. "I won't let it go a second time."

"I'm sorry, Natches. I know how they are. I should have expected it," she told her host, but she could feel her face flaming. "I apologize for the trouble I've caused."

It was their favorite way of ensuring she did as they wanted her to, like leaving a party, or any situation they deemed inappropriate. Her brother's father, Mac, was the only person who didn't use the tactic. And the only time they didn't try it was whenever he was around.

"And that's a damned shame that you feel the need to apologize for assholes," he said, his tone still cold. "Now get the hell out of her way, cousin."

Saul stepped to the side slowly.

"Look at it this way," she whispered painfully. "Once again, I'm leaving the gathering. As usual. You and Seth don't have to babysit anymore."

Isabeau pushed past him then. Keeping her head down, she prayed she was hiding the pure mortification she could feel sweeping through her.

It wasn't just the fact that others had witnessed the argument. It was that now they knew even friends didn't trust her ability to take care of herself in the simplest of circumstances; so how could anyone else?

Despite her anger, the feeling of eyes boring into her back, and her knowledge that once again she was the center of attention, she kept her steps slow, measured.

God, please don't let me trip. . . .

As though the prayer had been instantly heard, her vision cleared just enough, barely enough, that she was able to make out the path in front of her for several precious feet. Thank God, because one of the children had left a toy directly in the path. She let her cane tap it, feel around it, then adjusted her path for the large toy truck.

She wanted to cry but pushed the tears back, just as she always did.

At least she didn't have to worry about the twins calling her brother. She'd already called him, told him about the blowout, though she'd glossed over it, and she'd told him about Tracker.

Burke had been quiet, thoughtful, but hadn't seemed worried. Even if he was concerned about any of the information she'd given him, he wouldn't have shown it. But he would have demanded she come back to the ranch or told her if he was heading to Kentucky to assess the situation himself.

Her brother wasn't the least shy in letting her know when he thought she was in over her head.

He'd done neither.

Instead, he'd listened, and told her he would trust the twins to back any decision the Mackays or Angel's brother thought was best. He didn't know Tracker, he'd told her, but he'd met Angel and he knew the Mackays.

He didn't seem to either believe or disbelieve her claim that it was just a blowout, though she was certain Seth and Saul had already called and made their beliefs known.

She was so tired.

Isabeau admitted she'd grown tired of the near-fatal events, the constant moves and uncertainty even before she'd returned to Kentucky. She'd known there was more to the so-called accidents for years. She lived in fear of them. And she'd been daring a killer to strike again by the very fact that she refused to stay hidden.

Because no one had ever been endangered other than her.

Until Angel.

And if it wasn't for Tracker, she would have returned to the ranch. Once Angel had nearly been killed, she'd known her life was all but over. Her choices had become: let a killer finish the job, return to the ranch and hide, or trust Tracker to do what he said he was so damned good at.

At this point, she had no choice but to trust Tracker.

By the time she reached her room and closed herself in it, the headache was at that painful level that refused to be ignored.

She'd been expecting it. Those brief periods of sight always came with a price. But this last one wasn't as brief as in the past. She could still see several feet in front of her. Not clearly—it was distorted—but she could make out color, and furniture.

The heavy wood headboard and footboard with its intricate carved posts. Matching dresser and chest with the same intricate carving as well as bedside tables. A heavy multicolored quilt lay over the bed with ruffled white pillowcases over the pillows.

The lamps next to the bed were simple, the white lampshades emphasizing the splash of color in the quilt.

She wanted to go to the porch, stare out over the clearing behind the house, see the lake, but she knew better. She'd be noticed, especially by the twins, but even more, her head was throbbing forcefully now.

Opening her bag, she dug beneath her clothes and pulled free the medication her doctor had prescribed. Shaking out two pills, she put them on her tongue and then walked to the built-in fridge that held several bottles of water. Opening one, she took a drink and swallowed the medication.

Capping the water bottle, she placed it on the bedside table and sat on the bed, rubbing at her temples, wishing she'd come to her room first thing after her vision had cleared and she and Tracker had returned to the pavilion.

The pills made her drowsy, and to ensure the headache would be taken care of, she had to give in to that drowsiness and actually sleep for a few hours.

The periods of sight were getting more frequent and the headaches less severe. The mists that otherwise obscured her vision weren't as thick, and the blurred forms she glimpsed within them were becoming more detailed.

Her sight was definitely returning. She feared that with it, the past would as well. If it hadn't already been trying to. . . .

NINE

TRACKER RUBBED AT THE THIN LINE OF A SCAR THAT RAN along the left side of his jaw, the subtle itch just beneath it a warning. His gaze raked over the clearing from where he stood in the tree line above it, glaring down at the preparations for the evening party.

The wood for the bonfire was loaded and stacked in preparation to fire up; the band was performing its last-minute check. Snacks and sandwiches were placed under the pavilion and drinks set out in ice.

Everything looked just the way it should. No problems, no strangers. Reports from the hillsides surrounding the grounds on three sides were negative for any anomalies. The party was good to go according to more than a dozen Mackay cousins and in-laws.

So why the fuck was every internal warning instinct he possessed awake and active?

The dark core of violence and fury normally hidden kept pushing forward, despite his knowledge that allowing it could be disastrous. He hadn't let a woman affect him this much in a decade. Not since he'd learned how deeply one could betray a man, and how easily they could be used against him despite that knowledge.

Ghostly screams of agony echoed inside his head for a moment. His and a traitorous woman's, mixing with a monster's laughter. The remembered feel of blood leaking from his skin, the icy-hot sensation of a knife slicing his flesh, and the almost rabid hatred in the eyes of the woman he loved as he stared at her in agony.

No remorse. Her brown gaze had flicked with pleasure at his pain instead.

Yet, when it had been her screams he heard, he'd begged for her life.

She'd thought his enemy actually loved her. That the vicious warlord who convinced her to betray him would let her live.

Chained to a wall, weak, his body bruised, cut, and bleeding, he'd watched that bastard kill her as she screamed, cried for mercy. The things he and his men had done to her . . .

He forced the image away. Forced himself from the brutal memories that it did no good to relive. There was no changing the past or the man it had made him into.

And what the hell was he doing allowing a woman to bring those nightmares from the dark, bleak place he'd locked them into?

"Everything's quiet," Chance said from the shadows behind him. "The August twins packed up and drove out just after Isabeau went to her room. Supposedly heading out of town."

Bullshit.

Those two would have slipped back in and were no doubt in position with an eagle eye on the party below.

"They're here," he said, his voice barely a whisper.

"One overlooking the doors from the porch, one with a direct shot to the clearing," Chance agreed.

Tracker wasn't even going to ask how the hell Chance had managed to locate their nests.

"Anyone else?" he asked.

"Four Mackay cousins are in position to watch over the party," Chance stated. "No one unknown, each one reporting to Natches, Rowdy, Dawg, and Duke."

No wild cards.

"Something doesn't feel right," he murmured.

Goddammit.

Every scar on his body ached with a subtle warning.

And there were a lot of them.

"Natches has two cousins in the house; Duke and Dawg are on the porch," Chance reported.

Tracker shook his head, his gaze constantly moving, sweeping over the clearing and the lengthening shadows.

The Mackays could feel it too, he thought.

"Anyone have eyes on Isabeau's door?" he asked.

"In the bedroom across from Isabeau's, the door opened, one of those Mackay cousins have a direct view to it. Just to be sure until she wakes up. According to Angel she complained of a headache and went to lie down."

No doubt a direct result of the changes in her eyesight, Tracker guessed. Hell, how had everyone missed the fact that Isabeau had periods that her sight returned? Hell, he'd known her all of two days and he'd realized it.

"She can see, can't she?" Chance asked, his voice barely above a whisper.

Tracker gave a short nod. "Not all the time, but enough that it has someone scared, I think."

"No one else has noticed it," Chance pointed out. "J. T. and Mara don't believe her stalker is someone who's a daily part of her life."

"Doesn't matter," Tracker sighed, those screams from his past clawing in his chest now. "Someone suspects, or they've feared it would happen enough to take every opportunity to finish the job they started when she was fifteen. Unfortunately, the guests here this weekend aren't just local family. It would be impossible to tie anyone to her before she leaves tomorrow."

He could feel the scars on his back tightening. The warning becoming stronger.

"J. T. and Mara will have that suspect list soon," Chance promised. "I know they're working on it."

And they were damned good at what they did.

Still . . .

"It's getting dark," he told Chance. The need to see her, to have eyes on her and be assured of her safety, was overwhelming. "She'll wake soon. She doesn't want to miss the party."

And he was going to make damned sure he was at her side, covering her back.

Something was brewing, he could feel it in his gut, just as he knew Chance, the Augusts, and the Mackays could feel it in theirs.

And Isabeau was sitting in the bull's-eye.

"Go on, I've got this," Chance told him. "You watch her back, I'll have yours."

"What about you?" Tracker growled.

"Mine's covered," Chance assured him. "I always keep my back to a wall, you know that."

That was what his brother kept assuring him. Tracker could only pray he wasn't lying to him.

Keeping to the shadows, moving with a stealth he'd learned in a kill-or-be-killed arena, he made his way to the bottom of the hill, then skirted the clearing, heading for the house.

He could see Isabeau's window, the low light she kept burning a warm glow through the slit in the curtains.

As he made his way to the pavilion, the first indication of trouble was the light in her room that was suddenly extinguished.

Isabeau wouldn't have turned that light off.

As he neared her room, her scream suddenly pierced the dusk and sent rage exploding through his senses.

IT WAS A RARE OCCURRENCE THAT ISABEAU CAME AWAKE instantly. *Instantly* and *awake* weren't synonymous as far as she was concerned. But one second she was sleeping and the next she was awake, aware, and certain there was someone in the room with her.

Peeking through her lashes, she felt her heart racing faster as her gaze was met with nothing but pitch black. She always left a light on; the little glimmer of light that usually pierced the mists that covered her gaze was far easier to deal with than total blackness.

Was her sight reverting?

Or had the small light on the other side of the bed been switched off?

She could feel a heaviness in the air around her, a malevolence that grew more frightening by the moment. She wasn't alone in her room, and whoever was there with her wasn't there for pleasant conversation.

She remained still, silent, uncertain where the intruder was, but she knew he was close. Too close. She could feel a chill running up her spine, a knowledge that danger was breathing down her neck.

And now, when she needed to at least see the shadows, her vision was totally black.

She strained to hear something, anything. Thankfully, the party hadn't progressed to the music stage yet. The room was quiet, almost too quiet.

A second later, she heard it. A footfall against the hardwood floor as someone stepped from the carpet runner. Boots? It sounded like cowboy boots, the type worn by her brother's cowboys on the ranch.

Another step.

He was coming steadily closer.

If she screamed, would anyone hear her?

Didn't matter, she was screaming anyway.

That was one of the first things her brother had trained her to do in the event of an attack.

Scream.

And fight.

She let out a bloodcurdling scream as she rolled to the opposite side of the bed, threw the blankets back, and jumped from the bed.

A snarl of male rage sounded behind her as she threw herself to where she knew the glass doors should be and let out another piercing scream . . . even as she tripped on the rug between the door and the bed.

As she went down, the sounds of a gunshot, glass shattering, and screams from outside echoed around her. Sharp glass rained around her as she covered her head, crying out rather than screaming, expecting to feel a bullet hit her at any second.

She heard her bedroom door hit the wall as it was thrown open, boots banging on the wood from all directions, a distant sound of more glass shattering and orders being shouted out.

Chaos was erupting around her, and she couldn't see a damned thing. Her bearings were off, and each time she tried to feel for direction, glass cut into her hands.

"Isabeau!" Tracker's shout came a second later, her breath catching from the feel of his hands gripping her waist and pulling her to her feet. Into his arms.

Safety.

Warmth.

Her nails dug into his arms as she tried to get as close as possible. Panic was shortening her breath, adrenaline still pumping through her body.

Light suddenly flared around her, shapes and colored blurs whirling in a muted kaleidoscope as Tracker lifted her from her feet, and in the next second, sat her on her bed.

"Where's Angel?" he shouted, the tone icy.

"Safe," Chance yelled back. "How did that fucker get in?"

"He went out the glass doors in the room across from here. . . ." another voice shouted.

"Lost him . . . hit the lake . . ." Information was being shouted back and forth, relayed in an almost confusing sequence.

Isabeau dug her fingers in the blankets, gripping them, barely controlling the shudders that raced through her.

"Where's Isabeau?" Seth's voice cut through the raised voices.

His voice was concerned, deeper than she'd ever heard it, and had her panic rising.

She reached out for Tracker again, found his arm, her fingers gripping on to him, desperate to not be pulled from him. Seth, Saul, Burke. They always jerked her away from any hint of danger and forced her back to the ranch, away from anything or anyone that could represent a threat. Where she should be safe. Where she couldn't endanger anyone else.

"She's fine." Tracker seemed to move closer, to surround her.

He held her close to him as he eased onto the bed beside her, holding her close to his side.

THE VOICES WERE STILL ECHOING AROUND HER. THE Mackay family was now up in arms.

"We have to leave." She was on the verge of begging. "Please, Tracker. Before someone gets hurt. Just take me home. I don't want anyone here hurt."

There was no way to even express her regret to the Mackays that this had happened. That she was the reason trouble had invaded the family weekend.

"Well, at least it's just a door." One of the cousins laughed. "Jesse took a bullet in the shoulder, and Doc put close to twenty stitches in Kyle from the knife someone tried to gut him with—"

"There's a reason we don't allow children. . . ." Chaya's tone was heavy with resignation.

"One would think the lot of you would settle down in your old age," Chatham Doogan, a Mackay brother-in-law and former assistant director of Homeland Security, remarked drolly.

Isabeau could only shake her head.

No one had ever mentioned trouble of that sort at the lake house. She'd heard about the events since returning to Somerset. How much fun they were, how exciting, lively, and entertaining . . .

"Yeah, well, there's a reason we make sure the sheriff and you government types are invited," Natches grunted. "Keeps the rest of us out of trouble."

But it was going to be guaranteed to cause her more trouble because they were there, and she was going to have a lot of questions to answer.

ISABEAU WAS HOLDING ON TO HIM, BUT NOT IN DESPERation or fear from the attack. There was a difference. He knew what the other felt like, but he wasn't as certain of what he was sensing from her.

This wasn't like anyone else he'd ever protected. He had a feeling if he let go of her, then she wouldn't sway or collapse. She'd stand there, head held high, on her own, taking everything in as she was doing while he held her. But having him hold her, to allow her to settle against him, made her stronger in some way.

He'd test the theory, but he'd be damned if he'd let her go to do it.

Looking around the room, he caught sight of Seth—the older twin was watching them, his expression bland, but his eyes raged. With anger or regret? Tracker wondered.

As though he realized he was being watched, Seth turned away and spoke to Angel's husband, Duke. It was then that Tracker realized the other twin wasn't there.

"Does stuff like this happen often?" Isabeau whispered as the commotion finally began leveling off.

"Eh, at least once every gathering." He sighed. "Mackays draw trouble. Though it's usually other cousins or in-laws instigating it. Been a while since they had fresh blood to hunt."

The Mackays had settled down for the most part since their wild-assed youths. Well, they'd settled down some.

"At least a few years," he amended. This damned family drew trouble like a magnet, and the Augusts in Texas weren't much different as he understood it.

"You should take me home," she told Tracker again. "Before someone else gets hurt. I don't think my conscience could bear it, Tracker."

No, it wouldn't be able to.

"Still think it's just bad luck, baby?" He ran one hand up her back as he asked the question. "Someone's serious this time." He lowered his lips to her ear and asked so quietly that no one else would hear, "Who else knows your sight's returning, Isabeau?"

She froze in his arms for a long moment before lifting her gaze to his face and, just as quietly, said, "Who have you told?"

"Not a soul. But I think someone must have figured it out," he told her. "Don't tell anyone here. Keep it between us. Sheriff Mayes and Doogan are going to want a statement for their little reports. I'll be with you. Be brief. Be honest. But don't mention that."

She nodded, lowering her head, her fingers uncurling from his shirt. He didn't give her a chance to step back from him. He kept his arm around her, kept her at his side. He had a feeling she was more terrified for those at the party than for herself, and that would make it too damned easy for the Augusts to convince her to slip away and return to Texas.

"You know, if you run away, I'll just follow you. Right?" he asked her, realizing the thought of her running away actually made him angry.

She tensed further, giving a little shake of her head.

"Why?" she asked, turning to him once again. "Why would you do that, Tracker?"

"Because whoever did this endangered those I consider mine. He went too far this time. I'm going to kill him for it." And he had a feeling he just might enjoy doing it.

He'd kill the bastard for what he'd been doing to Isabeau alone. Years of believing she was somehow a bad-luck magnet or marked by fate. Someone was desperate to make it appear an accident that they'd tortured her for years. And if Tracker hadn't taken the time her brother and friends should have taken to convince her it was serious, she'd be dead right now rather than standing in his arms.

With her mussed platinum-blond hair and distressed violet eyes, she listened to what was going on around her, keeping her head down whenever possible to avoid revealing the fact that she could see anything at all.

Her sight wasn't clear, but neither did she live in the dark. And he'd understand that more fully once he got her to her house and away from so many listening ears.

He'd take her home in the morning. Until then, he'd be damned if he was leaving her side for a minute. He wouldn't take her safety for granted again.

Never again.

Thankfully, Doogan and the sheriff, Shawn Mayes, kept their questions brief. Natches hadn't had to give them Isabeau's background—they'd known since she'd returned to her home two years before. Mayes had checked into it when his father, a former sheriff, mentioned her parents' deaths. And Doogan knew simply because he was a nosy bastard like that.

But Tracker had watched their expressions and he knew they were drawing the same conclusions he was where the past so-called accidents and near-fatal events were concerned.

Isabeau had been in someone's crosshairs for a while.

Once the questions were over, he helped her move her things from her room to the one next to it. This one was minus a door leading to the outside, and he'd make damned sure she was safe while she was there.

And to that end, information was power.

Closing the door behind them, he took the hangers of clothes and rehung them in the exact same order in the new closet as they had been in the first, just as he'd promised.

When he finished, he strode back to the door and locked it as Isabeau stepped from the bathroom, where she'd carried her overnight bag.

"I need to shower and change clothes," she told him. "It shouldn't take long."

She rubbed at her arms with hands that had been scratched and torn in places on the glass that had covered the floor. Rowdy's wife, Kelly, had cleaned the cuts, but they were superficial enough that they hadn't required bandages.

"I'll wait for you here. We're going to talk before joining the party tonight. . . ."

"I don't think that's a good idea." She shook her head instantly, her expression mutinous. "You're going to keep pushing this, Tracker, someone is going to get hurt. Someone besides me or you. If that happened, it would destroy me."

He narrowed his gaze on her.

"You're getting ready to run, aren't you, little rabbit?" he drawled, his lips curling as mocking amusement shot through him. "Just like always."

She actually thought he was going to allow her to leave while a killer was stalking her ass? It was bad enough her brother and so-called friends hadn't managed to take care of this yet, but he'd be damned if he'd drop the ball on her too.

"I'm not stupid," she sneered, but he could see the fear in those intense violet eyes. "I can't afford you. With your skills and your line of work, you're no doubt more expensive than any schoolteacher could afford. . . ."

"So, why don't we just take my fee out in trade?" he drawled. "I'm certain I'll be more than satisfied with the bargain."

He watched the shock widen her eyes, but by God, that was arousal that flushed her cheeks and added to the heat in those violet orbs.

And he wasn't lying. He was so eager to get her beneath him that his cock was like a hot iron in his pants and had been since the first five minutes he'd spent with her in the truck after that dumbass attempt to make a bullet in Angel's tire appear to be a blowout.

"Tracker, I've heard the women at this party whispering about you. Any one of them would be more than happy to have sex with you. Don't pretend you have to bargain for it." Her hands went to her curvy hips as belligerence seemed to shimmer on the air around her.

"I'm not pretending to want you, sweetheart," he assured her, actually glad that she probably couldn't see his expression. He had no doubt he looked anything but pleasant right now. "I intend to have you in my bed. I am certain I'm going to eliminate the son of a bitch that thought he could kill you right beneath my nose. And I wouldn't take your goddamned money under any circumstances. Those are facts. Period. But if you're feeling beholden enough, a little head goes a long way."

Shock rounded her eyes as complete disbelief seemed to fill her expression. But that flush on her face was more than anger. Far more. She wasn't completely opposed to the idea.

Her gaze shifted away from him then, a hint of nervousness crossing her features.

"I don't know how...." She gave a helpless little shrug before pride suffused her expression and lifted her chin. "So once again, there's little compensation to be had for what's no doubt an exorbitant fee."

She didn't know how?

"Isabeau, it would be a really good time to tell me if you're a virgin or not," he suggested, fists clenching at his sides to keep from immediately releasing the raging hard-on torturing the fuck out of him. "This is no time for pride, sweetheart."

"No." The answer was brief, short, to the point. And infused with just enough anger that he suspected she was innocent enough, sexually, that she may as well be a virgin.

At any other time, he would have walked away. Any other woman and he would have left her that innocence and protected her anyway.

But Isabeau wasn't any other woman.

Before she could consider avoiding him, he had her in his arms, and in the next breath, beneath him in the bed.

Waves of curls spread around her head, and those brilliant eyes were almost glowing. With anger or desire, he was getting ready to find out.

"Get off me, Tracker." Her voice shook, and those pretty lips took on a sheen of moisture as her tongue swiped over them.

He stared into her eyes, certain she saw far more of him than she'd ever admit to, and pushed between her knees, slowly parting her thighs.

Her breathing became deeper, harder, the flush on her face extending beneath the light, sleeveless blouse she wore and spreading to the tops of her breasts.

Tight, hard little nipples tightened beneath her bra, pushing against the material covering it until he could clearly discern them beneath the blouse.

"Get off you?" he murmured, holding her hands pinned to the bed as he lowered his body until the erection beneath the light material of the pants he wore pressed snugly against her denim-covered pussy. "I don't think so. Not quite yet. But if you're really serious about it, just say no."

Her lips parted.

"And if that word comes out of your mouth, the next time, I'll make sure you're begging me before I touch you again, Isabeau. And I can do it."

He could feel that heat, the arousal filling her. She was going to go up in flames once he got his dick inside her and burn him alive.

She glared back at him mutinously, straining lightly against his hold, but she didn't say no, which would have stopped him immediately.

When his lips touched hers, brushed against them, her breathing became harder, but rather than parting the soft curves, she kept them stubbornly closed.

Releasing her wrists, he gripped the back of her hair with one hand, the other spanning her jaw, and her lips parted on a gasp as he laid into the kiss he'd been dying for since he'd been forced to release her earlier.

Deep, hot, her hips arched into him, grinding against the hard width of his cock through the layers of clothes. He released her hair and jaw, grabbed her hands, and pushed them to her breasts.

"Unbutton that fucking blouse," he snarled against her lips, satisfaction surging through him at the little gasp that escaped her lips. "Now, Isabeau. Give me a taste of you."

"Tracker." She whispered his name, and he swore he heard innocence in her voice.

"Do it," he growled. "Now."

He nipped at her, penetrated her lips with his tongue again, and told himself he was crazy for teasing both of them this way.

Finally, the edges of the blouse fell away. Isabeau was fighting for breath now, excitement and arousal shimmering in her face.

"The bra." He pushed for more. "Release it."

He leaned back, watching as slender fingers struggled with the front clasp for a moment, then released it.

He didn't bother demanding she push it aside; he did that for her. And swore he was going to come in his pants.

Smooth flesh, swollen and glistening with perspiration. Tight, pretty pink nipples. Like cotton candy. Damn, he'd always loved cotton candy.

"Lift one to me, baby," he growled. "Feed me a pretty nipple."

She hesitated, a hint of embarrassed uncertainty flashing in her face.

Rotating his hips, caressing that covered pussy, he watched her breath catch and pleasure suffuse her expression.

"Come on, we don't have much time left. Show me you want this." And he knew she wanted it. Wanted him.

Slowly, too slowly for his sanity, her fingers curled beneath one swollen mound as though offering him paradise.

And fuck yes. He was taking it.

Isabeau promised herself she wasn't going to let him kiss her again, wasn't going to let herself weaken.

She wasn't just weakening now; she was melting.

She watched, able to see more than shadow, but not the roughly handsome features she knew he possessed. Still, barely able to keep her eyes opened, she watched as his head lowered.

Then she was lost.

Moist heat covered her nipple, the slow, destructive suction he applied to it tore through her senses and shattered any thought she'd had of what his touch would be like. His teeth rasped, gripped the peak, then his mouth covered it again, drew on it, his tongue working her nipple like a favorite treat.

She knew her nails were digging into his upper arms just beneath the sleeve of his T-shirt, but she couldn't force herself to let him go. All she could do was arch to him and hold back what she knew would be screams of pleasure if she lost that last measure of control.

His hips moved between her thighs as pleasure raked her nipple. The pressure against her clit mixed with surging sensations rippling from her nipple to her womb, clenching in the depths of her pussy.

Oh God, she needed him.

She angled her hips to him, moaning at the exquisite sensations pressing into her clit as he moved to her other breast and treated it with the same hot hunger that he'd given the first one.

Her thighs clenched on his. Each sensation was piling atop the other, tearing at her senses, making her reach for more. She wanted to beg. Wanted to plead with him to strip her, to take her, no matter who or what could be making their way to her door.

"Please . . . Oh God, Tracker." Heated impulses of desperate need were rising inside her, pushing her, clawing at her.

When she felt the clasp and zipper of her jeans release, felt his hips ease back, her breath caught. His fingers slid beneath the material, pushed beneath her panties. She was so slick, so wet, there was no resistance when his fingers parted the bare folds, slid lower.

His lips surrounded her nipple again, sucked it hard, deep, and his fingers found her clit, swollen and pulsing with need. He did rake over it, didn't directly touch the sensitized bud. Instead, fingers gripped just beneath it, catching the thin flesh there that separated his fingers from the throbbing mass of nerve endings, and applied the most exquisite pressure. At the same time, his tongue flicked over her nipple, sucked it, and Isabeau felt ecstasy completely rupture inside her.

His lips covered hers just a heartbeat before she screamed, holding the sound between them as her hips tried to tighten and she fought to buck beneath him. The sensations were uncontrolled, the rapture like an ever-exploding force inside her. Out of control. Throwing her headlong into pure, exquisite sensation.

Oh God, she'd never known pleasure like this. Had never heard of it outside the books she listened to occasionally. But even then, it wasn't like this. Like pure, effervescent rapture.

It was liquid hot, destructive, and over far too soon. She collapsed beneath him, feeling his fingers ease back, his head lift, and she couldn't even make herself open her eyes.

Until a heavy knock came at the door.

"Isabeau?" Saul called from the hall as he tested the doorknob and found it locked. "I need to talk to you, honey."

He needed to talk to her?

Did she even remember how to talk?

Tracker eased from her, hurriedly clipped her bra, and helped her sit up on the bed.

"Isabeau?" The knock was louder this time.

"I'll be out in a while, Saul," she snapped, irrationally irritated with the disturbance. "I'll meet you at the party."

If she dared to open the door, he'd know exactly what she and Tracker had been doing. Or close to it anyway.

Silence met the demand.

"Tracker with you?" There was a note of resignation in his voice. "Forget it, I don't want to know. You have ten minutes and then I'm coming back."

Ten minutes?

Isabeau hung her head, breathing out roughly.

"Get your shower, sweetheart. I'll be in the front room waiting for you. Saul can talk to me if he tries to come back here," Tracker told her.

"No fighting, Tracker," she told him, suddenly tired, overwhelmed. "I can't deal with it."

"No fighting, sweetheart," he agreed, but she heard the deepening of his voice, and she knew no matter her wishes, the twins now had a boundary where Tracker was concerned. "If you promise to wear that pretty dress I hung up for you. The one with all the little blue flowers."

"Fine. Whatever," she sighed.

She liked the feel of that dress. Burke's sister had picked it out for her when she and Burke had come to Kentucky at the beginning of the summer.

Tiny buttons closed the bodice while the skirt fell almost to her knees. It was light and cool, and it made her feel feminine.

"Take your time." A kiss brushed against the top of her head. "If you need me, just yell. I'll hear you."

She just bet he would.

God, she was in so much trouble where this man was concerned, and she knew it.

If her stalker didn't hurry and show himself, then Isabeau was going to end up with a heart so broken, there would be nothing left to ever give another man.

And she knew Tracker wouldn't stay.

He never stayed, Angel had once said. No woman could hold a man whose heart had been destroyed in the wars and battles he'd fought. He'd seen too much, his sister had told her, knew too well the cost of caring for someone, and the ability to do that had been burned out of him because of it.

She sighed wearily as the door closed behind him, and she knew by the empty feeling of the room that she was alone. The overhead light was on, and her vision was clearer than it had been for some reason. She could see not shadows but shapes and color.

TEN

SAUL WAS WAITING IN THE FRONT ROOM, HIS BACK TO THE large picture windows as he watched Tracker step into the room.

He was a man on a mission, and Tracker knew it. And that did not bode well.

"What's on your mind, August?" he asked, the other man's dark scowl an indication that whatever it was, Tracker wasn't going to like it.

Saul rubbed at his jaw a second, his lips quirking wryly before he spoke.

"There's a story I heard years ago, didn't hardly believe it, but maybe I should've," Saul began. "A rumor that a very young Tracker Calloway was held for a week in a certain warlord's dungeon. Tortured past the point where you should have died. When your family finally managed to get to the secured cells in the underground bunker where you were being held, they found not just your lover dead but the warlord and six of his best soldiers as well. One of those soldiers survived, minus a hand, and the nightmare he swore you became shouldn't have been humanly possible."

Those screams echoed in his head; demonic laughter; Kawlee's laughter, then her horror; the warlord's demented screams of pain.

"Then, you and Chance disappeared for several years," Saul continued. "When you returned and took over your parents' rescue team, they say you earned the position in a fight that left most of your male family members lying in the dust, and a threat to kill your father if he didn't step down."

Yeah, that was the short version, Tracker admitted silently.

"Believe in fairy tales now, do you?" Tracker grinned back at him, feeling the ice growing in his soul as Saul's little story gave life to demons Tracker believed vanquished in the past years.

Saul's expression was heavy now, his gaze unyielding. "Isabeau isn't a lying little tramp that would betray her lover, and she doesn't deserve to pay for that woman's actions. You treat your women like sex toys and leave them lying when you're done. You rarely know their names and rarely acknowledge their presence if you see them again." Regret and concern shadowed Saul's voice now. "Don't do that to Isabeau, man. Not just for her sake, but for those who love her. You think you're a demon with a wound that can't be healed, then you haven't met Burke. And you have no idea how deeply Seth and I care for that woman."

Goddamn, he'd never had so much trouble trying to protect one woman, let alone trying to fuck . . . get one into his bed.

He almost betrayed his own inner shock that he couldn't finish that first thought in the same vein that he would have with another woman.

He fucked them. He didn't make love, had no fucking idea what that even meant. And Saul was right. He used the women he fucked.

War whores, his father called them. They'd known the rules just as he did. Knew and understood what he needed at the time.

Those women weren't Isabeau though.

"Is there a point to this?" Tracker asked, even though he knew there was.

"Yeah, there is." Saul nodded. "Seth and I made a mistake, and we realize it. Letting her go because we didn't believe she could handle what we needed from her wasn't the answer. Walk away. We'll take over from here. We love her, you don't."

He almost laughed at the other man.

"Tell me, is Isabeau the only one that isn't aware that the reason you walked away from her is because her brother would have killed you if he found her in bed with both of you?" This would be amusing if it wasn't so close to pissing him off. "Go to hell, August. You want her? See if you can take her. But I think this little chat is because you know damned good and well the chances of that were gone long ago."

"She loves Seth. . . ."

"She never loved Seth." Tracker shook his head, remaining relaxed rather than tensing to fight. "She had a crush. You're her friends, and the men she's allowed into her life because subconsciously she's so terrified someone else will get hurt that she's refused to allow herself to have a man."

The tightening of Saul's jaw and flicker of knowledge in his expression assured Tracker he was right.

"I'm going to finish this where the danger to her is concerned, and whatever develops other than that is none of your fucking business. So go join Seth wherever he's hiding, tell him this little chat didn't work, and don't make the mistake of bringing any of it to Isabeau." He stared back at the twin with icy determination. "While I'm in her life, keep your fucking opinions and your hands to yourselves, or you'll be the ones missing those particular appendages. And maybe a few more. We clear now? Or do we need to discuss this further?"

He could feel the rage threatening to escape, something he rarely had a problem with unless engaged in battle.

"I can't wait till her brother gets here." Saul's smile was pure anticipation.

"Stop the drama, man," Tracker ordered with an edge of pure irritation. Hell, Irk and Jerk were starting to get on his nerves. "Do what you do best. Hide and watch. Stay the fuck out of sight until that son of a bitch makes his next move. Better yet, give a real show of fucking leaving once this party is over. Let us fix this problem for her and worry about the rest later."

Later.

When he left. When she'd need someone to lean on, someone to love her.

That rage suddenly licked at his consciousness, white-hot flames scouring his senses before he jerked it back and barely, just barely refrained from taking August apart.

What the fuck was wrong with him?

"We have anything else to talk about?" The snarl in the words wasn't normal either.

Saul continued to just stare at him for long moments. Finally, he gave a slow shake of his head. "No. I think we've covered everything," he said thoughtfully.

"Good. Then go do whatever you and Seth do when you're not irritating the fuck out of me," Tracker told the other man. "And leave Isabeau the fuck alone tonight. Let her enjoy at least a few hours of this damned party before she has to face her past. That is, if you know what the hell's good for you."

He didn't wait for an answer but turned on his heel and stalked across the hall to the kitchen and the bottle of whiskey he knew the Mackays kept in the freezer there. Right now, it was either a couple of good, bracing shots or shoot an August.

He figured Isabeau would be pissed if he killed an August, so he'd go for the whiskey instead.

ELEVEN

THE EVER-SHIFTING STATE OF HER SIGHT CLEARED FUR-
ther as Isabeau dressed to join the party outside. A hot shower relaxed the small aches and pains from the previous attack. Using
practiced motions of the blow-dryer and her own fingers, she restored
the loose waves that it took very little effort to maintain.

No makeup. She'd learned how to apply it, but she'd never been
comfortable doing so. The one time she'd made the attempt, Burke's
uncle had laughed when he'd seen her, claiming she looked like a
clown.

She was certain she hadn't. Bill wasn't a nice person, and she knew
it. And Kenya had assured her she'd applied the makeup properly.

The fear of misapplying had lingered though.

Pushing away the memory, she pulled on another of the dresses
the Mackay girls had picked out for her. The one Tracker had asked
her to wear. It was a little short, but cool and feminine. The small
straps caused the bodice to drape over her breasts, barely covering
her bra.

But that was a requirement for her clothing. They had to be bra-friendly.

As she checked to make certain the dress was hanging properly, there was a firm, quick knock at the door.

"Ready to party, baby?" Tracker drawled from the other side of the door.

The sudden racing of her heart, the excitement, sense of pleasure, and sensitivity in every erogenous zone of her body warned her that her need for this man went deeper than she liked.

She was in trouble emotionally, and she knew it.

That didn't stop her from moving quickly to the door and opening it.

Isabeau scented a faint hint of whiskey drifting through the darker, natural male scent, and it was sexier than it should be.

HE WAS GOING TO GO TO HELL.

Tracker stepped into the bedroom, closed the door behind him, and pushed Isabeau against the wall. Before she could do more than gasp, he took the kiss he'd been dying for since the last one he'd had.

She was almost fucking addictive.

Almost.

Because he'd managed to deny himself after all. If a man could make it two hours, then he was good. Right?

Hell yeah, he was right.

He took her lips, his tongue pressing inside, fucking her mouth, driving himself insane with the taste of her.

His cock was iron-hard, his balls aching. Lifting her, he guided her thighs to his hips and pressed into her, grinding his erection against the soft flesh of her pussy.

God, he wanted nothing more than to tear her panties off her and thrust so hard and deep inside her that he didn't know where he began or she ended. There was little else he could think about or focus on.

Tearing his lips from hers, forcing himself from the taste of her, he eased back, pressed her legs down until she was standing on her own again. He laid his forehead against her, his breathing ragged, hard.

"Tracker?" She whispered his name, her breathing rough, her body humming with arousal.

All he could think about was how slick and wet, how sweetly responsive and completely immersed in his touch she had been just a few hours previously. The taste of her, the scent of her lingered in his head like the most potent drug or the sweetest aphrodisiac, and he was dying for more. As he stood there, telling himself to let her go, to step back from her, he felt her hands slide from his back to the taut plane of his abs and the buckle of his belt.

Ah hell.

"Isabeau . . ." He meant to stop her. He was going to stop her.

But fuck . . .

The button and zipper of his pants released. One soft silken hand gripped the raging flesh of his hard-on as the other pushed the shirt he wore up his stomach. Her lips pressed to his chest, an inquisitive little tongue licked at his flesh, shooting white-hot pleasure through his nerve endings.

Hell, he didn't think he'd ever felt that, but it was good. Damned good.

And she didn't stop there.

As those hot little kisses, sizzling licks, and tingling rasps of her teeth moved down his body, closer by the second to the sensitive flesh of his cock, Tracker leaned forward, braced his palms flat on the wall, and, forcing his eyes to stay open, watched.

Violet eyes slumberous, her face flushed with feminine hunger, she gripped the stiff stalk of his cock, those pretty pink lips parted, and her tongue swiped a trail of pure sensation across the swollen head.

A grimace pulled at his face, his teeth clenched, and it was all he could do to hold in a growl of pure, debilitating pleasure.

Then her mouth covered the crest, her tongue tucking into the sweet spot just beneath the head, moist heat surrounding it.

God damn.

He was ready to shoot like an untried teenager getting head the first time. Except he wasn't a teenager. He was a grown-assed man with a decade of steely physical control. Control that this woman, with her lips and tongue and hot-as-hell mouth, was fraying to the last thread.

The touch wasn't knowing or that of a woman who had learned how to please a man. It was hesitant, innocent almost, and it was making him crazy. Each draw of her mouth, the look of pleasure on her face, the drowsy sensuality, combined to destroy him.

He dropped one hand from the wall to thread his fingers into her hair but not to guide her. Just to touch her. He had to touch her, feel all those silken waves of hair in his hand.

Despite his best intentions, his hips moved against her mouth, fucking her lips by small degrees, and he groaned at the pure lash of sensation.

God, it was good. So fucking good.

Had he been too long without . . . Another thought he couldn't complete.

This had nothing to do with any faceless, nameless woman he could have at any given time. This was Isabeau. And those little cries that escaped her throat and vibrated on the incredibly sensitive head of his cock were almost his undoing.

His balls were drawn tight, aching with the need to release.

Hell, he'd been aching for release since he'd caught sight of this woman standing on the street with his sister and her friends. Laughing. Violet eyes so bright.

Eyes that stared up at him now, glazed with pleasure and desire as she stroked his cock with her mouth, her hands. It was the hottest thing he could remember seeing. Feeling.

"Fuck. Isabeau . . ." he whispered as the suckling pressure pushed him to that point of no return. "Baby. Pull back. I'm going to come right in that sweet mouth if you don't."

The sense of anticipation, of excitement that filled her expression was telegraphed through that wicked tongue and ecstasy-giving mouth.

His hand tightened in her hair, not restricting her movements, but ensuring she stayed in place at the same time.

Sensation raced from the head of his cock to his balls, jagged forks of heated pleasure as he felt the muscles of his thighs tightening one fiery second before the rest of his body followed suit.

He couldn't hold back the ragged groan that tore from his throat any more than he could stop the pure, fire-hot rapture from exploding through his senses.

Fuck.

It was a blow job, just a fucking blow job.

It shouldn't be pulling his release from him with so much pleasure that it exceeded even the hottest full-blown sex he'd ever had with any other woman.

Nameless, faceless, or otherwise.

Hell, it almost took him to his toes it was so fucking good.

It was dangerously good.

TWELVE

FINISHING HER COFFEE THE NEXT MORNING, ISABEAU stared out over the lake from the porch, her vision just clear enough to make out the boats on the water and surrounding hills with their thick forests. Color and light, but still, her vision wasn't clear.

And the nightmares had returned.

She hadn't awakened screaming, but she'd been crying when she awoke. This time, there were parts of the nightmare that she remembered though. Her father staring sightlessly at her mother as she lay mere feet from him.

Blood stained the wood floor. Her father's, her mother's, meeting between them, connecting them even after death. But as her gaze lifted to see her murderer, her sight had gone black, and she'd awakened with a start.

Her memories were returning.

But did she want to remember?

"We have a problem," Tracker announced as he stepped from the house to the porch and headed toward her.

Of course there was a problem. There'd been a problem since before her arrival.

She watched as he stomped over the porch until he stood in front of her, arms crossed as he leaned against the thick support post across from her.

Even with her vision still incredibly blurry, she could tell how tall, how strong he was. And as much as she hated the realization, she was far too susceptible to him. Both physically as well as emotionally. Because it hurt her heart to stare at him and realize that she couldn't please him.

"Is that problem the reason I'm sitting here on the porch rather than heading home?" she asked him.

Was it the reason she'd spent the night alone? The reason he'd stalked from her room while she was still on her knees last night?

Her face flamed at the thought.

Turning her head from him, she stared to her side. She could make out the porch, the yard stretching to the narrow beach, and a few lone houseboats still secured there.

"It's the reason," he agreed. "Chance drove to your house this morning and went through it. He found just what we suspected. Several devices equipped with video as well as audio capabilities."

She swung around to him once again, staring at him in shock.

"There was what?" She blinked back at him.

"One in the bedroom vent," he told her. "Just above your bed. One in the living room vent, one in the kitchen and a guest room as well as the basement. You've been under constant surveillance. That's how someone knows your sight's returning, isn't it?"

Isabeau could feel her breath coming ragged and sharp as panic rose inside her.

Cameras? Someone had been watching her?

"They've probably been there since I came home," she said, her voice coming out as a whisper as she felt her throat tighten. "And yes, whoever was watching me would know my sight is returning. And that I've been possibly remembering parts of that summer as well."

She'd celebrated during rare moments of sight, cursed it when the heavy mists returned. She'd had nightmares in her bed and discussed with a few close friends her suspicion that her father would have never killed her mother. And several weeks ago she'd told Mattie she'd remembered parts of the week before her parents' deaths.

"That explains why they made the attempt to blow the tire out and cause Angel's truck to go over the cliff." He turned, staring at her fully now. "It's why they made the attempt here by breaching the house. They're scared. That makes them dangerous. But it also makes them predictable."

He sounded so confident. So in control. She felt anything but in control and confident. She wanted to hide. To run away and find a way to escape. And there was no way to do that.

"What do I do now?" she asked him. "My sight's coming back, a little at a time, but it's still too blurry to be of any use in defending myself."

She couldn't go back to her house, and she couldn't return to the ranch. She had no idea who to trust.

Except Tracker.

She could trust him to protect her body, at least.

"I have the defending part covered," he grunted. "Before entering the house, Chance set up a jamming device, just in case," he informed her. "Whoever's watching will think the devices malfunctioned before he arrived, if they're watching. He'll stay put until we get there. He's deactivated them but left them in place. I suggest we return to the house as though we're none the wiser."

As though they had no idea who was behind it. Which they didn't.

She could feel her insides trembling as she fought to keep from shaking on the outside.

Someone had been watching her.

Watching her dress and undress.

Sleep and dream.

They'd seen her each time she stumbled, seen her when she'd sat and cried with loneliness.

She'd been violated in a way that left her cringing to her very soul.

And she doubted it was the first time.

"This is why the attempts have always been close," Tracker said. "Baby, you've been working your guardian angels overtime."

Isabeau lowered her head, staring at her hands for long moments before she pushed herself to her feet.

"Excuse me," she whispered. "I need to go in for a moment. . . ."

She needed to be alone.

She needed to make sense of it.

His voice hardened as he gripped her elbow, drawing her to a stop. "You're not calling those fucking twins or your brother. You're going to get in the truck, and I'm taking you home."

She shook her head, desperate to escape now.

Knowing someone was trying to kill her and knowing she'd been spied on to that extent was too much.

"I need to think. . . ."

"There's nothing to think about," he bit out, his voice graveled now. "You'll carry on, business as usual, and Chance and I will take care of the rest."

"There is not business as usual. Don't you understand that?" she cried out, swinging around to face him. "Someone has just been waiting on this. Waiting for my vision to return. Waiting for me to have hope that I could have my life back, just to plan to take it. How can anything be business as usual now?"

She reached up, running her fingers through her hair before gripping it for a second at the back of her head in a gesture of confusion.

"Because you're not alone anymore," he stated, the hard tone of his voice not in the least reassuring. "Because I swear to you, before I leave, the danger will be at an end. You'll have your life back."

Without him.

That thought smacked her senses, almost causing her to flinch.

God, at what point over this weekend had she allowed herself to care if he stayed or not?

She didn't care, she assured herself. She was just scared.

No, she was fucking terrified.

"I need to call Burke. . . ." she whispered.

She needed a voice of reason.

"Isabeau." His voice gentled. "How do you think someone knows where you are, knows your habits and when to strike? He doesn't just know you, baby, he knows your family. Telling Burke is the same thing as warning the person who wants to kill you that you're protected and we know he's coming."

Pain ripped through her.

Of course it was someone she knew. Someone who knew the family. How else did they always know where she'd moved to, no matter how quiet Burke tried to keep it? And she knew her brother was incredibly secretive.

She was alone in this, she told herself.

But hadn't she been all along, to some extent?

"Your bags are in the truck," Tracker continued. "Chance is in place and waiting for us, and I have friends watching our backs on the drive to Somerset. I'm not taking chances here. You're safe."

She was destroyed. Everything inside her was breaking apart, and she had no idea how to stop it.

"Yeah," she repeated softly. "Safe." Drawing in a deep breath, she gave a quick, sharp nod. "Let's go, then, and get it over with. Then you can have your life back too."

He could leave and pretend he never knew her. Had never touched her.

She didn't wait for him to respond. Unfolding the cane she carried, she made her way from the porch to the truck. Behind her, Tracker stayed close, his hand at the small of her back, subtly guiding her.

She could see enough to make her way but kept that to herself for now. Along with everything else she was keeping to herself. Not just her fear and pain, but her response to the man behind her as well.

She ached to turn to him, to feel his arms around her, to lose herself in the pleasure he could give her. A pleasure she couldn't give him evidently.

And she feared that would be her greatest regret.

HE'D MISCALCULATED THIS WOMAN'S EFFECT ON HIM.

Tracker admitted that, in some distant part of his brain, as he navigated the narrow route that led to the main road.

She affected him to a point that he knew she was far more dangerous to him than anyone, even the bastard who had nearly destroyed him years ago. Because she had the ability to remind him of every dream that had been shredded inside his soul.

Damn her.

When he'd stared down at her the night before, seeing the innocence, feminine need, and vulnerable emotion in her face, his breath had nearly stopped in his chest. She'd looked fucking radiant.

So goddamned beautiful she stole his breath. And she'd scared the shit straight out of him. To the point that for the first time in his life, he'd run.

He'd run from the one thing he craved more than breathing.

Touching Isabeau.

Because he couldn't remember a time when he'd needed anything as desperately as he needed her, and he knew she could destroy him with that need.

This wasn't a woman who understood the rules of the world he moved in. She had no idea how to wield a knife, shoot a gun, and he doubted she'd ever been in a fistfight in her life. She would be completely defenseless against her enemy, and even more so against the enemies he'd made in his life.

And it would break his soul if something happened to her.

That knowledge made him weak. Knowledge like that made a man too careful, because he had something to lose. Something that could suffer with his loss.

And he knew the horror she could suffer if he blinked.

Fuck.

Pushing his hand through his hair, he tried to push back the direction of his thoughts. He'd figure it out once he found the person trying to kill her. There was no sense in driving himself crazy with it now.

But it was driving him crazy.

From his hard dick to the ache in his chest and these damned unfamiliar thoughts. She was already making him crazy.

And what the fuck was with that ache in his chest?

Glancing over at her, he took in the composed features of her face and remembered the color of her eyes moments ago when she'd swung around to look at him.

Those violet eyes had blazed bright, a bit darker than normal as her expression reflected the turmoil rising inside her.

It was like he could feel that turmoil, that confusion and . . . help-lessness.

A sense of helplessness.

Yeah, he knew that feeling after all, long ago and far away. The horrible weight of knowledge that he was between the fires of hell and the devil's pitchfork. And he knew he'd never had that feeling reach out to him because another person was feeling it.

The clients he protected rarely felt such vulnerable emotions. They felt anger, even rage. Terror or uncertainty, but never help-lessness.

She wasn't angry, wasn't scrambling for a position of safety, even in her own mind. She was scared, but not terrified, and he couldn't blame her for the terror if that was what she felt.

This was a woman who had always found a road around the danger facing her, lived with the knowledge that even if it was just bad luck, death was breathing down her neck.

Until now.

No matter how hard she tried, she couldn't find a way to protect not just herself, but those trying to help her.

"I've spent my life protecting others, Isabeau," he told her, realizing the truth of it. "J. T. and Mara didn't believe in protecting their children, even as babies. It's one of the reasons I can't bring myself to call them *Mom* and *Dad*. We traveled with them, learned when to be quiet, how to fight, and before our teens, learned how to protect. There's nothing your stalker can do that I haven't learned how to counter."

Her head lowered, and from the corner of her gaze he saw the way her hands clenched on her cane.

"I trust you to protect me," she stated, her voice soft, certain. She wasn't lying.

But that feeling of helplessness still nagged at him.

What the hell was he going to do about her?

He ached for her until his back teeth hurt. His dick was so damned hard it was like iron in his pants, and he wanted nothing more than to hold her, comfort her, and fuck her until they both dropped in exhaustion.

Hell, maybe he was the one feeling helpless.

And if that was true, then he was up shit's creek. It meant she was starting to matter, and he had no idea how to make it stop.

He had no choice but to put a stop to it though. He couldn't, wouldn't allow himself to accept what caring for her might mean. To accept that he was giving anyone—not just the enemy, but her—that much control over him.

"My father didn't kill my mother, did he?" she asked as he pulled onto the main road and headed for her home. "Someone killed them. And then tried to kill me."

J. T. and Mara might have been lousy fucking parents, but they were damned intuitive when it came to profiling a crime. And they were certain Carmichael Boudreaux hadn't had it in him to hurt either his wife or his child. Not for any reason.

"That's what we think," he agreed. "Dawg and Natches knew your parents well, and they never believed he killed your mother or tried to hurt you. We believe the attempts on your life were made by the same person who killed them. Evidence suggests a reluctance to hurt you, but whoever it is is running scared now. Your sight's coming back, and something in your nightmares may suggest your memories are close to returning as well."

"Then I saw the person that killed them." It wasn't a question. "And it was someone I might have trusted."

She breathed out heavily and turned her head to stare through the window at her side.

"I think you've always known that, Isabeau," he guessed, glancing at her in time to see the subtle flinch in response to his words. "That's why you've kept running, kept refusing to accept that each attempt against you was an attempt to kill you. Believing it was bad luck made it easier to accept."

Human nature could be a bitch, especially on those who felt themselves to be defenseless.

"Maybe it will all be over soon," she said, her voice so soft he barely caught it.

"It will be. I promise."

HE PROMISED.

Those words were still ringing in Isabeau's head as Tracker pulled into the driveway beside her home. Sunlight spilled around the house, and she could almost see the way it sat on the little rise above the street, the steps that led from the house to the grassy yard, the shade the huge oak tree cast around it.

The covered porch with its lazy swing, the tall privacy fence that enclosed the generous backyard. The ranch-style house had been her mother's pride and joy. The large open living room, dining room, and kitchen had been perfect for entertaining dinner guests, and her mother had done so often.

The whole house was roomy and welcoming. When she'd returned, she'd felt that welcome as soon as she stepped into the house. Like warm, ghostly arms surrounding her.

She felt it every time she came back.

Moving in behind Tracker, she felt that warmth, sensed it. It was a home that had only known love, and that love had infused it.

The love her parents had felt for each other, for her, and for the life they'd lived. They'd been happy, just as she remembered. Her father hadn't been the monster he'd been portrayed to be. He'd been her father, tall, proud, and full of joy.

"Chance will get your bags in," he told her.

She nodded at that. "I think I'll lie down for a while. I'm tired."

Exhausted. Scared. Fighting to accept that someone she knew, and probably cared for at one time, had destroyed her life and was still trying to destroy it.

"Isabeau." He caught her arm as she turned toward the hall leading to her bedroom. "About last night . . ."

"No." She jerked from him as she lifted her hand in a stopping motion. "We're not discussing last night."

She couldn't bear the thought of it.

Humiliating heat rushed beneath her skin even as the need for him seemed to intensify.

"Isabeau . . ."

"You made your wishes clear, leave it at that," she snapped, the anger and hurt she felt escaping that place she'd pushed it to just to deal with it.

"Did I, now?" The deepening tone of his voice sent a surge of pure hungry need to strike her senses.

"Yes. Leave it alone, and I'll make certain I do the same. Now if you'll excuse me, I'm going to shower and rest for a while." She escaped him as fast as possible, not even bothering to use the cane now that she was in the house.

Where she'd once believed she was safe from spying eyes.

It didn't even matter anymore. She may as well call the doctor and set up that appointment to have her eyes checked, to see exactly what was going on.

It wouldn't matter if anyone suspected now. Someone had been watching and listening anyway. They already knew the danger she represented to them.

Folding the cane, she tossed it on her dresser as she stepped into her room. Catching the door with her other hand, she pushed it closed, perhaps harder than she'd meant to if the crack against the door-frame was any indication.

Her breathing hitched, and before she could stop it, moisture filled her eyes.

Not that it fell.

Hell no, she wasn't crying because she couldn't please a man; that was something she'd already known. It was the reason why she rarely dated, why she was so alone.

Breathing deeply, she pulled her phone from the small crossbody purse she carried, then lifted the purse's strap from her and placed it next to the cane on the dresser.

Inserting one of the earbuds from the small attached case, she activated the phone.

"Call Jakob," she stated quietly.

A second later she heard the ring of the other phone through the earpiece.

"Hey, girl, what's doin'?" Jakob's deep voice came over the line, as somber as always.

"You owe me a favor," she reminded him. "I'm collecting."

Silence filled the line for long moments.

"This is gonna get my ass kicked, right?" he sighed on a heavy breath.

"I just need you to try to keep Burke home," she told him quietly. "And if he heads to Kentucky, I need you to let me know immedi-ately."

Jakob was Burke's best friend. If anyone could keep him out of Kentucky, then it was him.

"What's goin' on, girl?" he demanded. "I know you had another accident. You in trouble?"

Trouble? Isabeau didn't think that accurately described the situ-ation.

"I'm not in trouble." Yet. "But I need you to do this for me. Come on, Jakob, you owe me," she reminded him firmly.

He was silent again. Thoughtful, that was Jakob. But it was tearing her nerves apart.

"Mac and Fiona are gone, and Bill left yesterday," Jakob told her, a bit irritably. "The fact that no one's at the ranch to make decisions should keep him busy until he heads to California. If it doesn't, I'll holler at ya."

It was obvious he didn't like it though.

"I'm not in trouble, Jakob," she told him again. "Don't sound so grouchy."

Jakob snorted at that. "Girl, you are trouble. But if the situation changes, you let me know. We'll fix it. You hear me?"

"I hear you, and I promise I'll call." She crossed her fingers on that one.

She wasn't really in trouble though, she assured herself. Tracker was here. He was protecting her.

So she wasn't lying. Right?

She assured herself that was the case, disconnected the phone, and forced herself to the shower. She just wanted to sleep, wake up, and find out it was all just a crazy, messed-up dream rather than her reality.

That was all she wanted.

JAKOB DISCONNECTED THE PHONE THEN SHOVED THE device into the side pocket of his pants while meeting Burke Weston's predatory gaze.

The other man was one pissed fucker. Not that Jakob could blame him, but the anger sizzling on the air around him could become a problem.

"I can't believe she actually made that fucking call," Burke cursed before turning back to the window and staring out.

"I can't believe she lied to me so easy." Jakob shook his head.

The apartment was on the second story, sheltered by the limbs of the tree growing outside it, and with a perfect view to the front of Isabeau's house.

"I wasn't able to reactivate the video feed," Burke stated, his tone clipped. "Either one of those infernal internet resets hit it, or Chance found the bugs."

Jakob was betting Grogan found the bugs, but he didn't say the words. There was already one hole in the drywall from Burke's fist; they didn't need another one.

"Her sight's returning; her nightmares indicate her memories won't be far behind," he reminded the other man. "All we have to do is stay out of sight and wait."

Because if she remembered, every Mackay in the county as well as law enforcement would show up at Isabeau's house. Once that happened, things might get ugly.

"Get hold of our contact," Burke ordered then. "I want to know what the fuck is going on and find a way to get a fucking bug in that house. When this happens, we'll have to move fast."

Fast wasn't the word for it.

Walking from the living room to the bedroom of the apartment, Jakob made the calls. Once he was finished, he stepped to the wide window and, lifting a slat on the shade, looked out to the Boudreaux home.

So far, the Augusts hadn't made an appearance after supposedly leaving the party and heading back to Texas. But if they showed up at the August ranch, he'd know it. Someone was waiting for them if it did happen.

Chance Grogan had left several hours before and hadn't returned.

Word was he'd hooked up with some piece of ass from the party at the Mackays'.

And, so far, they still had about zero information on Tracker Calloway.

Born to J. T. and Mara Calloway, residents of Bermuda. He traveled between there and Kentucky often because of his sister, Angel. No information on her either, other than the basic born, raised, educated, etc.

Tracker and Angel Calloway had been raised with Chance Grogan and worked as technical specialists for a variety of companies over the years. Computer work mostly, though Angel Calloway had also worked as a companion of sorts to a few high-profile families.

Nothing indicated they could be a problem except for the fact that somehow the too-rough, too-scarred Tracker Calloway had taken up with Isabeau at that party and, by all reports, had become her lover.

Seth and Saul August had confirmed that piece of information. And surprisingly enough, warned Burke that Tracker was probably one of the most dangerous men they knew.

Hell, he'd met Calloway and Grogan in a little Mexican border town several years ago in a bar that none of them should have been in. They were big, muscular men. Scarred, well-traveled, possibly military, but once talking to them, he hadn't considered them a threat. They'd all been at the wrong place at the right time when a cartel fight had broken out.

Calloway and Grogan had handled themselves, but Jakob knew a lot of men who could do that without being part of the dangerous underworld he and Burke visited far too often.

There was more to Tracker Calloway than they could find though, evidently, and Jakob couldn't help but think the other man was a problem. A serious problem.

And one that would have to be dealt with.

THIRTEEN

HER VISION WAS DEFINITELY RETURNING FOR GOOD.

A week later Isabeau stepped from the ophthalmologist's office, her heart in her throat and hope clawing at the sense of futility she'd felt since returning from the party with Tracker.

After a battery of tests and an MRI the doctor had ordered two days before, he was now certain the blindness had either healed or reversed. The impact of the bullet to her skull and resulting injury to her brain had been the cause of the blindness. Several fragments of her skull had been dug out of her brain at the time, and the doctors had feared the damage to her sight was irreversible.

Isabeau had feared it was irreversible.

According to the specialist, there was a marked change to the damage that tests taken a year after she'd been shot had showed, indicating the changes were permanent.

Holding her prescription for protective sunglasses, Isabeau stepped back into the waiting room.

Everything was still incredibly blurry, and according to the doctor it might be for a while yet, or her vision could return in an instant.

It was blurry. Too blurry to distinguish features, but form and color were becoming clearer.

As Tracker rose to his feet, she could tell he was wearing black cargo pants and a black T-shirt. He was tall, with broad shoulders and dark hair, and she could distinguish the hint of blue eyes.

She knew he carried a scar on his face, and several on his hard stomach and thighs. She'd felt those during the few times she'd been able to touch him and knew the wounds that caused them must have been horrible ones.

"Ready to go?" The dark tone never failed to resonate through her senses like a stroke of pleasure.

Isabeau gave a brief nod. "I need to stop down the hall and choose a pair of prescription sunglasses. He said you can't miss it," she told him as they stepped from the office. "It shouldn't take long."

"Take your time," he assured her patiently.

"Will you pick a pair for me?" she asked, keeping her voice low. "Everything's still really blurry. I'd like to have a nice pair."

"Of course," he agreed.

Tracker glanced down at the top of Isabeau's head, that ache in his chest irritating as hell.

Her hand lay against his arm comfortably, naturally, as he guided her down the hall.

She walked more confidently now, not that she hadn't before, but he could see the difference now that her eyesight was improving.

"The doctor's certain the changes are permanent," she told him, and he could hear a thread of fear and of hope in her voice. "He guesses, according to the changes and what the MRI showed, that I could actually return to normal before winter."

Excitement filled her voice as she looked up at him, and it sparkled in her eyes. For a moment, the reality of the danger she faced was pushed back, and happiness filled her face.

And fuck, she was so damned pretty it was all he could do not to push her against a wall and kiss the living daylights out of her.

"Here's the door," he told her, pausing to open it and allow her to move in ahead of him. "Let's try some on, see how they feel, and go from there."

The smile she gave him was a little shy but filled with hope and a glimmer of happiness. That happiness was something he hadn't seen in the past week.

After an hour going through glasses, trying them on, working through different styles, and Tracker describing to her what each of them looked like, Isabeau settled on a pair that would protect her vision and compliment her face.

The dainty wire frames were light with a hint of rosy color around the dark lens. The prescription was in stock, and after several hours' wait, they were able to return for the glasses.

Tracker used the time to take her to lunch and give Chance the opportunity to try to identify whoever had followed them.

The fact that they'd been followed was a certainty. The who and why were the questions Tracker wanted answers to. Unfortunately, whoever it was knew what the hell they were doing, because Chance was unable to identify them.

It was dark by the time he escorted Isabeau back into her home.

Chance's arrival ahead of them ensured there were no bugs active in the house even if someone could have found a way past the other man's electronic video and audio surveillance. Unlike Isabeau's stalker, Chance knew how to hide his electronic eyes and ears.

"I need to return a few calls," Isabeau told him as she moved for her bedroom. "I'll likely be a while."

"Isabeau." He stopped her as she turned away. "I know you're getting impatient, but now's not the time to worry your brother or try to leave."

"I know that." She gave a quick nod of her head. "But if I ignore his call, he'll just head out here anyway. He worries."

He tried to protect her, but as he often told her, he couldn't protect her against her decisions.

"I know he does," he said softly, feeling his fingers curl into fists as he fought to keep from touching her. "I have a sister too."

And he knew he'd have been in Kentucky within twenty-four hours of that so-called blowout if it were Angel being targeted. The fact that Burke Weston hadn't showed up bothered him.

It bothered him more than he wanted to admit.

"I know," she whispered. "It's why you're here, remember? To kill whoever endangered her when they tried to kill me."

His jaw clenched.

Vulnerable, uncertain. The look on her face had the power to make him ache to deny those words. Angel wasn't the only reason he'd decided he was going to catch the bastard. Anyone who thought torturing Isabeau was acceptable needed to die.

"Yeah," he agreed, his gaze sliding to her lips as if he could feel them against his, taste her kiss against his tongue.

It was all he thought about anymore, all he dreamed about. When he could sleep, that was.

"Get away from me," he growled, knowing if she didn't move, if she didn't get the hell away from him, he was going to end up fucking her against the wall. "Right now. Go."

The change that came over her expression was fascinating, the slight widening of her eyes, the way her face tightened. Then her eyes narrowed, and he swore he watched a flame leap to life inside the violet color.

"Get away from you?" she enunciated clearly, all but slapping him with the words. "No one's holding a gun to your head, asshole. Move yourself if you find my presence so offensive to you."

The clear challenge and confrontational attitude were enough to have his dick pounding and his balls aching for release.

Damn her. She had no idea just how iffy his control was right now. And the problem was, he couldn't force himself away from her.

"I won't fall in love with you," he informed her, desperate to send her running. "Do you understand me, Isabeau? I'll fuck you until we're both exhausted, and when it's over, I'll walk away with no regrets."

For a moment, anger and hurt flashed in her expression before just as quickly it was gone.

"No regrets, Tracker?" she questioned him then. "Who are you trying to fool, me or you? I have no doubt you'll walk away, but unlike the women you've walked away from before, I won't be forgotten so easily."

The feminine anger and aroused gleam in her eyes were mesmerizing.

"You're wrong." He was bluffing and he knew it. "You're going to end up hurt, Angel will get pissed, and the Mackays will piss me the fuck off. And it won't change anything."

"Then walk away, Tracker." She had the temerity to actually dare him as she stared up at him. "It's a big house. And you don't order me to move, or to get away from you when you have two working legs, and from what I saw that last night at the lake house, you damned well know how to use them."

At the lake house, when he'd spilled his release into her sweet mouth while watching the pure, unadulterated pleasure in her expression. And he'd known, in that moment, Isabeau could destroy him.

It had taken everything in him, every fucking ounce of self-control he possessed that night, to leave her kneeling on the floor and stalk from the room.

He'd called himself every kind of bastard possible, and kicked himself a thousand times, even knowing it was the kindest thing he could have done, for both of them.

He'd had the strength to do it then. He didn't have it now.

Before he could debate the action or stop himself, he had his hands on her. Whirling her around, he turned her face-first against the wall. The surprised little gasp she gave only fueled his arousal and did nothing to dampen the lust beginning to overwhelm him.

He palmed her neck with one hand, pulling her head back as he lowered his lips to her cheek. Her hands were flat against the wall, her breathing harder now, as he felt her pulse racing beneath his fingers.

"I could take you like this," he growled against her cheek. "Push those pants to your ankles and fuck you until you're screaming with your release. Is that what you want, Isabeau?"

He watched through narrowed eyes as her tongue peeked out to lick her lips slowly.

"It doesn't matter if that's how I want it," she panted. "I wouldn't be able deny it any more than you were able to walk away."

Tracker slid his other hand between the wall and her stomach, pushed it beneath her top, and slid upward until he could cup her breast. It was swollen, firm, her nipple hard beneath his thumb.

A whimper escaped her lips, pushing him closer to that edge where control was lost and nothing else mattered but the lust.

"You want gentle touches and flowery words," he sneered despite the regret tugging at him. "Sweet romance and candlelight. You'll never have that with me. Ever."

His fingers tightened marginally at her throat to emphasize his statement.

"I didn't have it that last night at the lake either," she snapped back, trying to ignore the need burning between them. "I assume you're capable of at least allowing me a chance to orgasm this time?"

The sarcastic little question had disbelief surging through him.

She hadn't asked if he was capable of making her come, but if he'd give her a chance to come. As though she would be the one to control her orgasms. The pure, sweet innocence in her question was almost his undoing.

"Isabeau, tell me the fucking truth," he snarled, his hand moving from her breast to the thin little belt cinching her soft capris. "Are you a virgin?"

She looked back at him, lifting to him as he undid the zipper of her pants.

"Are you?" She stared back at him challengingly. As though her question was all he needed for an answer.

And perhaps it was, because they both knew he was no virgin.

He pushed her pants from her hips and slid his hand between her thighs, cupping her pussy and feeling the dampness that met his fingers through her panties.

Fuck, she was wet. So slick and hot that the thin material did nothing to contain it.

She needed.

He eased his fingers beneath the material, his body tightening at the helpless little cry that escaped her.

"Fuck. So slick and wet, baby," he groaned. "I bet you taste like the sweetest candy."

He sank one finger inside her, his eyes closing at the snug confines and wet heat that spilled at his penetration.

Sliding back, he lifted his hand, crossing it over her breasts as he brought his finger to his lips and tasted her.

Sweet summer heat met his taste buds. Pure feminine sugar, he thought, amazed that he'd never tasted anything so tempting. A pure heated taste he knew he could become addicted to.

And he needed more of it.

Jerking back from her, he turned her again, pushed her back against the wall, and went to his knees in front of her. He pushed her legs apart, lifted her knee with one hand and pulled her leg over his shoulder, laying his lips to her glistening folds.

"Tracker . . ." She cried out his name, her hands gripping his hair as he shoved his tongue inside her, desperate for more of her.

Fucking his tongue inside her, Tracker released his pants and freed the hard length of his cock, his fingers gripping it and stroking up to clench around the throbbing head.

Fuck, he was going to come to the taste of her. Like an untried kid at his first taste of pussy.

The taste of this pussy was exquisite though. Female nectar. And too damned good to walk away from again.

Isabeau fought to breathe, to remain standing, to hold on to the lightning-fast strikes of sheer ecstasy long enough to orgasm from the wicked, hungry strokes of Tracker's tongue. Instead, the sensations built and gathered until she was shaking, trembling with the need for release.

A release he seemed in no hurry to give her. No matter how she begged or cried out in demand, he refused to allow her to slip over that edge.

He licked, thrust his tongue inside her, and sent flames raging straight to her womb, only to pull out and lick and sip with hungry intent around her clit before returning to send his tongue tunneling inside her again.

She wanted to scream out in need but couldn't find the breath to force the sound out. She had to concentrate to just drag enough oxygen into her lungs.

"Tracker, please," she panted, her hands clenching in his hair as she strained toward him. "Oh God, please let me . . ."

She needed to orgasm. She needed to orgasm so bad she was shaking with it. She could feel the edge just out of reach as he played with her body.

And he was playing with it.

With every lick of his tongue, every caress of calloused fingers against her thighs and brush of his hair against her skin. His tongue stroking around her clit, flickering against the little bundle of nerves and driving her insane as he built that need higher. Each thrust of his tongue inside her, each little lick and deep male groan . . .

"Did I give you enough time to come, baby girl?" he growled as he pulled back and surged to his feet.

Isabeau's eyes flew opened and widened in shock. Her lips parted to cry out in protest when he gripped her rear, lifted her, and pushed her against the wall as he guided her legs to his hips.

"Damn," he groaned. "No condom."

Isabeau shook her head, desperate, pleasure tearing through her as the wait seemed agonizing.

"I'm protected," she gasped. "The pill . . . Don't stop."

He wasn't stopping.

"Is this what you want, baby?" He moved one hand to grip his cock and rub the head between the sensitive folds as he held her with the other arm.

Isabeau stilled. The feel of his cock pressing against her entrance, stretching her with erotic heat, had her breath catching. She was too inexperienced. She hadn't had sex in years.

But that didn't stop her from moving against him, her body desperate for the pleasure pain beginning to burn inside her.

He penetrated her by slow degrees, stretching her inner flesh as she cried out with the sensations ricocheting through her.

Fire and ice, pleasure and pain.

"Hold on, baby," he whispered at her ear, his lips moving to her neck in an erotic little bite.

Her hands clenched on his shoulders, and she felt him pause, felt his muscles bunch as one hand clenched on her rear, the other at her thigh, and in one smooth thrust, he pushed fully inside her.

Her back arched. A long, low moan escaped her as she rolled the back of her head against the wall.

There was no escaping the fiery sensations or the throbbing flesh buried inside her. Stretching her, filling her to the point that pleasure and pain combined in a mix that raced through her system like wildfire.

"That's it, Isabeau," he crooned, his voice dark, wicked. "Take all of me."

He held one hip securely, his hips shifting in slow, destructive little thrusts that stroked her inner muscles and encouraged her slick response to spill around him as he let her body adjust.

Not that there was much room to adjust. She knew she was inexperienced, but she also knew the two lovers she'd had before weren't nearly quite so blessed either.

"Tracker." She moaned his name, moving helplessly against him as her knees tightened at his hips. Each stroke inside her body, each slow invasion sent those flaming lashes of sensation tearing through her.

She felt her shirt rip, the clasp of her bra releasing between her breasts, and then Tracker got serious about destroying her mind. His head bent, and he caught a nipple in his mouth, drawing on it hungrily as each retreat of his cock lengthened, each thrust inside her becoming harder, quicker.

She could hear the harsh cadence of his breathing as she gasped for air, the inferno rising inside her until she knew that when it took her, she'd never be the same.

His tongue flicked at her nipple, his mouth suckling her, and the sounds of her own sharp cries retreated in the distance as each heavy thrust inside her had her clawing for more. Each brush of his flesh against her clit, each draw of his mouth on her nipple, had her reaching harder, more desperately for the chaos growing closer and threatening to explode inside her.

"That's it, baby girl." The sound of his voice was more a snarl. Her body tightened, clamped down on his cock as he moved inside her, in an attempt to hold him still when she needed him to move harder, faster. "I have you. Just like this."

She tried to scream as he began fucking her harder, faster. His iron-hard flesh pumped inside her, and she swore he swelled further, hardened more, and the pleasure pain of his possession intensified until she felt herself exploding with such an overload of ecstasy that she wasn't certain she could survive it.

She arched, jerked in his arms, cried out his name, and sank her teeth in his shoulder as a sense of madness whipped through her. Maddening, overwhelming, irresistible rapture fragmented through her until she was certain, clear to her soul, that she would never be the same again.

And just when she thought it was over, when she thought she could breathe, she heard a wicked chuckle at her ear.

"Oh, baby, we're not quite finished yet."

Tracker knew the second he began pushing inside the fisted little channel that nothing would ever be the same. He'd never take another woman without thinking of Isabeau.

He'd spilled into his hand before he'd ever finished licking at the sweet syrup raining from her. His cock hadn't softened though; if anything, it had become harder, his need for her more powerful. But what it had done was give him just a bit more control. It hadn't eased the overpowering hunger for her. It had deepened it, made him more determined to mark her soul as deep as she was marking his.

Holding her against him, he moved from the hall, barely making it to her bedroom. He didn't bother with the bed, but propped her on the top of the dresser, pushed her back against the mirror, and, angling her hips to suit him, held her beneath her knees and watched the sweet invasion of her body as he pumped inside her.

"Tracker?" She sounded shocked, but her response was slick and hot.

"Fuck." He was fascinated by the sight of smooth, flushed pink flesh parting, hugging his cock, slickening further with each impalement.

Her pussy sucked at him with each thrust inside her, tightened, rippling along the head of his shaft until he had to clench his teeth against the overwhelming urge to blow inside her.

He hadn't come inside a woman since he was a brick-dumb twenty-one-year-old. Hadn't wanted to take that risk since. But he wanted to now. He wanted to fuck inside her until he was drowning in her then fill her with every fucking drop of his release like a man crazed for the feel of a woman.

She was protected from pregnancy; he already knew that. He'd made it his business to know. He was clean, he'd ensured that over the years. He could do it. Fuck her naked like this until he gave her every drop of himself.

The thought of it destroyed him. His cock swelled with the tempting hunger, his balls drawing tight as he felt the first warning heat building at the base of his spine.

Clenching his teeth, he kept his gaze on her pussy, watched as her little clit became more swollen, flushing to a ruby red as he felt her pussy slickening further, felt her gathering for another release.

God yes.

Fucking her was sweet. So goddamned sweet.

He heard himself growling. A low, almost animal sound as sweat gathered on his forehead, a rivulet tracking down the side of his face.

"Come for me again, Isabeau," he demanded, moving one hand

until he could play along the side of her clit, stroke it, push her deeper into the pleasure he could hear in her sharp little cries. "Now, baby. Come for me now...."

She arched to him, her pussy clamping down on him as he swore he felt the top of his head explode with the power of his release. He buried his cock inside her, hard. Felt the force of his seed erupting from him in furious, blinding pulses of complete rapture.

He moved against her as though he could possibly sink completely inside her, past her body, her heart, and into her soul. Mark her. Brand her until every being on the earth knew the hell it would unleash if it dared touch her.

As he felt the last, blinding ejaculation tear from his body, he knew to the bottom of his soul that even after walking away from her, he'd want to kill any man that dared to try to touch her.

Tracker Calloway didn't claim anything as his own but the brother and sister—not of blood, but of the heart—who had been raised with him. He didn't ask the world for anything, didn't expect anything of it.

But he knew as he collapsed against Isabeau, his body still possessed by hers, that he claimed her. Silently. Secretly. But claimed nonetheless.

FOURTEEN

HE'D FUCKED UP.

He'd known he was going to do it with the first taste of her lips, and he'd known it before he touched her the night before.

Slipping from her bed before daylight, he glared at the hardened state of his cock, cursing the unreasonable need he had for her, and forced himself from her room.

Of course, he'd had to compound the mistake of touching her by sleeping with her. By marking her.

He'd seen the faint bite marks on her neck, her breasts. Hell, he'd been like a man starved for touch. Never had he known such need for a woman. Even as he stepped into the shower, he knew the hunger he felt was unreasonable. It hadn't been that long since he'd had a woman before heading to the lake house. He was highly sexual and enjoyed sex.

This craving for one woman's touch, for her kiss, wasn't a familiar feeling though. And he knew, to the soles of his feet, that walking away from her would destroy him now.

Protecting her was more important than his wants.

And it was time to see to eliminating the danger in her life. Her stalker hadn't made a move since the lake house, but that didn't mean Chance hadn't been busy ferreting out information.

According to him there were suddenly two major players in a very dangerous world who appeared to be watching Isabeau. One of those players he'd suspected was aligned to the Mackays already, while the other he knew as the merciless, drug-running cutthroat he was.

John "Weasel" Costas headed a small, Louisville-based gang that was aligned with major criminal organizations, but he was also rumored to take some serious side jobs of the cleanup sort. The fact that he'd been sighted in Somerset was seriously concerning.

If anyone had the information he needed about the other group, then it was Zoey Mackay's husband, Doogan. The former Homeland Security assistant director had served in so many different agencies in Washington that Tracker doubted there was a player Doogan wasn't aware of.

Pulling Chance into the house rather than overwatch in the rental house next door, Tracker left before Isabeau finished her shower. He didn't dare wait until she left her room. He may not be able to keep his hands, his lips, or his dick off her.

Before he met with Doogan, there were a few other things he needed to take care of. Dawg Mackay had been a friend of Isabeau's father, and Tracker needed information of the more personal sort where they were concerned. Dawg would know the Boudreauxs' friends, and possibly anyone they had considered enemies as well.

J. T. and Mara needed additional information to form a reliable suspect list, and to get that, they needed to know more about the Boudreauxs. And some of that information was quite surprising. And only added to the mystery surrounding Isabeau's family. It made the meeting he'd arranged between him and Doogan that afternoon even more important.

Tracker stepped into the Doogans' front door nearly four hours later, those final moments in Isabeau's room still bothering him. Something was off, not quite the same with her. He just couldn't put his finger on what.

It wouldn't let him alone.

What had been different?

Hell, the sex had been damned great. She burned him alive. And he knew damned good and well it had affected her just as much as it had him.

But as though she was as desperate to avoid the morning after as he was, she'd rushed to the shower away from him.

"Have you had lunch?" Chatham Bromleah Doogan III, Doogan to friends and enemies alike, asked as he closed the door behind Tracker.

Tracker nodded at the question, his lips tugging toward a grin at the sight of a child's toys littering the floor and family pictures scattered around the room.

"Life's treating you good, I see." He glanced back at the other man, not really surprised at the satisfaction that filled Doogan's Irish dark features.

"Zoey makes sure of it," Doogan chuckled, leading the way to the kitchen and the coffee teasing Tracker's senses.

Tracker could only shake his head at the response. As part of the ever-growing Mackay clan, Zoey Doogan ensured her husband's life was never boring, at least.

"She's not here?" Tracker asked, looking around the well-appointed kitchen with its wide windows and gleaming countertops.

Doogan glanced back to him as he reached the coffee maker.

"Lunch with Natches's, Rowdy's, and Dawg's daughters," Doogan said, grinning. "I guess Annie's having some kind of crisis. I thought they got over those when they hit eighteen?"

Tracker grunted at the comment. "Angel's only got worse."

His sister, Angel, had been worse than a hellion at eighteen. The first fifteen years had been a breeze comparably.

Doogan poured coffee and carried the cups to the marble-topped kitchen island, where Tracker stood.

"The rest of the team made it in?" Doogan asked, sipping at this coffee. "You have everything you need?"

Tracker gave a brief nod to the question. "They've been here for the past two nights. Before they arrived, Chance caught sight of a few other interesting parties." Taking his smartphone from the pocket of his shirt, he opened it and pulled up pictures of the two men Chance had identified. "Jakob Marx, VP of a Beaumont-based MC, the Reapers. And John 'Weasel' Costas. Head of a little gang in Louisville rumored to be behind several suspected killings for hire in the tristate area."

Doogan stared at the pictures, frowning at the information.

"I know of Jakob," he murmured. "Dealt with him and the Reapers a few times when they've ridden into Somerset on a run. Costas." He stared at the picture. "That one I don't recognize."

He was a rather plain-looking man. Nearing his forties, brown hair, brown eyes, brawny. Nothing about him stood out except his rap sheet and his connection to organized crime.

"He and two of his men have cruised past Isabeau's house in a plain, four-door Ford sedan. Jakob has taken an apartment on the second floor of a building across the street from the house. Chance hasn't confirmed it yet, but he thinks there's someone staying there with him."

"Girlfriend maybe?" Doogan asked, taking a sip of the coffee.

Tracker's lips quirked at the response. The other man was good, damned good. But Tracker's instincts for trouble were honed in ways Doogan's hadn't been.

He'd allow the little subterfuge to stand for the time being, but he

knew the former agent was hiding the fact that he knew exactly who
was in that apartment with Jakob.

"Should I be concerned that the VP of a very dangerous little MC
appears to be watching Isabeau?" he asked Doogan instead.

Doogan's lips thinned, his jaw tightening at the question.

"Maybe," he finally sighed. "I'll check into it today, as well as Costas, and let you know what I find."

Tracker sipped at his cup again, watching Doogan thoughtfully.
He didn't know what the hell was going on, but he had managed to
piece a few things together.

"I don't deal with surprises real well. You know that," he reminded
Doogan. Chance's connection into the Reapers swore Jakob and Doogan
were some sort of allies. Knowing the man, Tracker didn't doubt the
information.

Doogan's lips quirked. "I prefer to keep my sources quiet for the
moment. I'm sure you understand."

"Oh, sure I do," Tracker agreed with a mocking nod. "But maybe
a few of those sources should stay out of sight a bit better. I might have
to make a little visit. Just to be neighborly, you know?"

Doogan frowned back at him. "Jakob and his brother, Jango Marx,"
he finally revealed, his tone resigned. "They owed me a favor."

"They did, or their boss does?" Tracker grunted. "Forget it. I don't
want to know." He gave a hard shake of his head. Some things he
was just better off not knowing. "Make sure they stay the hell out
of my way, if you don't mind. I'd hate to get on their boss's bad side by
killing two of his men."

The leader of that particular MC wasn't someone he wanted to
piss off. They'd crossed paths a few times, thankfully with the boss, a
man they just called Black, owing him and Chance rather than the
other way around.

"What the hell's going on, Doogan, and what part does Isabeau play in it?"

Doogan grimaced. "Isabeau doesn't play a part in why the MC's in the area, other than the fact that the Marx brothers are doing me a favor by lending a hand in watching out for her."

"I don't need your help," Tracker snapped. "No one jumped in to help her before, and you're just going to get in my way now."

And they were friends. Of a sort. But he had a method when he worked, and Tracker didn't need Doogan adding to it or messing it up.

"Isabeau's a friend to Zoey," Doogan told him. "And she's a fine woman. Whatever's going on, she doesn't deserve it. She's been through enough in her life."

"Her father was one of your contacts," Tracker said, watching Doogan carefully.

It wasn't a question for a reason. J. T. and Mara had found the connection, and the very fact that there was a connection between the two men at one time assured Tracker that Isabeau's father had once been one of Doogan's "watchers." Men and women who reported back to Doogan on various criminal individuals and groups.

It hadn't been that hard to figure out, Chance had assured him, once they had the proper information. Carmichael Boudreaux had been a known MC member in Baton Rouge before running off with Mac Weston's former wife just after she'd stayed in town on vacation. Not long afterward, the entire MC Boudreaux had been a member of had been brought up on charges of drugs, murder, mayhem, and a little bit of homeland terrorism.

It made it all the worse that Doogan hadn't figured out who had killed her parents before now. And it just pissed Tracker off more as well.

Doogan looked down at his cup at that point, a heavy sigh leaving his chest.

"Tell me, did her parents die because of their association with you?" It made sense. Retaliation could be a bitch.

"No. They didn't. Her parents, Carmichael and Danica Boudreaux, weren't in a position to report on anyone who would have known of their connection to the agency or to me. Whoever killed them knew who they were after though. Nothing was stolen from the cabin, and the doors were unlocked. Evidence suggested they knew their murderer. And Isabeau has never remembered so much as a moment of that night."

Tracker wondered about that though. She hadn't told anyone her sight was returning; why would she tell them if she'd remembered anything about the person or persons who destroyed her young life? At least, not until she remembered enough to ensure they paid for the crime.

"How are you and Isabeau getting along?" Doogan's brow arched. "Zoey seems to think Angel's worried about you breaking her heart."

Angel and Zoey obviously talked too much.

Tracker gave Doogan a hard, flat stare.

His personal business was damned sure none of Doogan's business.

"Damn." Doogan breathed out heavily, and Tracker saw the suspicion in his eyes. "Don't play with that girl, Tracker. She's not Kawlee."

"This meeting's done." Pushing back his coffee cup, Tracker stepped away from the kitchen island.

The problem with men like Doogan was that they simply knew too damned much about a person without a word being said. Spooks and spies. Bastards.

"You're sleeping with her, aren't you?" Doogan remained in place, his coffee cup in hand, his expression dark, forbidding.

"None of your business." Sleeping with her. Holding her. Burning the night down with her. Still, none of Doogan's business.

Doogan shook his head at that, the thick black strands brushing over his forehead as he stared back at Tracker.

"Not mine," Doogan agreed. "But someone else could come after you later if you break that girl's heart. Someone you don't want on your ass."

Yeah, that's why she was unprotected and nearly killed.

"Then that someone can pony the fuck up and watch her back, and I can get back to my regular paying gigs," Tracker grunted.

Not hardly.

As that thought passed his mind, an imperious alarm went off on his phone. Jerking it from his shirt pocket, he stared at Chance's message in disbelief.

Café. Now. Attempt made.

At the same time, Doogan received his own alert.

"Fuck!" Disbelief strained the other man's voice, but Tracker was already moving for the door.

What the hell was she doing at that damned café?

FIFTEEN

TRACKER WAS CERTAIN IT WASN'T FEAR THAT RAGED through his system and heightened his senses. He knew he broke every posted speed limit in the county to get back to Isabeau though, and put the Harley through hell on the ride.

The rage he'd admit to. It tore through his system, fed every muscle in his body, and thundered through his brain.

She was fucking blind. Defenseless. The thought that someone would dare to continue to terrify her was like shards of glass tearing through his brain.

He was barely aware of the fact that Doogan's SUV, sirens blaring, was racing behind him. All he cared about was the fact that traffic was parting and getting the fuck out of his way.

Once he hit town, he was forced to slow down, but the sidewalks were clear in the more congested areas, and he made use of them.

It seemed to take forever to get to the small café at the end of Isabeau's block. There, he was forced to haphazardly park the bike before jumping from it and racing up the street to the café.

Racing like a madman. Like a man terrified he was losing something important to him. He knew what it looked like and couldn't stop.

The area was congested with Mackays. Damn sure, Chance wasn't comfortable with that one. Not that Tracker had seen him yet.

"Isabeau!" He yelled her name as he neared the restaurant, pushing at the men who seemed to want to block his path, to stop him before he could get to her.

When two broad male bodies suddenly blocked his path intentionally, holding him back, his fists came up, adrenaline and fury gouging at any self-control he may have had left.

"Tracker. Stand down, goddammit!" His fist was caught in a ham-sized hand before he was pushed back, the harsh male tone breaking through the haze of red clouding his senses. "She's fine. She's safe. Man. Chill the fuck out!"

Dawg Mackay stood in front of him, his cousin Natches backing him. The two middle-aged men, fierce and hard despite their advancing years, refused to step aside.

"Get the fuck out of my way, Dawg," he snarled.

He hadn't seen her yet, hadn't touched her. He wasn't certain she wasn't harmed.

He should have never left her. Chance was just one man, a damned competent man, but just one.

"Tracker. She's fine." It was his foster sister, the girl he and his family had raised and loved, who finally brought him to his senses.

Focusing on Angel, he drew in a deep, hard breath.

"Get these two off me, Angel, before I have to kill one of them," he warned her.

Worried, concerned, she stared back at him for a long silent moment before stepping back herself.

"Let him go to her first," she directed the men. "He's not going to listen until you do."

Pushing forcefully past them, he didn't give them or the others standing around a chance to object further.

As he neared the door to the café, it pushed open and Chance met his gaze, waving him inside.

"What the fuck happened?" he snapped at the other man as he caught sight of Isabeau sitting among a Mackay family reunion on the other side of the room.

"I didn't know she was leaving until the Watts girl showed up to get her," Chance muttered. "Warn me next time, why don't you?"

Tracker ignored the demand, striding to Isabeau and trying to force back his fury.

Tall, dangerous in-laws as well as a few "outlaws" to the Mackay family surrounded the women sitting with her, creating a human blockade that would have been impossible to get past unless they allowed it.

"Isabeau." He spoke her name as he neared, letting her know he was there.

"Tracker?" Hesitant, still resonating with fear, Isabeau called out to him, rising from her seat in a jerky movement as he moved for her.

He didn't wait for Chance's explanation any more than he'd been willing to wait for the Mackays' or for Angel's.

He ignored the men standing around her, as well as the sheriff standing close to her table. He was aware of the glares, frowns, and disapproving looks and didn't give a damn.

Pulling her into his arms when he reached her, he pressed her head to his chest, his hand covering the back of her head as he held her close with the other. Her hands tucked between them, pushing beneath the light riding jacket he wore and clenching in the material of his shirt.

She was shaking.

The feel of her slight body trembling against him was almost more than he could stand.

"I have you," he whispered at her ear, his head bent over hers, creating as much of a haven as he could provide her. "I have you, Isabeau."

He wanted to pick her up and carry her out of there, get her home and away from any threat of danger that could still exist.

It took every ounce of strength he possessed to remain still beneath so many eyes and just hold her as she shook like a leaf in a storm against him.

"You need to sit down." But he'd never let her fall, not as long as he could hold her up. "You're still shaking, sweetheart."

Long, silken waves of hair rippled down her back as she shook her head and her fingers clenched at his shirt tighter.

Just a minute longer, he told himself, then he'd let her go, get her to sit down, and he'd figure out what the hell happened.

Instead, he found himself picking her up and sitting himself in the chair she'd vacated. He couldn't force her to move, to let go of him. He could feel the fear still rippling through her body, and if he had to let her go while she trembled with such vulnerability, he'd never face himself in a mirror again.

Facing himself now would be impossible as it was. If he hadn't left her, hadn't felt he needed to meet with Doogan himself, then he would have been here.

"I need to go home." Her voice was so low he doubted anyone else heard her. "I just need to go home."

Tracker looked up, found Chance, and met his gaze as he gave a brief nod to the door. He couldn't take her back on the bike, not this time. He couldn't take that risk.

"You're not leaving yet, Tracker." Natches Mackay stepped forward, his cousin Dawg behind him.

Hell, if those two didn't make a formidable picture, despite their ages. Over six feet tall, still broad and powerful, the two men were county legends in many ways. And it was never a good thing to go against them. Not that Tracker really gave a damn.

"Isabeau wants to go home. You need to talk to her, you can come by later. Right now, I'm taking her home, where she knows she's safe," he told the two men, rising with Isabeau still in his arms.

She tightened her grip around his neck and kept her head buried at his shoulder.

At least she wasn't shaking as she had been moments before.

"Dammit, Tracker," Natches griped, following behind him as Tracker walked past them. "We need to question her."

Tracker didn't answer.

As he pushed the door open, a pickup eased in next to the curb, and Chance reached out and threw open the passenger-side door. Tracker stepped into the vehicle, Isabeau still cradled in his arms, his arms tight around her. He loosened his grip only long enough to slam the door behind them.

"Get us to the house," he ordered.

"Gotcha. The cousins are going through it now. Everything's clear so far. No bugs, no one watching the house," Chance assured him.

A slight shiver raced over Isabeau.

Tracker wanted to hit something, preferably whoever was behind this.

"What happened?" He could hear the rage in his voice and couldn't do a damned thing to cover it.

"Two trucks and a sedan," Chance stated, turning the truck down Isabeau's street. "The trucks were a distraction. They collided with each other in front of the café with enough commotion to distract everyone. Two men jumped out of the sedan and tried to grab her. Somehow, she managed to duck and jump back as they reached her. It gave me that extra few seconds to get to her. They raced off with two of the café's customers in pursuit. The two men didn't look familiar, but their rides were Harleys."

Chance pulled into Isabeau's drive.

"Anyone able to ID the would-be abductors?" he asked.

Chance shook his head. "Not that I know of, not so far, but I'm laying my money on Costas for the attempt. It looked enough like him at the wheel of the sedan that I wouldn't care to make the bet. I suspect the two men who followed are associated with that MC we identified before, but they weren't wearing colors and didn't advertise themselves."

It didn't make sense. The Reapers MC wasn't all about damsels in distress or poking their noses into something like this, even for a man like Doogan, so the riders shouldn't be part of that club.

"House is clear," his brother said as he checked his phone. "The boys say it's nice and undisturbed."

And the "boys" would know. The two cousins he'd pulled in were experienced and highly trained.

As Chance moved from the truck, Tracker waited until he came to the passenger side of the vehicle, watching the street, before Tracker got out of the truck, Isabeau still in his arms.

Thankfully she'd stopped shaking so damned hard. Those tremors cascading through her body had made his self-control ragged.

"I can walk," she assured him, but her arms were still wrapped around his shoulders, her face buried at his neck.

"And I can carry you just fine." He heard the darker tone of his voice and almost winced at the sound.

Stepping into the house, Chance at his back, he strode through it to her room and pushed the door open firmly. He paused only for a moment, making certain the room was empty before carrying Isabeau to her bed.

Laying her down, he didn't give her a chance to protest. Tangling the fingers of one hand into the long, soft strands of hair, he tugged her head back and took complete advantage of the little gasp that left her lips.

They immediately parted farther, her tongue meeting his, her body slackening, becoming pliant within his hold. Lust rose like a demon inside him, hardening his body, his cock, stealing his mind for precious moments. Nothing mattered but the woman, this kiss, and marking her as his own.

If he marked her, there would be no doubt who she belonged to, and his enemies would remember the heavy toll he'd exact if anyone dared to harm her.

It was that thought that had him quickly pulling back, breaking the kiss and staring down at her.

Her lashes lifted, brilliant violet eyes staring directly up at him, pupils expanded, the color darker than normal.

Those eyes. They drifted lower, to his lips, the heavy lift and fall of his chest as he fought to bring his breathing back under control, then back to his eyes.

"Your vision's better," he stated.

She blinked up at him again, a hint of uncertainty filling her expression. "It cleared up a bit more overnight. It's still blurry, but I can pick up details better."

"Did you see who tried to take you?" He kept his gaze narrowed on hers, watching her pupils, the shifting color in her eyes.

"It happened . . ." She cleared her throat. "It happened too fast. My gaze isn't clear enough yet to identify details quickly or faces."

Tracker straightened, lifted his knee from where it rested on her mattress, and stared down at her.

Self-conscious now, she sat up on the bed and swung her feet to the floor.

"Does anyone else know?" he questioned her.

She gave a slight nod. "Burke's father, Mac, called just after you left this morning." She bit her lip nervously. "The eye doctor contacted my specialist in Beaumont for records. They called the ranch and spoke to Mac to confirm I was in Kentucky. I don't know what my doctor in Beaumont told him though, so I just kept to the truth. My sight's incredibly blurry but improving." She looked up at him, her expression worried. "Burke's uncle Bill called bitching about Burke being in California and wanted to know if I knew why he was there. I told him Burke called the other night from California and I hadn't heard from him since." She was talking fast, her nostrils flaring with nerves and fear. "Kenya called, she has a new boyfriend and wanted to talk. . . . Then Annie and the girls showed up, and I thought it would be safe. . . ."

And it should have been.

He crouched in front of her, his hands bracketing her face as tear-filled violet eyes stared back at him.

Son of a bitch. Someone was going to die for this. Painfully.

"Did they say anything at all when they tried to grab you?" he asked, watching her expression carefully.

She shook her head, her expression uncertain.

"Someone's going to end up hurt," she whispered, glancing away from him. "Everyone keeps trying to protect me, and I'm terrified that all it will accomplish is someone else dying. I can't stay—"

"Finish that sentence, Isabeau, and I swear I'm going to paddle your ass." He'd had enough of it.

Disbelief filled her expression for one breathless moment.

"Is that a threat, Tracker?" Her nostrils flared as her hands pressed into the mattress, lifting her marginally closer to him, as though she would dare to challenge him.

The very thought of her taking that route had his dick thickening, hardening immediately. Lust slammed into him like a runaway train. Never, not once in his sexual life, had he ever had such an immediate, overwhelming response to a woman.

"You can bet your sweet ass it is," he promised. Leaning forward, he let his lips brush against her ear before taking a quick, gentle nip of the lobe.

Startled, a gasp left her lips, and her nipples peaked beneath the soft material of her bra. As he pulled back, he caught the rapid, heated flush beneath her cheeks and the dilation of her pupils.

"Want to test me, baby girl?" he asked softly, his lips almost—but not quite—touching hers. "Want to see how fast I can make you beg me to paddle that pretty ass?"

Her tongue flicked out over her lips, dampening them as her breathing increased, causing her breasts to push temptingly toward him.

"You couldn't . . . You wouldn't . . ." she whispered, her eyes widening, whether in disbelief or fascination he wasn't certain.

What he did know was those hard little nipples made their presence known beneath the sleeveless summer tank top and the bra she wore beneath it. A light flush mounted her cheekbones, and he could tell she didn't know whether to be outraged or turned on. Though it seemed she was a little bit of both.

"Oh, I damned sure could," he promised her, letting one hand grip her neck firmly. "And if you keep daring me, nothing will give me greater pleasure."

She just stared at him for a minute before her brow furrowed, a thoughtful look coming over her face.

"Tracker, I don't know whether to be offended or turned on," she finally stated consideringly.

"Well, baby, when you figure it out, you just let me know, then I'll answer accordingly." He couldn't help the grin that edged at his lips or the need to push her back on that bed and fuck her until she was screaming his name. Again.

Damn her. Less than a minute ago she had him ready to stomp around in rage, and now he was grinning. She was probably the most dangerous woman he'd met in his life.

"Tracker. I need you out here," Chance called out from the hallway beyond the door, putting an end to the activities he was planning.

Isabeau sat back once again, and though she didn't back down, her position was no longer challenging.

"I need to shower . . . change clothes." She changed the subject as though he wasn't about to paddle her ass for holding back on him. Or for making him so damned hard his cock was like iron.

Instead, she ran her hand through her hair, grimacing as she encountered evidence of its tangled state.

He hadn't paid enough attention to how she'd been dressed until that moment. Her soft white cotton capris were dirt-streaked, the sleeveless top torn in several places, and her white sandals scuffed.

She pushed the sandals off even as his gaze strayed to her delicate little feet.

Dammit.

He was losing his fucking mind. He swore she had the prettiest feet he'd ever seen.

"Good idea." Forcing himself to step back from her, Tracker blew out a hard, silent breath. "I'll see what I can find out about the attack while you're in the shower."

Her head jerked up, surprise showing on her face.

"You'll tell me?" she asked, as though the idea were somehow a foreign concept.

"Unless you don't want to know." He had to fist his fingers to keep from reaching out to touch her as she gave a small, uncomfortable shrug.

"Everyone seems to think the details shouldn't concern me." Her smile was tight, and hurt flashed in her eyes. "They never want to talk about the so-called accidents."

And they made finding the details impossible for her, no doubt. The pain in her eyes went deep though, deeper than just a few supposed accidents.

"Your parents?" he asked her softly.

She inhaled slowly, her lips curling bitterly.

"Burke still refuses to tell me what he learned after the investigation into my parents' murders." She pushed from the bed, walking tensely to the dresser, where she pulled out a drawer to collect another outfit. "It's been ten years, and I'm still not certain exactly what happened. Newspaper articles are brief, and the police report even briefer."

And it haunted her.

Tracker had heard that tone in other clients' voices, seen that expression on their faces. Not knowing was often more horrifying than the facts of a traumatic event.

"Then it's about time someone told you," he decided. "I'll find the report for you, Isabeau. I promise you that. And I'll give you every detail it contains."

She seemed to freeze in place for long moments before giving a short little nod.

"Thank you," she whispered, closing the dresser drawer and heading to the shower.

And it was in that very moment that Tracker knew Isabeau was touching a part of him that no one had managed thus far. Because his heart literally melted in his chest as he watched her back and shoulders straighten and her expression fill with determination.

She was vulnerable, and though her sight was improving, she was still basically blind. She was being terrorized and threatened. But Isabeau Boudreaux wasn't about to bow down to any of it, not even for a second.

Hell no. She was too damned strong for that. Too damned stubborn and filled with life to lie down and die for anyone.

That strength both broke his heart and filled it with admiration. This was a woman who would kill to protect her own. She'd never lie down with the enemy. . . . Fuck, he wasn't doing this. Trust no one, believe in no one unless they'd been through the flames with him. And only two people had done that. Chance and Angel.

He forced the thought back, forced himself from the room, away from her.

It didn't matter how strong she was or wasn't, or who she was or wasn't. He knew life, and he knew how vicious it could be, how destructive.

Stepping into the hall, he followed Chance into the kitchen when the other man motioned him to follow.

"The Marx brothers were the two bikers who went after the sedan. My contact just got back with me," he said, his voice low, his green gaze flat and hard. "The vice, Jakob, wants a meet after dark tomorrow. Says it's important. Their prez wants to talk."

He wasn't sure why Jakob and his brother had a hand in this, or why the Reapers' president suddenly wanted a meet, but Tracker was starting to suspect several different scenarios.

"Set it up," he ordered. "Make certain the cousins are here before we leave, as well as Duke and Angel. You and I will make the meet."

Chance nodded and left the house through the back door, leaving Tracker to stare into the sunlit kitchen. Isabeau was in the shower. The thought of joining her was tempting as hell.

The thought of her, the water from the shower flowing over her, caressing her breasts, nipples, the smooth skin of her thighs, had him grimacing, his body tight with need.

But hell, he stayed hard because of her.

She was messing with his head, weakening him. He'd raced after her today with no thought to the consequences or of approaching a little less dramatically to be certain who was watching.

He'd been reckless. Thoughtless. Then he'd pushed his way past the Mackays and his sister like a wild man. No wonder Angel had stared at him like he was insane. He was acting insane.

He was acting like a man who had lost his mind.

Or his heart.

Grimacing at the thought, he gave his head a hard shake. His heart was intact, he assured himself. Nothing wrong there.

It was fine.

The ache in the center of his chest had nothing to do with Isabeau. He didn't know why it was there, but it wasn't because of her.

SIXTEEN

A SHOWER AND A CHANGE OF CLOTHES, THIS TIME ULTRA-soft cotton lounging pants and a matching top, the hint of navy blue pleasing to her newly awakening senses, and Isabeau was ready to face Tracker again.

Her vision was a little better, details becoming a little clearer. Just not clear enough yet. She hadn't been able to see the men who had tried to grab her clearly enough. Not enough to identify them.

That wouldn't be a problem for long though, she assured herself as she pushed her feet into a pair of ballet slippers and left her bedroom. She followed the low murmur of male voices through the house until she neared the kitchen, where they abruptly went silent.

"Isabeau." It was Chance who greeted her as she stepped into the kitchen.

She saw him turn toward her briefly before once again facing Tracker. There was something about his movements, the way he held his body that seemed very, very familiar. Which was odd, considering it had been ten years since she'd seen anyone turn or move in any way.

"Give me a call if you need me," he told Tracker, his voice low. "I'll see what I can find out."

Tracker didn't say anything, but she could feel his gaze on her, intent and probing as she turned to him.

"Mayor Mackay." There was the faintest hint of mockery to his tone. "Called while you were in the shower. His wife's brother is chief of police."

Isabeau nodded at that. "Alex Jansen. I remember him and Christa. Alex used to visit with Father along with Natches and Dawg. They were friends."

She could still remember the tall, handsome soldier her father had once argued politics with. She remembered he had been one of the few men her usually taciturn father had laughed with.

"Yeah, well, one of his detectives, Samantha Bryce, will be here soon. Detective Bryce is in charge of the case and has a few questions."

"I know Sam." She nodded. "She's a friend of the Mackays' as well as Doogan's. Her wife, Carrie, owns the café actually."

"Figures." His tone carried a resigned sigh that almost had her grinning.

"Sam's cool," she told him, though she didn't know how comfortable she would be with the other woman questioning her.

She didn't know Sam as well as she knew Alex and the Mackay cousins Natches, Dawg, and Rowdy. She'd grown up with the three men in the periphery of her life. They'd been friends of her parents' and visited often when they were at the lake.

Her father had been incredibly picky about the people he socialized with, but he'd seemed to enjoy the Mackays' company.

"Sam's a pain in the ass, but she comes by it honestly," he grunted. "Her father was once director of Homeland Security, before Doogan's time. Arrogant bastard, but a good guy."

She didn't know Sam's father, but she liked Sam. The woman had a dry, funny sense of humor despite her toughness.

"There's not much I can tell anyone." The thought of being questioned made her nervous too. "I couldn't make out details or identify anyone."

She couldn't afford to allow anyone besides Tracker and Chance to know that her sight was returning, not yet. She was just waiting for the day that it was clear enough to go back to the cabin, where she hoped, prayed her memories would return.

Her breath caught in her throat a second later as she felt his fingers at her neck while he pushed her back against the wall behind her.

Her neck arched into the hold, sensual weakness washing through her. It became harder to breathe, but not because of the slight pressure at her neck.

Excitement. It rushed through her, wiping away anger, uncertainty, and self-preservation. She wanted to see his face, however she could see it, but her lashes refused to lift fully, insisting on dipping and nearly closing instead.

"Damn you." His voice was a growl at her ear as the fingers holding her in place flexed against her neck in a firm caress. "I could have lost you today, Isabeau. I'm not happy about that."

"Tracker . . ." His name escaped, but whether it was a plea or a protest, she wasn't certain.

"Don't think that I don't sense the fact that you're keeping something from me, baby. I won't allow your need for secrets to risk your life any longer. Play whatever games you think you can play with Sam. But when she leaves, you have to deal with me."

He didn't give her a chance to protest or to deny the accusation. As her lips parted, his head lowered, and she forgot the fact that she even had anything to deny.

His lips covered her, possessed, stroked against hers, and built a need in her there was no denying or fighting against. Her hands gripped his waist, feeling the hard muscles beneath and wanting to get closer. Skin to skin. Melting against him.

A deep, possessive kiss, one that assured her that Tracker intended to own her. Heart, body, and soul. If he didn't already.

She became aware of the firm knocks at the door only when his head jerked up, turning toward the front of the house. His hand slid slowly from her neck in a lingering caress as he stepped back from her.

"Company," he murmured. "Get ready, baby, the inquisition is here."

She saw his face clearly, briefly. Mockery, concern, and an emotion that had her heart tripping before accelerating further. There was more there than just worry, mockery, and lust. Something with a darker, harder edge. As quickly as it reflected in his expression, it was gone though.

Turning away from her as her gaze once again blurred the details, he stalked silently to the door, not making even the briefest sound as he crossed the hardwood. A quick check at one of the side windows and he was opening the door.

"Sam, Natches, Chaya, and Zoey," he greeted. "Where's our esteemed mayor?"

"You love reminding us all of that title," Natches seemed to growl. "Still can't believe he's playing politics. Someone needs to knock some sense into his ass before it's too late."

Isabeau couldn't help but grin. The Mackay cousins were always fussing at one another over something. It had been like that for as long as she could remember. Even as a girl she'd witnessed some of their more heated arguments.

Natches especially had been a hothead.

The cousins had mellowed out over the years though. She remembered noticing it as a young girl, after Chaya had come to town. Her father had remarked to her mother several times that Natches was calmer, happy even.

And the man Isabeau had gotten to know in the past two years was mature, mostly calm and levelheaded, and a wonderful father to his daughter.

His wife, Chaya, a former Homeland Security interrogator, was quite intelligent and intuitive. Several times she interjected her own questions into the conversation with Sam or asked her to clarify her answers.

Not that Isabeau had many answers for them. She hadn't been able to identify her attempted abductors, and they hadn't spoken to her. She'd seen someone jumping for her and reacted by jumping back. After that, chaos had erupted.

Thankfully, the questions didn't last long, and the three rose to leave.

"Chaya, are the girls all okay?" she asked before they could head for the doors. "They weren't talking much at the café after the commotion."

"The girls are fine, Isabeau," Chaya promised her. "Concerned for you, angry that the attempt was made, but fine. I'm sure they'll be calling or visiting soon."

Isabeau licked her lips nervously. "You should have them stay away until this is over," she told the other woman, hating the fact that she was a danger to her friends. "This is twice that someone else could have been hurt. I don't want there to be a third time."

The room was silent for long seconds, and she could feel all their eyes on her.

"We suggested that after the party," Chaya finally admitted wryly. "Annie stated that was what your stalker wanted, Laken gave a little unladylike snort, and Bliss smiled. And I have to admit, that smile scared me. She resembled her father way too much in that moment."

There were chuckles from the others.

"Be good, sprite," Natches said fondly. "We'll be seeing you again soon, I'm sure."

Sprite.

Her father had always called her that, and the Mackays had picked up the habit when she'd become a teenager.

"God, sprite, why are you here . . . ?" Agonized, filled with pain.

As quickly as the sound of that voice was there, it was gone. But she'd known it. She'd walked out of her bedroom at the sound of gunshots, shocked, frightened, and staring at . . . who?

Who was it?

The knowledge was there, so close and yet still hidden.

But he'd called her sprite. There had been so few people who called her that. Her parents, her brother. A few of her parents' friends.

"YOU OKAY?" TRACKER ASKED, HIS VOICE QUIET AS HE locked the door behind Natches and the three women.

"Tired," she sighed, rubbing at her temples and the ache building there.

Tracker watched her, that tightness in his chest intensifying.

She was killing him slowly.

When he looked at her, he simply couldn't see her as he had women in the past decade. He hadn't caught her lying to him, deceiving him, or attempting to work him. She was often uncertain, scared, and he suspected she was holding something back in regards to her memory, but she wasn't manipulative or deliberately deceitful.

What she was was scared. She thought about things, analyzed them, tried to make sense of them, before revealing what she was thinking.

When he looked at her, he didn't hear his own screams in his head or feel the agony of a blade slicing at his flesh. When he held her, there were no monsters rising in his mind to destroy him.

What he saw instead was what those monsters could do to her.

She was unprotected, and with or without her sight, an innocent to the dangers of his world.

If he didn't walk away, then he'd be dragging her into his world. Or he'd be forced to step away from it completely. And even that didn't ensure her safety. He'd always have to be diligent, watchful. And every man ended up blinking at some point.

"Sometimes it feels as though it's all a dream," she whispered bitterly, her hands falling to her sides as she stared back at him. "A horrible nightmare. And, at other times, too farcical to be real."

"Once we have his identity, it'll get easier," he promised her.

Once he knew who it was, the bastard was going to die.

"Chance said you left this morning to chase down some leads?" she finally asked. "Did you learn anything?"

"So far nothing but suspicion." He frowned back at her. "And you shouldn't have left the house while I was gone."

Her head tilted a bit, her brows lifting at his response.

"You didn't inform me that I shouldn't leave the house," she pointed out defensively. "Not that I will again, but perhaps you should inform me of the rules of this game so I can act accordingly."

"I'd have thought the rules were pretty straightforward," Tracker grunted at her response. "Someone's trying to kill you, Isabeau. Until I can figure out who, you stay put and stay safe. That means staying in the house when I'm not with you. And likely while I am with you as well."

Isabeau heard the demanding tone of his voice and could barely make out the arrogance of his features. Thick black hair lay along his face in a shaggy cut, his blue eyes piercing the veil of blurriness. And every indication that he was in autocratic domineering mode was plain to see. Blind or not.

"No, Tracker, the rules are not quite that clear," she argued. "Except to you perhaps. Maybe you should inform Chance that when I'm about to break one of these unwritten rules, he should speak up. Otherwise, I'm a little clueless here."

"Oh, I intend to have my little talk with Chance." He crossed his arms over that wide chest, and she could feel him glaring down at her. "Until then, I want to make it clear to you. If I'm not with you, you don't leave."

She'd be damned if she'd make that promise. Promises should be made with the intention of keeping them, she'd always thought. And she knew, once her sight cleared a bit more, she had a trip to the cabin to make. One without him or Chance.

She'd never be able to think in his presence, she knew. Whenever he was around, her body was too aware, her senses too muddled with arousal and need and regret.

Regret that once this was over, he'd be gone. That he'd ride out of her life and likely never return.

What was it Seth and Saul had told her? He didn't like to acknowledge past lovers or meet up with them again. He'd avoid her, for whatever reason, and when he couldn't, he'd pretend he didn't know her.

And she didn't know if she could bear that either.

It would break her heart over and over again.

"We suspect the men that tried to take you are part of a low-level criminal organization out of Louisville, known to take kill contracts in the tristate area. Two customers in the bar went out after them, members of a motorcycle club from Beaumont, Texas. Jakob and Jango Marx. Recognize the names?"

She gave a surprised start. "Jakob and Jango? You're certain?" Concern and confusion creased her expression as she stared at him.

"Know them?"

"They're friends of Burke's," she stated hesitantly. "I know they ride motorcycles. Jakob and Burke have been friends as long as Seth and Saul."

"Is Burke part of an MC?" he asked her.

"A motorcycle club?" She shook her head. "He hasn't owned a bike in years, that I know of. And I never heard anything about a club. I just talked to Jakob the other day. He didn't mention being in Somerset. Maybe he just showed up?"

"He and his brother have been staying in an apartment across the street for the past month. . . ."

Isabeau fought the racing of her heart and the sheer panic that began burning through her mind.

"A month," she whispered.

She knew Jakob. He'd always been kind, always been a friend. She and his sister, Octavia, were close.

"Burke didn't mention he was here." She clasped her hands, twisting her fingers together as she fought the fear rising inside her now. "When I talked to Jakob, he acted as though he was still in Texas. He didn't mention being in Kentucky."

"Would your brother have him come in to watch you?"

"God, who knows." She was shaking now, and she hated it. "I would have said no twenty minutes ago." She breathed in deep, fighting not to cry when the tears tightened her throat. "You said they went after my attempted kidnappers?"

"They did. Natches has a few cousins out searching for them, and they haven't returned to the apartment. I'm hoping to chat with them when they come back."

Chat with them. "Like you chatted with Seth and Saul at the party?"

"If need be," he answered. "I'll try to begin cordial. I know how to be."

He didn't sound like it was his top priority though.

"I would appreciate it," she whispered.

"Jakob another admirer? Like Seth?" he asked, as though the thought made him angry. He moved to her slowly, deliberately. "Another possessive asshole with no reason to be?"

Her eyes narrowed on him. She couldn't completely make out his expression, but from what she could see of it, he wasn't pleased.

"Not that I'm aware of," she snapped, uncertain why he even gave a damn. "But what difference does it make? According to you, you're not sticking around anyway."

"Until I'm gone, by God, you're mine! That's the difference it makes. And I'm sick of dumbasses getting in my way." His tone hardened, became deeper, huskier.

The sound of his arousal.

A shiver raced up her back, and heat flushed through her body.

Hadn't he spent the night driving her from one orgasm to another? She was tender in places she had never been tender in before, and still, she wanted him.

"And until you're gone, are you mine?" she questioned him, her breath catching as he pulled her into his arms, flush against his body.

"Do you see another stubborn-assed princess determined to make me crazy?" he snarled.

But he didn't give her a chance to answer him.

His lips covered hers in another of those hot, demanding kisses, and her body ignited. Sliding her hands to his shoulders, she gripped them, feeling the hard muscle beneath flexing, rippling with power.

She needed him. Like she'd never needed anything in her life, and not just because she was in danger. Because he was Tracker. Because his kiss, his touch, could make her forget the world around them.

Because he paid a band to play a slow song she could dance to, because he described the lake house to her even though he was angry.

Because when he held her, she didn't just feel safe, she felt wanted. And because he let her make him crazy.

He could have walked away at any time, left her to anyone else's care once Angel was safe, and no one would have blamed him.

Instead, he was kissing her as though she were his lifeline rather than the other way around. Guiding her backward, lifting her and taking her to the bed, his lips never leaving hers.

She moaned as his hand pushed at the elastic band of the lounging pants, brushing them from her hips as his lips lifted from hers enough to slide to her neck.

"Tracker," she whispered, delirious with pleasure as she arched her neck to his rough kisses.

"Get rid of this." He pushed her top to her breasts, leaned back, gripped the hem, and pulled it over her head.

Within minutes she was naked and lying back against the pillows as she watched him tear his own clothes from his body. She could see enough to admire bronzed skin, the breadth of his shoulders, the blue of his eyes.

"You're fucking beautiful," he whispered, coming over her. "All silky and hot. I'd kill one of those bastards if they tried to touch you."

Before she could respond to the threat, he pushed her thighs apart, his fingers trailing over the sensitive mound he found.

"You taste like summer, Isabeau," he groaned, his head lowering. "Sweetest fucking taste . . ."

She gasped as his tongue licked the swollen folds, his hands pushing her thighs farther apart, pushing beneath her rear and lifting her to him.

Her fingers clenched in the blankets beneath her, her lips lifting to him as the need grew. Sparks shot through her bloodstream; pleasure burned over her nerve endings.

She'd never known anything so good, so hot in her life.

His tongue was wicked, hungry, smoothing around her clit, igniting her flesh with patient, hungry greed. And he was owning her senses.

She shuddered, crying out with the intensity of sensation as she spread her thighs wider for him.

She'd never known pleasure like she'd found in his touch. Never imagined it could exist. And in a distant part of her mind she wondered how she was going to live without it once he was gone.

For now, she let the pleasure have her, let him have her. With each lick, each heated draw of his mouth on her clit and penetration of his fingers, she came undone.

The inferno built with destructive force until she was begging, pleading with him for the release he was holding just out of reach.

Until his lips surrounded the swollen bud, his tongue flickering over it, around her, driving her hard and fast into an explosion that ripped through her senses and sent her spinning into ecstasy.

As the pleasure peaked inside her, Tracker rose between her thighs, and a second later the blunt crest of his erection was forging inside her pussy. Pulsing and iron-hot, his cock worked inside her, stretching her, filling her.

"Ah hell, Isabeau," he groaned, his voice sounding tortured. "So sweet and hot . . . I love watching that pretty pussy open around my cock . . . watching you take me . . ."

Her inner flesh flexed, little explosions erupting inside her and making his cock feel harder, hotter.

"Like that, baby?" he asked her, his tone graveled. "Like hearing how damned good you feel?"

Her nails bit into his shoulders as she felt him grip beneath her knees, pushing her legs back as he sank deeper inside her.

"Yes," she moaned out. "Oh God, Tracker . . . Deeper. Take me harder."

His hips jerked against her, almost driving his full length inside her as she strained against him, desperate to feel the burning pleasure that only came when he took her fully.

Need raced through her in violent arcs of heat. Her heart was racing, need clenching her pussy around him, pulsing through her veins, and sending more slick heat to meet the intrusion even as he began drawing back.

"Tracker, please . . ." she cried out. "Please . . . harder . . ."

A second later he drove inside her once, twice, until he was buried fully inside her. White-hot pleasure ripped through her. A blinding shock of such sensation that she could only arch to him as she felt ecstasy circling around her.

Harder. Faster. He thrust inside her, his cock forging inside to the hilt and causing her pussy to clench, to ripple around each penetration as she felt her muscles tightening. Each impalement raked across sensitive nerve endings, stroked hypersensitive flesh, and finally sent ecstasy imploding inside her.

She tried to scream as her body jerked, arched to him, and the detonations of sensations inside her stole her mind.

Her heart.

She was flying on waves of pure rapture, crying out his name as she felt him thrust inside her in one final hard push, before he gave in to his own release.

Each hard surge of his release echoed through her flesh, prolonging the chaos of her orgasm.

Tracker came over her, his arms surrounding her, his touch gentle now, soothing as she shuddered in the final throes of her orgasm.

And in that moment, Isabeau knew what love was. It was his arms surrounding her, his hands gently stroking her back, that knowledge that no part of her would ever be the same.

Even knowing the heartbreak to come and the loneliness she'd feel once he was gone, still she opened herself that final bit and let him have her, all the way to her soul.

SEVENTEEN

THE NEXT EVENING, TRACKER SAT IN THE LIVING ROOM, several files open on his tablet, all too aware of Isabeau in her office doing whatever class plans actually entailed. He had a feeling she was hiding though. Just as he had been hiding when, before she awakened, he'd left her bed, dressed, and escaped to find Chance and the coffee in the kitchen.

Something had happened the night before. Every time he touched her, each time she orgasmed in his arms, he felt something he'd never felt before, and he had no idea how to explain it or how to deal with it.

She'd touched him, he thought. Not physically, but inside, where he'd sworn he'd never let a woman touch him.

He'd learned at a young age how caring too much for one person could destroy a man. It had destroyed the young man he had been, and he'd promised himself he'd never let it happen again.

Isabeau had done last night what no other woman had ever managed to do. She'd touched his heart, slipped inside it, and now he had no idea how to push her back out.

Hell, he had no idea how she'd gotten inside him to begin with. He hadn't known she was there until that moment of realization the night before. As he came inside her, matching her release, feeling the heat and pleasure of her. That was when he'd felt it. That ethereal sensation, like heat sinking inside him, and that heat, that warmth, whispered of Isabeau.

Goddamn, he needed a psych ward or something the way he was shooting flowery phrases around.

"Tracker." Chance stepped into the living room, his gaze going around the room, making certain Isabeau wasn't there.

"She's in her office," Tracker assured him, keeping his voice low.

"Jakob said ten tonight. He'll text the address thirty minutes before the meet. Said Black will be there as well."

Tracker gave a short nod. "Get everything set up. I want her completely covered while we're gone."

"Duke and Angel will be in the house, the cousins outside," Chance agreed. "Seth and Saul are lurking around here and there as well. They keep moving, never staying in one place."

They kept trying to hide from Chance, in other words.

"It shouldn't take long to figure out what the hell Black's men are up to," he stated, closing the tablet and sitting back in the couch. "Let J. T. and Mara know and see if they've made any headway on that suspect list."

"Something else." Chance drew his attention back. "They found Costa and two of his men. Looks like they had a disagreement and shot each other at a deserted cabin outside of town. All three are dead."

Looked like . . .

Tracker's lips curled into a sardonic smile. "You believe it?" he asked his brother.

"Fuck no," Chance drawled. "Black's men know what the hell they're doing. It's that simple."

"That's what I figured." Tracker sighed. "Get hold of J. T. and Mara. I'll meet you outside at nine."

"See ya then," Chance agreed, and turned and left the room.

Tracker made his way to Isabeau. The one place he'd wanted to be and refused to allow himself. He didn't have to refuse any longer; he had a reason to go to her.

HER VISION WAS CLEARER. THE BLURRINESS WAS BARELY there now, but it wouldn't be long before it receded completely, and it was all she could do to keep that knowledge to herself. With the added clarity of her sight, her memories were becoming clearer as well.

She hadn't seen who had killed her parents, but sensed the knowledge, just out of reach. It would take next to nothing, she knew, to put the pieces together. Perhaps no more than that last misty veil easing away.

Agitation raced through her, making it impossible to stay still.

Someone wanted her dead because they feared what she might remember.

She feared what she might remember.

What she was trying to remember.

Rubbing at the ache in her temple, she paused at the corner of her desk, a sense of racing panic surging through her. Too much was happening at once, giving her nowhere to turn, no way to make sense of the images that flickered through her head. Or the suspicions.

She needed to find out why Jakob and Jango were there, and why Jakob wasn't answering her calls now. Why Burke wasn't answering his. If those two were here, then that meant her brother wasn't far behind. She knew that much about their friendship. If one needed help, then the other two were always close enough to provide it.

She should have known Jakob would never really warn her if Burke was headed to her. They were too tight, too close. She had believed, hoped, that the favor he owed her would balance the scales though.

But regardless of whether they were here, she needed to deal with remembering on her own. She was just waiting for her sight to return enough that she could navigate by herself.

It was so close that she felt if she concentrated enough, tried just a little harder, then it would completely clear up.

But she'd been trying most of the day, and still, that faint mistiness remained.

Smothering an irritated snarl, she turned back to the desk, intent on throwing herself into her chair out of sheer frustration, when a firm knock sounded at the door.

Tracker.

A hint of outdoors and the dark scent of a male, dominant and in his prime, drifted to her as the door opened and his tall, broad form entered.

Only Tracker carried that scent. A natural, unique scent that teased her senses and reminded her of the pleasure only he had ever given her.

She could see enough to detect the scar on his face; she could see the strong, rough features enough to know that he wasn't traditionally handsome but savagely good-looking. Strong. She already knew there wasn't an ounce of spare flesh on that muscular body, but now she could see it. Almost.

"Your would-be abductors seem to have gotten into a disagreement in a cabin outside town. It appears they killed each other," he told her as he closed the door and stood watching her.

"They seem to have?" She crossed her arms over her breasts and stared back at him, disbelieving.

"That's what the scene suggests, or so I was told." He leaned back against the door, watching her.

It was all she could do to keep from meeting his gaze, from betraying that she could see more today than she could yesterday. She couldn't risk him figuring out her plan.

"I thought if I left Texas that I'd be safe," she said softly, staring at his neck, the tough, tanned flesh that she wanted to just nip and lick.

"You're safe now," he promised, the confidence in his voice soothing her panic marginally.

Only marginally.

"Do you have any idea who's behind all this yet?" she asked, trying to control her fear, and her suspicions.

"J. T. and Mara are still working on it. They think another twelve hours at the most. We should have a short list by then."

A short list. "Is there a long list?" She shifted, bracing her feet fully on the floor, steeling herself for the answer.

"If there is, neither J. T. nor Mara have told me about it," he stated, a bit amused. "I only hear about the short list."

"Wonderful," she muttered.

"No one is going to hurt you, Isabeau," he promised, his voice low as he moved to her, his arms wrapping around her and pulling her against his chest.

How warm he was, how strong. But he wasn't made of steel.

Isabeau shook her head. "I hate it that you and Chance are in the line of fire. Angel's my friend, Tracker. If either of you are hurt, she'll never forgive me."

He chuckled at that, causing her to frown at the disregard.

"This is probably the least dangerous assignment I've had for years," he assured her, the humor in his tone more dark and deadly than she would have expected. "Whoever's behind this has nothing on warlords, terrorists, and extremists determined to murder influential figures or their spoiled-ass heirs. But that aside, Angel would never blame you for anything. She would know better."

He rested his head atop hers, refusing to release the grip he had on her.

It made her feel good, the way he held her. Secure. Safe. Wanted.

Had she felt wanted in her entire adult life? In that moment she knew she hadn't, not really. But Tracker made her feel not just protected but wanted too, needed.

"I wasn't supposed to be at the cabin that night," she admitted to him, feeling him tense as he held her. "I was supposed to be at a sleepover with friends. But one of the girls had started dating a boy I liked and I was angry, so I didn't go." Tears filled her eyes as the fear spiked inside her. "I convinced one of the other girls to take me to the cabin. Mom and Dad were out, so I went to my room, closed the door, and lay down on the bed. I don't remember anything after that. But I hadn't remembered that much until recently."

Until the dreams she'd had as he held her the night before.

Her mother wouldn't have wanted her to remember their deaths, she knew.

"Do you think they died because of something I saw that night?" she asked him.

She'd always feared that had been the case.

"If you saw something you shouldn't have, then that was on them, not on you," he told her firmly. "You wouldn't have seen anything if they weren't doing something that endangered you."

They *had* been doing something. She didn't remember what, but she remembered the arguments, the accusations, and her father's fury. She'd never heard what they were arguing over, just the little eruptions over simple things. A purse her mother bought when she went shopping. Things that made no sense then or now.

"Have you checked the house again for listening devices?" she finally asked when the silence became too much to bear any longer.

"Chance takes care of that several times a day," he assured her. "But yes, he went over it again today, to be certain."

"I don't like this," she said, the fear she was trying to battle back rising inside her again. "I don't like friends being in danger and all this subterfuge."

"It won't last much longer," he assured her.

She'd either be dead or he'd figure out who was trying to kill her.

The slow ache she could feel building in her temples became stronger.

"I'm sure it won't," she agreed, breathing in deeply and stepping away from him.

No, it wouldn't last much longer. Whoever wanted her dead wasn't wasting much time between attempts.

As she turned once again, Tracker caught her arm, pulling her back around and into his arms.

Those dark violet eyes opened wide, a little gasp leaving her lips.

He couldn't resist taking those lips, sinking against them with his own, his tongue forging past, staking ownership, and trying to brand her senses with him. He wasn't a stupid man. He knew himself. And he knew exactly what he was doing with every kiss, every touch.

Just as he knew before he ever pulled her back to him that it wouldn't end with just a kiss. She was too sweet, too tempting, and he was too damned hard for her. Before he left the house, he was going to have her. And waiting wasn't going to happen.

Pushing one hand beneath the soft top she wore, he unclipped the lacy bra and captured a silken, swollen breast in his palm as his finger and thumb encased the hard point of her nipple.

Isabeau lifted to her toes, a strangled cry leaving her lips and meeting his.

Lifting his lips no more than a breath, he looked into her flushed, aroused features, and once again found himself surprised by her instant need for him. Just as his own hunger for her surprised him.

"That's it, Isabeau," he growled against her lips. "Burn for me, baby."

He pulled back just enough to turn her and bend her over until she braced her hands against the cushions of the chair next to them.

"Tracker?" she asked, excitement lacing her voice, excitement and a bit of shock as well.

"I'm not waiting," he informed her, one hand at the small of her back to hold her in place as he released the belt and snap of his pants.

Freeing the iron-hard length of his cock, he pulled at the elastic band of her lounging pants, eased them over her hips to her thighs, then let his fingers graze the slick, hot flesh between her thighs.

"And neither are you." The guttural tone of his voice shocked him.

Had he ever wanted a woman with a ferocity that affected every part of him like this?

He didn't think he ever had. Hell, he hadn't believed it possible, let alone experienced it.

He'd figure it out later, he told himself, parting her thighs as he heard her faint, needy little moans.

Goddamn, she turned him on, made him crazy to have her, made it hard to think of little else but taking her, feeling the pleasure and pure rapture she alone gave him.

Moving into position, knees dipping, he guided his erection to her silken, moisture-laden folds and began pressing inside.

His cock throbbed, the crest expanding further as he forced his way through the snug tissue and heavy feminine moisture. Hot and tight, her vagina clenched on the sensitive head, her hips shifting, moving against him, taking him deeper.

He gripped her hip with one hand but didn't restrain her little movements. It felt too fucking good to hold her back, to keep her still.

Her sheath clenched, fluttering against the thick shaft invading her, taking him until he could barely breathe for the pleasure.

"That's it, baby." He groaned the words, fighting to keep enough of his senses to remain on his feet as he fucked her. "Fuck me back, just like that."

She jerked against him, the explicit words increasing her arousal if the rush of slick heat against his cock was any indication.

Gritting his teeth, he let his lips curve in satisfaction.

"Sweet, hot little pussy." He thrust against her in one hard, impaling push of his hips, burying fully inside her.

Her back lifted, her body jerking in response as another shattered cry met his ears.

"Oh God, Tracker . . ." The cry had sensation racing down his spine as her vagina became tighter, slicker.

"Like that, baby?" he groaned, pulling back slowly until only the throbbing head remained inside the flexing grip. "Let's see if you like this." He tightened his hand at her hip. "Let's see if that hot little pussy likes it."

He pushed in hard, deep. Still, it took two thrusts to forge inside her fully. She gripped his dick in a sensual vise he had no desire to escape.

As he tunneled inside her, she lifted closer, her hips moving, each tight, inexperienced roll of her hips shattering his self-control until there was nothing left of it.

He was lost in the race to the pleasure he knew awaited both of them now. He couldn't speak, couldn't do anything but hold her in place, ensure he didn't hurt her, and fuck the hottest little female he'd ever held in his arms.

Sweat ran in rivulets down the side of his face, stung his eyes, and the heat surrounding them, infusing them, rose by several degrees.

His lust was raging out of control, but so was hers. As though each of them fueled the other's pleasure.

He'd let it mess with his mind later, he promised himself. And it would mess with his head.

For now, there was just Isabeau and keeping them both on their feet amid the most pleasure he'd experienced in his life. Moving inside the snug heat of her body, feeling her response, her rapid rise to release and her need for it, was more than he could bear for long.

Second by second the threads of his control slipped, worn down by her response, by the little gasps and moans that came from her.

He fought it, held back, immersed in how damned good it felt, moving inside her, possessed by her as he took her. He could have made it a few seconds longer, maybe. If she hadn't reached back, those little nails gripping his thigh, pricking at the skin with an added sensation that simply pushed him over the edge.

Two hard thrusts, the feel of her tightening, her orgasm shattering her, and he was done.

Burying deep, he felt his release explode from his cock, filling her, the tightening of her sheath increasing the explosive pleasure until he wondered if his knees would give out.

It took too long for his senses to return, for his brain to suddenly snap a little common sense back into place.

He eased from her, clenching his teeth as her pussy tightened as though to hold him in. Tearing off the shirt he wore, he bent to one knee and, holding her in place, cleaned their combined release from the flushed, bare folds of her sex and from her trembling thighs.

When he finished, he fixed her clothing, then straightened and lifted her in his arms. The way she curled against him, drowsy and sated, caused something in his heart to melt, and he didn't want to know what. Not right now.

"I just want a nap," she sighed as he laid her on her bed and pulled the light blanket over her.

"Nap," he ordered gently. "I'll have something sent from the diner for dinner."

"I need my aspirin. I think I'm getting a headache," she muttered, partially sitting up and reaching for the drawer in the nightstand, fumbling sleepily.

"I have it." He pulled the drawer open and froze.

The picture that lay in the drawer sent a chill chasing down his spine.

"Did you find them?" She covered a delicate little yawn.

Quickly extracting two aspirin from the bottle, he placed them in her hand and handed her the glass of water she kept on the nightstand.

When she placed the glass back on the table and snuggled into her pillows, Tracker picked up the picture and stared at it as anger began to vibrate through him.

He knew the man in motorcycle leather standing next to a Harley with his arm around a younger Isabeau. His fucking features were damned distinctive.

"Isabeau?" He kept his voice low, tried to hide the anger he was feeling.

"Hmm," she muttered, eyes parting drowsily as she stared up at him.

"Who's in this picture with you?" he asked.

A fond smile shaped her lips, but she didn't open her eyes. "My brother, Burke. His sister Kenya gave it to me just before I left, along with pictures of her and the family. She said every house should have pictures, but she wanted me to know for sure which one was of Burke because I hadn't seen his features since I was a teenager, so she wrapped it separately. When I unpacked, I put it in my drawer."

Son of a bitch.

He quickly snapped a picture of it with his phone, then replaced the frame carefully, certain to put the aspirin on top of it so Isabeau could find them easily.

He forced himself to ease back, to leave her lying alone in the bed, drifting off to sleep while he stalked back to his room and changed into his riding gear.

Hell.

He was going to kill the bastard.

Checking the time on his phone, he quickly sent a message, then stalked through the house to the back porch, where Chance was waiting. His sister, Angel, and her husband, Duke, had just pulled up the drive. Within seconds they were at the porch.

"She's in bed sleeping," he told them. "Chance is with me. This might take a while. I'll message when we're on our way back."

"Be careful," Angel told him softly as she patted his arm. "We'll take care of Isabeau."

And they would. He'd not just helped raise Angel, he'd helped train her. And he knew her husband, Duke Mackay, was a deadly enemy.

He stalked through the shadows of the backyard as he and Chance made their way to where the bikes were parked several houses down, under the eagle-eyed watchfulness of Ramble Calloway, the oldest of the two cousins who had flown out to provide backup.

"What's up, Track?" Chance muttered as they checked the bikes over, just to be certain no one had managed to get to them.

Removing his phone from his jacket, Tracker pulled up the picture he'd hastily taken of the photo in Isabeau's drawer and showed it to his brother.

Silence filled the night for long seconds as Chance stared at the image.

"Fuck." He finally gave a heavy sigh. "She know who her brother is?"

"I don't think she does." He tucked the phone back in place, then straddled the bike before looking back at Chance. "I'm damned sure she doesn't. But I'm betting Doogan and Zoey know. I sent a message to J. T. and Mara," he told his brother. "I want everything they can pull up on Burke Weston, aka John Black, before dawn."

He'd given the team a month here, mostly because the past year had been a busy one with several back-to-back jobs. He hadn't thought it would take as long as it had to at least find a suspect, though he could feel that suspect getting ready to show himself.

Ensuring Isabeau was safe when that happened was of paramount importance.

"What are you gonna do about her brother?" Chance asked.

Looking at him, Tracker smiled. A cold, hard smile.

"I'm gonna beat the fuck out of him."

EIGHTEEN

THE WAREHOUSE AT THE EDGE OF SOMERSET WAS DARK, a deserted relic of days gone past, now overgrown with ivy and the pitiful weeds trying to grow through the cracked and crumbling asphalt surrounding it. The dim bulb above the front entrance flickered in a feeble attempt to shed its weakened light, but only a small glow pierced the foggy darkness.

From one side of the forested hill surrounding the warehouse, Tracker listened as the growling rumble of a dozen Harleys eased into the small valley. Lights pierced the darkness, like the glowing eyes of stalking beasts, illuminating the area and piercing the shadows with a heavy sense of foreboding.

As they idled nearer, a shadow moved at the end of the warehouse and a gaping darkness opened slowly, the nearing lights revealing the derelict condition of the interior.

Tracker made his way from the hill to where he and Chance had parked their bikes behind a heap of rusted unused beams and sheet metal, keeping a careful watch on the area.

The Reapers hadn't sent a scout ahead, nor had they left anyone outside the warehouse to alert them to his arrival.

Stepping to his brother's side, Tracker pulled his weapon from his back and locked it in the metal saddle bag at the side of the bike as Chance did the same.

"This is dumb," Chance growled. "Going in unarmed like this. I know this crew, and they're never unarmed."

"They have enemies we don't." Tracker shrugged. "I'm here for a reason, Chance. That reason has nothing to do with guns. But you can watch from here if you like."

Chance snorted at the offer, locked the saddle bag he'd stored his weapon in, and straightened. Throwing his shoulders back and lifting his head, he stared down that half inch he had on Tracker broodingly.

Damn. That fucker looked far too much like his natural brother for Tracker's peace of mind.

"Jakob believes in a fair fight," he reminded Chance. "He'll make sure the rest of them follow suit."

He caught the roll of green eyes.

"Let's go," he ordered, rather than entertaining more of Chance's observations.

They stepped from behind the discarded metal and walked the distance across the parking lot, giving the now dismounted riders plenty of time to see them. The Harleys were silent now, but the lights were aimed directly toward the opened doors, glaring bright and malevolent at Tracker and Chance's advance.

Stepping into the silent interior and past the blinding light, Tracker gave his eyes a few seconds to adjust. When the dark shapes of the riders could be picked up, he looked around, his gaze landing on the man he knew commanded the hardened, secretive motorcycle club.

Most of these men didn't even have pictures in the files some law enforcement agents had on them. That included the president, John Black, known as Burke Weston to others, as well as his vice, Jakob.

"Tracker," John greeted, never moving from where Jakob and the hulking mountain known as Jango Marx covered him.

"Black." Tracker nodded to the other man as the sound of more advancing bikes could be heard nearing the warehouse.

"Friends?" Tracker asked. "Let me guess, Mavericks and Renegades."

He caught a brief flash of teeth as the echo of more than two dozen additional riders joined the party. The Harleys roared into the warehouse, surrounding the Reapers, and fully lighting the interior of the warehouse. Four bikes stopped at the entrance, riders dismounting, and moments later the heavy doors closed once again.

The furious, echoing growl of the motorcycles abated, shutting down a few at a time, until the interior was once again silent.

"Hell of a welcoming party, Jakob." Tracker addressed Black's vice, the man Tracker had arranged this meeting with.

"Not often someone with your rep demands a meet with our president." Jakob smiled confidently. "We know about your invisible little group, Tracker. Better to be safe than sorry, right?"

These men took the protection of their president seriously. And evidently, so did the two supposedly friendly rivals that the other two gangs were rumored to be.

Tracker nodded slowly and held his hands out from his sides. "I said I was coming in unarmed and accompanied only by Chance. I don't break my word."

He and Chance stood still as several of the riders moved forward quickly and checked them for weapons. Then for wires. With the formalities taken care of, they nodded back to Jakob and returned to their bikes.

"What's the meet about?" Black spoke this time, stepping from between the two men covering him.

"How many of these men do you trust with your life?" Tracker asked then. "I'd advise keeping only your nearest and dearest inside. I'd send the rest out."

Silence met the suggestion. Black stared at him, his gaze piercing before looking around the warehouse.

"I trust them all," Black assured him, and Tracker knew better.

"Well, I don't," Tracker retorted, hardening his tone. He didn't trust anyone with Isabeau's life outside his own family, but this man, he had no choice but to trust. "This concerns my client, so out of respect, nearest and dearest only."

Black never shifted nor indicated the tension Tracker could suddenly feel emanating from him.

"Jakob, Jango, Tiggan, March." He named off the very men Tracker had known he'd name. "The rest of you, step out."

It took a minute, but the warehouse slowly emptied of all but Black and the men he named. When the doors closed behind the other members of the three motorcycle clubs, Tracker met Black's gaze once again as the four men moved closer.

"How much do you trust these men?" Tracker asked.

Black's lips quirked. "Let's say they know my secrets," he answered.

Tracker nodded and let all the fury he felt toward this man escape when he spoke. "Do they know why I'm kicking your ass before I leave here tonight, or do you want to tell them? Because when I leave here, one of us is going to understand the other real fucking well, asshole."

Black grimaced, his hand lifting to rub over his face in frustration before he stared back at Tracker once again.

"I'm not fighting you, man," he sighed. "Both of us need to be in top form if we're going to draw this bastard out. And if I step forward, if I make any move to show my awareness of the danger she's in, then he'll go into hiding again and we'll never identify him."

Tracker clenched his fists, rage eating inside him like acid now. Because the son of a bitch was right.

Tracker could hear the torment, the sense of futility that Isabeau's brother felt, and the rage the leader of a deadly motorcycle gang felt.

"Who do you suspect?" He had to have an idea where the danger was coming from.

"Everyone," Black snorted, pushing his hands through his overly long black hair as he shifted restlessly. "Except those here now. We've tried to cover her, take turns whenever she's away from the ranch. Then I found out the so-called accidents had been happening there as well. For years I've tried to figure this out." He bared his teeth in a furious grimace. "Why the fuck do you think I agreed to allow her away from the one place she should have been safe?"

Betrayal. Tracker heard it in his voice, saw it in his face.

"Family," he said softly. "You suspect someone close to you."

"Not our men." Tiggan spoke up, his dark, savage features creased with worry. "We've been trying to figure this out for nearly a year now. We've laid in false information, rumors, anything we thought would draw out a traitor in our crews. Nothing's blipped. Not even a hint. But we're still careful."

"Yeah, association with that contact of yours could make life dicey in your little trades."

Jakob gave a snort of laughter. "Our crew is specially selected, Tracker. Trust me, they know of that association. They'd do us little good and be more a threat than anything else otherwise."

Son of a bitch, Doogan had his own little mini army set up in three motorcycle gangs with more rap sheets than a prison. How the fuck did he do it?

"It started with one little girl who risked her life to save two friends from rival gangs," Black stated softly. "Zoey Mackay. That's when the loyalty pact began. Over the years its pared down to only those members we trust implicitly. But that's beside the point and has nothing to do with Isabeau. This has to do with our mother's murder and what Isabeau saw that night. I know that much for a fact."

Unfortunately, Tracker agreed.

"I really want to beat the shit out of you, Black," he muttered, shooting the biker a fulminating look.

"Yeah, well, considering you're going to walk away from the sister I suspect is already half in love with you, according to Jango, I can feel your dilemma there, Tracker." Black gave a mocking laugh. "I know you, I made it my business to know you when Angel first showed up in Somerset. I knew you were the best man to protect one of two women I'd die for. I also knew there was a chance you'd break her heart."

And what the fuck could he say to that? He couldn't deny it, couldn't reassure the brother that the sister's heart was safe. No matter how much he wanted to.

"Doesn't help that you're sleeping with her," Jango grunted, his ruined voice a harsh growl. "Fucker!"

"Jango. Stop." Black seemed to remind the other man of something as he shook his head wearily. "She's not a kid anymore, as you and Jakob like to remind me. You can't treat her like one now."

Jango's noncommittal grunt could have meant anything.

"I've played uncaring and unconcerned with Isabeau and Kenya, hoping to keep them safe. So far, I succeeded where my enemies are concerned. But Isabeau is another story."

"I have her covered." Tracker glanced at Chance and saw the empathy his foster brother felt for the club president.

"As far as anyone else is aware, it's just you, Chance, and one other man," Black told him. "We're getting reports out of Costa's crew, and from what I hear, whoever's funding this little job is getting pissed, but Costa didn't reveal who it was. Shit will hit the fan when Costa's boss learns three of his best men killed each other."

Jakob's and Jango's smiles were pure, cold vengeance.

"We kicking his ass, or what?" Chance asked with feigned boredom then. "If not, Angel just messaged. Isabeau's having nightmares."

"Fuck! Get back there," Black snarled. "And get ready, Tracker. I suspect her sight is improving, and I know she's getting ready to remember what happened that night. When she does, our mother's killer will strike. God help us all if he succeeds."

NINETEEN

ISABEAU CAME AWAKE, A GASP OF FEAR ON HER LIPS, eyes wide as she stared into the dimly lit bedroom, confused and fighting to adjust from the dream to reality.

Swallowing tightly, she snapped her eyes open again, realizing in that moment that her vision was clear. Each detail of the room was clear, shapes and colors coming together without the edge of blurriness in her periphery.

Her vision was perfectly clear.

In the same moment, she knew she'd awakened herself with her screams. She always knew, because her throat was raw. But she wasn't alone in her room either.

As her lashes lifted, the bedroom door slammed open and Angel and her husband, Duke Mackay, rushed in, weapons held carefully at their thighs.

She could see them.

Angel, petite and blond, her pretty inquisitive features a perfect complement to her darker-haired husband with his harder, more dangerous expression.

"Did I scream?" she whispered as they discreetly reholstered their weapons at the smalls of their backs.

"Yeah, you did." Angel approached the bed cautiously, her expression concerned. "Are you okay, Isabeau?"

Was she okay? Physically she was fine, she knew. But she was suddenly scared, terrified of the memories she could now recall.

"I'm okay," she affirmed, still feeling off-balance and trying to adjust to the sudden clear sight. The ability to see everything as it was in perfect detail.

"Are you sure, sweetie?" Angel frowned at her from the other side of the bed. "You don't look okay."

Didn't she? She wondered if she looked as frightened as she felt.

"Angel," Isabeau all but whispered, irrationally terrified of being heard. "I can see you. I mean, all the way see you. Clearly."

She hadn't intended to tell the other woman that her vision was clear. She had intended to keep that to herself when it happened. But the fear driving her now was so instinctive, so strong, that the words slipped free.

Angel froze, her pretty gray eyes widening momentarily before her gaze snapped to the side to glance at her husband.

"I can see him too," she admitted, feeling the tears threatening to build in her eyes.

"I assumed so." Angel smiled gently. "But are you okay, honey? Do we need to call a doctor?"

Isabeau shook her head.

"I'm sorry I screamed." She held the blankets to her, aware she was naked beneath them. "I need to get dressed."

She needed to be alone, to process everything, to make sense of it.

"Will you be okay?" Angel asked, her concern evident.

Isabeau nodded, glancing back to Duke Mackay. He wasn't looking at her, but there was no doubt he was aware of every move she made.

"I'm fine." She licked her dry lips nervously. "Will Tracker be back soon?"

She shouldn't have asked, she knew she shouldn't have, but she was off-balance—no, she was scared. She was so scared, she was cold with the fear, and she needed him there.

He was always warm. Maybe he'd hold her, just for a moment, give her that sense of security she felt with him so she could find her balance.

"I can check," Angel offered. "Get dressed, Isabeau. I'm sure it won't be much longer."

Isabeau nodded, watching the couple warily as they left her bedroom. But it wasn't the two of them concerning her. It was the memories suddenly filling her head. The emotions, the fear, the panic that had overwhelmed her that night.

She remembered the bedroom at the cabin, sparsely furnished with a bed, dresser, and easy chair. She'd awakened at the sounds of loud voices, male and female.

There were two men. It wasn't just her father, but someone else.

It was someone she knew. Isabeau was aware of their identity but that knowledge was just behind the mists that still filled her mind.

Her mother was crying, begging. . . .

She remembered the sobs and the fact she'd never heard her mother cry. Ever. She'd heard her angry, regretful, apologetic, but never had she heard her frightened or sobbing.

Isabeau's heart was racing now, fear clogging her throat at that memory. Just as it had been that night.

Hands shaking, she pushed them through her hair, clenching on the strands at her scalp for long moments.

She heard her mother pleading with someone to please stop. *Please don't hurt them. . . .*

She fought for the memory, trying to remember what the other voice sounded like, who it was. Because she knew she had known that voice in her dream.

Isabeau forced herself from the bed, though it took several seconds to make her unsteady legs work. Her hands were shaking, her lips on the verge of trembling, and she wanted to sit down and let the tears fall. Instead, she walked unsteadily to the dresser, pulled out the drawer, and stared at the outfits stacked within it.

She pulled a pair of jeans and T-shirt free, moved to her chest, and collected a matching bra and panties. As her head lifted, she caught sight of herself in the mirror and stood still, staring at her image.

She hadn't seen her own image since she was fifteen. She'd forgotten what she looked like. The color of her hair, of her eyes, the shape of her face.

Lifting her hand, she watched as she stroked her fingers over her high cheekbones, the pouty curve of her lips. Stepping back, she stared at her naked body, her fingers going to the marks Tracker had left on her flesh. At the base of her neck, her breasts, on her hip, the inside of her thigh.

He'd marked her as though he owned her.

She shook her head at the thought. He'd warned her this wouldn't last past the discovery of whoever threatened her.

Her lips trembled again, the knowledge that she'd lose him soon causing her breath to hitch, the tears to threaten once again.

Turning away from the mirror, she quickly dressed, adding socks and sneakers to the clothes. Once she finished, she brushed out her hair, pulled it back into a ponytail, then walked to the window.

Pulling the curtain aside, she stared into the darkness, saw the stars shining overhead, the shadows that twisted and turned among the trees and brush separating her house from her neighbors'.

The shadows . . .

She stared into the rippling areas of those darker shadows, remembering how dark and alone her world would be if her vision retreated again. If it went away before Tracker returned, before she could see him, memorize his features so she'd always remember them.

She backed away from the window, then turned and stared into her dimly lit bedroom, her gaze falling on the bedside table and barely opened drawer.

Tracker had found the picture earlier. She'd forgotten she'd put it there until he asked her who it was.

Burke. A smile trembled on her lips as she rushed over, kneeling on the floor in front of the table and opening the drawer fully. Reaching in, she lifted the picture free and stared down at it.

She stood next to a tall, dark-haired man in jeans with leather riding chaps, a black T-shirt, and a black leather vest. His arm was around her, and she was smiling, but he wasn't. He looked somber, sad, alone.

He was five years older than she was, but the look in his eyes was older, bitter.

She stared at the photograph, seeing how he was turned to her, his back partially to the photographer, and her gaze was caught by the patch on the back of his vest.

A scythe, blazing fire, and the end of a word above it: *ERS*.

Reapers. She knew it was Reapers. Tracker had asked her about the Reapers, if she had heard of the motorcycle club, and that they weren't very nice men.

She stared at that vest, and she remembered it. Remembered

seeing the back of one fully. The fiery scythe, blood dripping down it, the word *REAPERS* emblazoned above it.

She dropped the picture, pushing herself quickly to her feet as it landed on the thick throw rug next to her bed.

It wasn't Burke she remembered wearing that vest. She could feel the memory, like a forgotten name hovering on the tip of her tongue, and she knew, knew to her soul, that whoever she hadn't yet remembered, she was frightened of.

"Isabeau?" Angel called out, knocking lightly on the bedroom door. "Are you dressed, sweetie?"

She hurriedly picked up the picture and shoved it back in place, closing the drawer with a clumsy move of her hands before turning to the door.

She cleared her throat and quickly dried away the evidence of the tear that tracked from one eye.

"Yes," she called out. "You can come in."

The door opened slowly, pushing wide, and Angel stepped just inside the room.

"I was worried," Angel told her with a gentle smile. "I hadn't heard anything from you."

"Getting my bearings." She rubbed at the side of her leg, still not certain she'd managed to do that. "Did you hear from Tracker?"

Angel shook her head. "Not yet. But he'll be in contact soon."

She wished he'd hurry. She was so damned cold. Maybe she should have taken a hot shower, she thought. There had been times that the water had helped chase away the chill. But Tracker was so much better at it.

"I need to go to the cabin." The words passed her lips before Isabeau realized the thought was in her mind. "I need to, Angel."

She had to go there. Now. While the memories were so close, just almost visible, remembered. She couldn't wait for Tracker, even though she knew she should.

"Tracker will be here soon, Isabeau," Angel promised. "I can't let you leave until he gets here. He'd hurt Duke really bad, you know. And I like that man's body as is." Her tone and her smile asked for understanding.

Isabeau did understand. Tracker would be angry, she admitted. He'd be all kinds of pissed, but she needed to go now. She needed to remember, and what if her memory as well as her eyesight retreated before Tracker's return?

Isabeau nodded as though accepting the fact that leaving wasn't going to happen.

"Can I be alone a little while longer, Angel?" she asked. "I just need to get my bearings before he gets here."

She didn't elaborate; she refused to allow the nervous excuses that hit her head to pass her lips. She took a deep, hard breath and glanced away, terrified Angel would glimpse the truth in her eyes. And that she couldn't allow.

"I understand, Isabeau." Compassion filled Angel's voice. "I'll send Tracker in when he gets here."

Isabeau nodded. When Angel left and closed the door behind her, Isabeau all but ran back to her bedside table and jerked her smartphone from where it lay next to the lamp.

Mattie.

Mattie would come get her. But she didn't dare use the voice control feature on her smartphone, she was too scared someone would overhear her.

She texted her friend quickly instead, waited, biting at her lip in fear that Mattie could actually be busy. When the reply came, Isabeau nearly lost her breath in relief. Now, how to get out of the house when the doors were either watched or equipped with motion detectors?

She knew her window, for certain, held one of the devices. It was on the inside of the window though, and she'd heard Chance tell Tracker he'd placed the window alarms on the inside to ensure they couldn't be tampered with. Because a flat piece of metal slid beneath it before opening the window would trick the alarm system.

Thin piece of metal.

Moving quickly to the window, she studied the device for long moments before hurrying to the closet where she kept her purse. It took a moment, well, maybe a few moments, to find a thin hair barrette at the bottom of her bag. The drawer of her bed table revealed a roll of gift tape.

It wasn't easy, but she managed to work the thin metal back of the barrette free, then push it between the metal strip and the detector with the tape secured to the back.

Pushing the tape into place, she then worked the window open, and a few heartbeats later she was shimmying out and running the short distance to the hedge between her property and her neighbors.

She found her way to the end of the block just in time to catch Mattie turning the corner next to the café.

"Isabeau?" Shock creased Mattie's expression as she slammed the car to a stop.

Without an explanation Isabeau pulled open the passenger-side door and jumped into the car, sliding low in the seat as she closed it once again.

"Just drive, Mattie," she hissed.

"You can see?" Mattie still wasn't moving.

She stared at Isabeau as though she were some unknown specter.

"Drive. I'll explain once we're past the house. Now hurry," Isabeau pleaded, almost breathing a sigh of relief when the vehicle began moving.

As they passed the house, she saw several men running for it, the front door opened, and Duke and Angel came onto the porch, yelling out to someone.

"Keep driving," Isabeau ordered her friend. "Don't even slow down."

Mattie glanced at her warily as Isabeau all but hid in the floor of the little sedan.

"Explain, girlfriend." Mattie wasn't happy. "And this better be good."

TWENTY

ISABEAU HADN'T REALIZED HOW LATE IT WAS. IT WAS nearly midnight before Mattie reach the graveled drive that led to the lakefront cabin her parents had owned. She didn't know if she or Burke had inherited it, maybe both, but she knew it had never sold, despite the offers her brother had received.

Mattie was still in shock that Isabeau had regained her sight and uncertain about the request she'd made.

"Isabeau, look, this might not be a good idea," Mattie said, not for the first time. "Let's go back and get Tracker. He's there for a reason."

"Tracker isn't there." She shook her head, staring at the road Mattie's headlights illuminated. "When you get back to town, stop at the house and tell whoever's there where I'm at. I'll be fine waiting for him."

She'd forgotten and left her cell phone on her bed in her haste to get out of the house. Thankfully, Isabeau didn't have Tracker's number. Mattie had suggested Isabeau use her cell several times and call him herself.

"I don't know about leaving you here alone," Mattie said, worried again. "It doesn't feel right. Maybe I should go in with you. Wait on you or something."

"That's because you're a worrywart," Isabeau told her when Mattie pulled the car to a stop at the short sidewalk leading into the cabin. "Go back and stop at the house. Someone will be there."

Opening the door, Isabeau stepped from the car, then leaned back inside to meet Mattie's gaze again.

"I'll be fine. I promise," she assured her friend. "Go now. I need this time alone, Mattie."

She didn't know what she was going to remember, but she could feel the answers coming closer, mixed with her mother's screams of rage and pain.

"Isabeau . . ." Mattie began.

"Go!" She stepped back, slammed the door closed, and gave her friend a determined wave.

Thankfully, Mattie backed up, turned her car around, and drove away from the cabin.

Walking slowly up the walk to the front door, Isabeau bent to the abandoned flowerpot and pushed her finger into the dirt that still filled it. Along the side, just an inch in the dirt, the key to the house was still hidden, protected by the porch overhang.

Pulling it free, Isabeau slid it into the lock with shaking fingers and unlocked the door.

The cabin was dark, the furniture covered with sheets. Isabeau flicked the light switch next to the door, thankful to see the lamps positioned on the low tables next to the couch across the room glow with a soft, warm light.

She'd been so angry when she'd arrived there ten years before. Angry at her friend and at the boy she'd had a crush on. She'd stomped to her bedroom and thrown herself on her bed, where she'd gone to sleep.

It had been dark when she'd awakened.

Moving into the living room, she came to a slow, painful stop, staring at the floor. The golden oak floor was darker in the center of the room.

Blood flashed before her gaze, the sound of her own screams filling her ears as she sank to her knees next to where her mother had lain.

She'd screamed out for her mother. Over and over again. Her father lay several feet from his wife, a neat little hole in the middle of his forehead as blood pooled beneath the back of his head. Her handsome, quiet father. She'd watched him as he watched others. He was picky about his friends and was loyal to them. But his wife and daughter had meant everything to him.

Her mother had been shot in the chest.

She was still alive when Isabeau knelt beside her, sobbing, begging her mother to please, please be okay.

There had been so much blood, she remembered. Her mother had stared up at her, her lips trembling.

"Why are you here, baby? You shouldn't have seen this," she whispered. *"You shouldn't have ever had this memory. . . ."*

Isabeau was only barely aware of the tears that soaked her face now and dripped to the floor.

Her mother hadn't wanted her to remember it, but she'd known, just as Isabeau had, even then, that she probably wouldn't leave the cabin that night alive.

Her eyes lifted, widened as a man stepped from the bedroom across the room. Tall, his black-and-silver hair cut close, wearing jeans and a black vest.

At first, it was part of her memories, right down to the sight of the gun he held in his hand, the black of the short barrel gleaming in the dull light.

His hair hadn't been silver then, she thought inanely. It had been black as night. He'd been younger, her father's age, and, she guessed, considered handsome. And she'd known him then, just as she knew him now.

Her brother's uncle. Bill Weston.

"I knew, when you remembered, you'd come here," he sighed, his pale blue eyes like ice. Devoid of emotion. Without a conscience. "Just as I knew you'd remember, Isabeau. I always knew."

Hadn't he said that more than once over the years? Always with a low laugh, as though he had faith in her, cared for her.

She'd always known better. She'd always known that Bill Weston cared for no one but himself.

"And I'm still alive," she whispered. "Why didn't you finish it when the first attempt failed?"

She stared up at him, knowing he hadn't meant for her to survive that night. But he'd had ten years to kill her since. Why hadn't he?

"You're like a fuckin' cat," he sighed, his thin lips quirking with an annoyed look. "Nine goddamned lives or more. I shot you in the head, and I was certain I killed you. How the hell that bullet just grazed your stupid hard head, I have no clue."

He shook his head as he sat in the chair directly across from her and looked down at the floor, at the dark stain that had once been her mother's blood.

Isabeau was shocked at the sadness that flickered across his expression for just a second. She'd never imagined his narcissistic little soul would know how to feel such an emotion.

"She was beautiful," he said softly. "I loved her from the day I met her, whore that she was. Lyin' fuckin' tramp." He sneered then. "And you." He shot her a look filled with resentment and anger. "You just had to look like her. Beautiful and wild and so damned pretty it made my heart hurt to remember."

Sentiment?

He wasn't known for sentiment.

"You have a heart?" She fought the rage burning inside her. "Excuse me if I call you a liar. You don't murder the woman you love, asshole. You damn sure don't attempt to kill the child she loved. Just isn't done, Bill."

And he laughed at her.

"Just like her," he said again, his finger resting on the trigger a little too firmly. "This time I'll make sure you're dead." He stared at her, his gaze like steel.

"And Burke?" she asked him, desperate to find a way to survive now. "He'll figure it out, Bill. This time, he'll find you."

He chuckled at the warning. "Burke will have to die as well. You see, he holds the one thing I covet above all others. He commands the Reapers. A very dangerous little group of men. With him gone . . ."

"No one who follows Burke will ever follow you, Bill," she informed him, feeling the deadline on her life nearing.

She had to distract him, had to find a way to keep this from happening.

Bill glared at her. "I know what I'm doing."

"Anyone who's loyal to Burke will never be so with you. You know they won't be."

"They don't have to be," he told her with a smile, a curve of self-satisfaction that terrified her. "Burke may have their loyalty, but I have enough information on each one of them that I can make certain I get what I want. Once I do, the rest will take care of itself."

Isabeau forced herself to sneer at his confidence despite the fact that she was terrified.

"You assume the men who follow him are that weak," she said

softly, as though she knew something about what the hell they were talking about. "Burke isn't that weak, and you know it. He'd never gather weak men around him. If there's even one that you can't control, then you're doomed."

Was that doubt that crossed his expression for just a moment?

"Strong men don't back down when the person they follow is murdered," she pointed out softly. "They wait, they watch, and when they strike, you can't avoid them."

He jerked to his feet, those icy blue eyes of his glittering with fury.

"Do you know how I met your mother?" he suddenly demanded.

Isabeau shook her head warily, watching as he turned his back on her and paced a few short steps away before whirling back once again.

"Mac led the Reapers then. A motorcycle gang. A very lucrative one actually." He rubbed at his stubbled cheek, his gaze pinned on her. "We were in Biloxi on a drug buy when Mac stopped in at a diner she was waitressing at. She was beautiful." His voice dropped, reverence filling it for a moment before it hardened once again. "When we left the diner, she was on the back of his bike. Before I even had a chance...."

Isabeau eased from the floor to sit on the couch as he watched her, keeping the weapon he held carefully in her periphery.

"But Mom didn't stay," she pointed out. "Let me guess, she found out drugs were involved?"

Isabeau reminded Bill that she wasn't just someone he needed to get rid of. She looked like the woman he claimed to love, and though he'd killed her, it was obvious she was an obsession of his.

He stared at her now, his expression quiet, reflective.

"Mac took her straight to the ranch, married her a few months later." He rubbed at the back of his neck. "Yeah, she found out about the drugs when that little twit son of hers and Mac's was about two." He shot Isabeau a mocking smile then. "She ran away. Left the kid so

Mac would let her go. That was their agreement. To keep their son, Mac swore Burke would never ride with the Reapers and Mac would never come after her."

Isabeau had never known why her mother had given up custody of her son. It was obvious when Burke visited that their mother loved him.

"I didn't know where she was for years, after she left Texas. Not until Burke began visiting her, just after you were born." He paced to the bar, stepped behind it, and, keeping his eye on her, placed his weapon on the top of the counter as he poured himself a drink.

"They didn't trust you?" she said knowingly. "Go figure."

His lips quirked in amusement. She'd hoped to piss him off.

"Mac knew how I felt." He shrugged, lifting the whiskey he'd poured to his lips and taking a healthy drink of the strong alcohol. "I think he worried I'd go looking for her."

He finished the drink, placed the glass back on the table, then laid his hand on the gun once again.

God, she had to find a way to distract him. She had to get away from him because she knew he had no intention of allowing her to leave the cabin alive.

"How did you find her?" There was no way Burke would have told him if he'd known Bill was a threat of any kind.

He grunted at the question. "By accident. We were in Somerset about twelve years ago during a weapons buy to some national liberty yahoos." He chuckled again, as though he found selling weapons to homeland terrorists amusing. "And there she was, trying to duck into some store to hide from us." He shook his head, his expression perplexed. "As though she could ever hide from me. After that, it was easy to find her."

He poured another drink, remaining silent for long moments, the gun within close, easy reach as he seemed locked in some memory.

"Why did you kill my parents?" she asked, unable to hold the question back. "If you loved my mother, how could you kill her? What did she do to you, Bill, to make you hate her that much?"

"She refused to come home," he said absently, glancing at the drink a moment. "I came back to Somerset that summer, found her, and told her how I felt." There was regret, but not enough, she knew. "She'd left her son when he was still a baby, as well as her husband. But she refused to leave that bastard Boudreaux or you?"

There was hatred in his gaze when he stared across the room at her now. "You weren't even a baby. A fifteen-year-old little bitch with no more sense than to not stay home when you were told to, right?"

Right.

She hadn't stayed home. Her parents had allowed her to go to the sleepover she'd begged to go to when normally they wouldn't have. And she'd left that party and come to the cabin when she normally did as her parents told her to do.

His hand tightened on the gun, and she knew her time was up.

TWENTY-ONE

HALFWAY BETWEEN THE WAREHOUSE AND ISABEAU'S home, the emergency signal on his phone went off. Angel wouldn't use that option except in the most dire of circumstances.

And only Isabeau could possibly be considered dire.

"Angel?" He activated the Bluetooth on his helmet and answered the call.

"She's gone!" Angel snapped. "She could see, Tracker. Called someone to pick her up. Ramble's trailing them, and they're heading your way."

Glancing around, he quickly signaled Chance and Isabeau's brother before pulling to the shoulder of the road.

"How?" he snarled furious. "How did she get out of the house?"

"She jimmied the alarm on her bedroom window and slipped out," Angel stated quickly. "Ramble contacted me the second she slipped into an unknown female's car and they drove away. I suspect Mattie Watts. She wanted to go to the cabin, but you weren't here. And you had Jase watching the cabin? He said there's someone else there. Burke Weston's uncle."

Tracker was aware of Weston standing next to him, his expression suspicious as he watched Tracker.

"Tell Ramble to pinpoint my location and pick me up," Tracker snarled. "We go in eighteen bikes deep and she's fucking dead."

He was going to paddle her ass for this little stunt. If he managed to save her.

"He has your location, and he's heading there," Angel confirmed.

Disconnecting the call, Tracker pulled the helmet from his head, glaring at the other man furiously.

"What the fuck is your uncle doing in Somerset?"

Something akin to terror flickered over Weston's face.

"He should be in Texas." He gave a hard shake of his head.

"Get ready to leave your bike here. There's enough room in the truck for you and one other man. No bikes, Weston, because I have a feeling Isabeau's dead if one is heard nearing that cabin she raced off to."

"Why would she do that? How could she . . . ?" Confusion filled his face, his voice.

"Her sight's been returning for a while." Dismounting the bike, Tracker placed the helmet on the seat. "My men will come in and get our bikes if you're riding with us."

"Isabeau can see?" Weston shook his head. "I suspected it was improving, but . . . She didn't tell me she could see. . . ."

"She didn't tell anyone but me," Tracker snapped. "She didn't trust anyone, goddammit. And you weren't around enough to give a damn, were you?"

The biker flinched, his expression hardening as he turned to one of the other two leaders.

"Jakob and I are going with you. Two-door cab truck?" Weston turned back to him, all emotion absent from his voice.

"Dual cab." Tracker nodded.

"Then you have room in the truck bed," Weston's second, Jakob, decided abruptly and motioned to the two other presidents. "Room for six others."

Bikes were moved farther from the side of the road, orders given, and, as Tracker watched, weapons prepared. The single motorcycle trailer on the back of one of the bikes held, of all things, automatic weapons.

Son of a bitch, how these bastards didn't get caught with their illegal hauls was a fucking miracle.

"When did Bill show up?" Weston demanded as Tracker stood aside and watched everyone preparing for Ramble to arrive.

"I don't know when. I just know he's there." Tracker had to forcibly keep himself from putting a fist in Weston's face. "John Black," he sneered, addressing Weston by the identity he used as a cutthroat, drug-dealing, arms-selling motorcycle gang leader. "Hell of a double life you're leading, isn't it?"

"Some days," Weston snapped. "Though yours isn't much safer, is it?"

He was going to put his fist in the bastard's face for sure, Tracker thought.

"Here's Ramble," Tracker called out as the signal pinged his phone. "Get ready to load up."

The second the pickup pulled to a stop, seven men loaded in the back with weapons, while Tracker, Weston, and Chance quickly entered the cab.

"Jase just reported." Truck tires squealed as Ramble hit the gas. "It's definitely Bill Weston at the cabin, and he's holding a gun on Isabeau. What do you want Jase to do?"

"Jase have that rifle of his?" Tracker snapped the question, aware of Burke's fists clenching where he sat in the back seat with him.

"That's how he's watching him, but he doesn't have a shot yet,"

Ramble answered as he navigated the speeding truck easily. "We're a good six minutes from the cabin if we rush in, ten if we ease in."

"That's if you take the main road," Weston snapped. "There's a logging road that's a hell of a lot quicker and you can use the lights until you're almost at the back door."

"Direct him." Tracker nodded. "Ramble, connect us with Jase. I want this coordinated. Isabeau is the main priority."

He let the biker direct Ramble as he listened to the reports Jase was giving. He hadn't found a position to get a clear shot on the elder Weston yet, but he was getting closer.

He wanted the threat against Isabeau neutralized at first chance. He didn't give a damn about a confession or explanations; he did care about her survival.

"That bastard's dead, Weston," he warned Isabeau's brother, not even attempting to cover the fury in his tone. "And God help you if Isabeau doesn't survive."

Because losing her would destroy him.

"SO, MOM DIED BECAUSE SHE DIDN'T LOVE YOU?" ISA-beau asked as Bill stared at the gun he'd laid on the bar before turning back to her. "Because she loved someone else?"

"The two of you remind me daily of your mother's betrayal. She should have been mine. I loved her." He shouted the last words, his hand now gripping the gun where it lay on the bar in front of him. "I loved her, you little fuckin' bitch. And she knew it. She left Mac while I was gone. She ran before I could stop her."

Her poor mother, Isabeau thought painfully. To learn the man she loved was involved with drugs and guns, part of the criminal element, and the only way out was to give up her child and run?

She remembered now, how her father had yelled back at her

mother that leaving her child hadn't been the answer. And she remembered her mother crying. Sobbing.

None of this made enough sense.

Isabeau shook her head. "And you think no one will know it was you?" she asked him, fear building within her. "Tracker doesn't work alone, Bill. The friend that dropped me off will have called, at the very least, a Mackay before she was out of the driveway."

Indecision flickered over his expression now. "No one knows I'm here."

"Doesn't mean no one will know," she told him. "How did you get here? You had to have driven. The Mackays are everywhere, and they're my friends. And you assume one of Tracker's men didn't follow me and my friend here. I was only fast enough to get away from them, but my ride wasn't fast enough to lose anyone that followed us."

Bill's gaze moved to the window behind her.

"I've been watching you." He narrowed his eyes on her. "There was two of them; that was it."

She shook her head at the observation. "There were just two in the house with me. There was also someone watching from outside. And I'm pretty sure we were followed to the turnoff on the main road. You won't have a chance to take anything from Burke. He'll be waiting on you when you get back to the ranch, along with Tracker. You might kill me this time, but I promise, they'll make you pay for it."

Once again, his eyes shifted to the window then back to her.

"You didn't love my mother," she whispered. "Love doesn't kill, Bill. You just couldn't stand the fact that she didn't want you."

He shook his head. "You should have died with her." His expression was somber now, rather than tinged with the madness of moments before. "I didn't want to hurt you, Isabeau, but we don't leave witnesses."

"Then do it right this time." She felt a tear fall down her cheek. "Don't leave me in the darkness again."

Something nearing regret creased his face, and he turned his head from her, lifted his hand from the gun, and covered his eyes.

Isabeau didn't wait; she didn't think. The second he turned his head, she knew it was the only chance she was going to get. She launched herself from the couch, racing for the front door, knowing it was the only way to safety. As soon as she cleared the couch, he didn't have a shot from behind the bar.

He was older.

God, let him be slower.

And it had been so long since she'd run.

She almost made it. Her hands were reaching for the door when something latched on to her hair, jerking her back with such agonizing pain she screamed.

She was thrown back into the living room as she heard a bullish bellow of rage. As he released her, she hit the wood floor painfully, sliding several feet across it. She fought to get to her knees to scramble away, despite the searing pain from her body colliding with the floor.

"You whore!" Bill screamed, and before she knew it, she was thrown to her back, his heavy body straddling hers, his hands going around her throat.

At least this way, she'd be dead dead, not just blinded without the memory of how it happened.

That didn't mean she wasn't going to fight.

Curling her fingers into claws, she reached for his face, raking it with as much force as she could muster, glaring up at him as the pressure at her neck had her vision dimming. But her nails dug in deep, taking flesh with them as they tore into his skin.

His howl of rage and the sudden release of pressure left her dizzy until a blow to her face nearly rendered her unconscious.

"I've hated you," Isabeau cried out as his fingers latched around her neck again. "I hated you. And so did she."

Isabeau glared up at him, crying from the physical as well as the emotional pain.

"Hate this, you fucking whore." His hands tightened again, the pressure horrifying as she tried to scratch at his hands, his arms.

He ignored it, and she knew her last sight would be Bill's enraged, bulging eyes as he killed her.

The sudden release of pressure had her gasping, her lungs suddenly drawing in sweet, precious air.

She felt Bill fall from her, heard male shouts, curses—were those motorcycles thundering outside? She coughed raggedly and her eyes blinked open as she was suddenly pulled into Tracker's arms.

"Isabeau." He buried his face in her hair while she was still trying to process what was going on. "God help me. Isabeau . . ."

She wasn't even going to try to process anything else.

Isabeau closed her eyes and let herself lean into the warmth, the security, the sheer delight she felt whenever Tracker held her. Chance must have Bill restrained, she thought as she sank into Tracker's hold. It didn't matter. She didn't care.

This would be the last time Tracker might hold her. Bill was captured, Tracker's job was over. That meant he'd be leaving her soon.

Too soon.

Just for a little while longer, she needed him to hold her.

BURKE WESTON BENT A KNEE TO THE FLOOR NEXT TO HIS uncle's fallen form. The sniper had taken the perfect shot, straight through the center of the forehead.

Bill lay on his back, his bulky body spread-eagle where he'd been thrown back by the force of the bullet, his expression still pulled into lines of rage.

Hell, they'd all known the bastard was certifiable. It was the reason he'd been retired from the MC years before. The man was delusional and paranoid, but no one had guessed he was murderous as well.

"We need to roll." Jakob squatted next to him, his tone filled with a warning. "Let Tracker take care of this."

Burke looked over to where the other man had a hold on Isabeau like he'd never let go of her.

It was going to take a minute for Tracker to loosen that grip, Burke thought.

"Have one of the men alert us when law enforcement gets close," he ordered his second. "I have to talk to Isabeau first."

It might be his last chance for a while. Hell, once she recovered, she probably wouldn't ever want to see him again. Not that he could blame her. Looking at himself in the mirror was hard most days; it would be impossible now.

She had to know that he had cared, that he had tried to protect her. He hadn't known her vision was returning, not because he hadn't wanted to have time for her, but because he was fighting so hard to protect her and to discover the identity of the threat she faced.

"They're already close," Jakob hissed. "You have to get out of here. We'll slip into the apartment across from her and go to the house when things quiet down. Staying is too dangerous for both of you."

Burke knew he was right. What they were a part of was too damned important at present, and far too vulnerable to discovery.

Grimacing, he wiped his hand over his face before straightening and staring at his sister one last time.

Tracker held her as though he held life itself in his arms. Her head was tucked beneath his chin, her long hair flowing over the arms surrounding her. The side of her face that he could see was already bruising heavily; the blow Bill delivered hadn't been an easy one.

Hatred seared his soul, but not for the first time. He'd tolerated the bastard for as long as he could remember. Mac had tolerated him because he was his brother; neither of them had believed he was really dangerous.

Until now.

Isabeau had been fifteen, nearly dead, so fucking tiny she looked like a child as she'd lain in that hospital bed. And when she'd awakened, she'd been blind, unable to remember or to identify the man responsible for killing her parents or trying to kill her.

Burke had always been ambivalent where his mother was concerned; she'd run and left him behind when she knew the criminal activities the Westons were involved in at the time. She hadn't taken the little boy who had loved her as only a child could.

"Black." Jakob used the alias to regain his attention, to force Burke to focus.

He gave a sharp nod, turned, and strode for the back door, where several of the Reapers' higher-ranking members waited for him. Their hard gazes took in everything, and the weapons they carried were locked and loaded.

"Contact Witchy and that bastard husband of hers," he muttered as they hurried from the cabin to the pickup they'd arrived in. "This will add to their case. I want that fucking ranch locked the fuck down and eyes on Mac and his wife, Fiona, at all times. Nothing is to happen to them. And make damned sure Kenya keeps her ass at school until this is finished. If she doesn't, heads are going to roll."

He didn't give Jakob the opportunity to insist on driving, but took the driver's seat himself with the others rushing into the vehicle behind him. He could see the flashing lights, hear the sirens as he quickly turned the vehicle around and headed back down the roughened track, lights out, to the main road.

Leaving his sister there without at least telling her he was sorry, that he loved her, was the hardest thing he believed he'd ever done in his life. He'd sacrificed his life, possibly his own future, to ensure the two young women he loved so fiercely, Isabeau and Kenya, were protected, no matter what happened around them.

For Isabeau, it had been protecting her against the son of a bitch who had murdered her parents and tried to murder her. For Kenya, it would be keeping her out of the mess that would be falling on the Weston ranch if Bill's connection to the Reapers was revealed by the press. So far, he'd managed to keep the Reapers and the Weston name separate, just as his father had done before Burke took over.

"Stop, man," Jakob muttered from the passenger seat, his voice low, hard. "Torturing yourself won't help either of those girls. We made this decision, and now it's too late to regret it."

Regret.

No, he didn't regret what he'd done to protect the girls. He regretted the necessity of it. And he hated the fuckers behind the need for it. He had promises to keep though. Promises that would keep his father from prison and the evidence of crimes committed before Burke's birth hidden. Promises that would make the world safer for both his sisters.

Now that Isabeau was safe and the threat that kept his attention divided was over, he could concentrate on finishing the job he'd taken for Doogan a decade ago.

Then, he'd either be dead, or he'd be free. And some days, he wondered if it mattered to him how it ended. Dead or free, as long as his family was safe, he didn't really give a damn.

TWENTY-TWO

THOSE BRUISES WERE GOING TO LAST AWHILE.

Isabeau caught a glimpse of them, again, as she left the bathroom after her shower, two evenings later. One side of her face was swollen and colored a deep purple from her forehead to her chin. It looked horrendous.

But she could see. Her vision was still crisp and clear, her sight working perfectly, to the amazement of the specialist who had arrived in her hospital room that morning.

Of course Tracker, a dozen Mackays, and various friends who had raced to the cabin that night had insisted she leave in the ambulance that had followed the sheriff and two deputies to the cabin. The EMTs had insisted she was concussed, and the doctor waiting at the hospital had concurred.

Bill's fist had come close to actually breaking her face, the doctor had reported. The deep bruising extended into the bone and would take weeks to heal.

Ignoring the mirror, she entered her bedroom and dressed in a light sundress that just brushed over the bruising along her side, hip, and thigh where she'd hit the floor after Bill had tossed her like a ball back into the cabin's living room.

She could hear voices through the house, the mix of Mackays, Tracker's team, and only God knew who else. She'd been questioned officially by the sheriff, the FBI, and Natches's wife, Chaya. Of them all, Chaya was damned scary. That woman had a stare that was damned spooky as she posed each question and observation like a surgeon working with a scalpel.

When the questions were finished, Chaya had sat back and let a smile drift over her expression, and it was like seeing a completely different person but with the same facial features. And Isabeau realized Chaya had pulled information free that even she was unaware of. Not just what had happened the night Bill attacked her, but details from the years she'd spent on the ranch as well.

Tucking her hair behind her ear on the undamaged side of her face, she lowered her head, staring at her toenails. The light, cotton-candy-pink color mocked her attempts to distance herself, to prepare herself for what she knew was coming all too soon.

Tracker would leave.

Her breathing hitched at the thought. She'd overheard him earlier giving the others orders, directing everyone to pack their equipment and prepare the plane. Chance had asked him if they were all leaving, and Tracker had confirmed they were.

She wouldn't cry, she promised herself. She'd let him leave knowing he was leaving her in a far better place than the one he'd found her in.

She loved him.

She didn't want him with her because she cried, or out of guilt. If he stayed, it had to be because he couldn't do anything else.

Drawing in a deep breath, she pushed her feet into leather sandals, drew the strap over her heel, and left the bedroom. It was time to face everyone for the last time. She wanted her home cleared out by the masses that didn't belong.

Tracker and Chance were staying at least until morning, she knew from what she'd heard earlier. She knew they were flying out from Lexington tomorrow afternoon and heading to another job.

No tears, she told herself again as her breathing threatened to become shaky. She was going to get through this, and she was going to be okay. She had her future stretching out ahead of her; she could see; she could have her life back.

If that life seemed a little empty without Tracker in it . . .

She forced the thought back.

She stepped into the living room, her gaze caught, not for the first time, by Chance and Natches. They stood on opposite sides of the room, one older, one a good twenty years younger. They could be father and son, and she was certain she wasn't the only one who noticed it.

The two men weren't looking at each other, but like her, they were receiving plenty of looks.

"There you are." Zoey Doogan stepped from her handsome husband's side and strode to her.

Her long black hair, the riotous curls flowing around her, and her pretty green eyes gave her elfin features an ethereal look. Zoey was anything but ethereal though. She was bold, willful, and incredibly stubborn according to everyone who knew her.

"Oh, sweetie, your face." Compassion welled in Zoey's gaze as she touched Isabeau's shoulder gently.

"It'll get better," Isabeau promised, but she didn't dare try to smile. Even talking wasn't completely comfortable.

"It will." Zoey nodded, her expression turning somber as Tracker stepped into the room. "You going to be okay?"

"Fine," Isabeau promised, sliding her hands into the pockets of her sundress and looking around at those in the room. "I'm just really overwhelmed."

Zoey chuckled at the statement. "You're tired of your home being filled to capacity, aren't you?"

Once again, Isabeau stifled a smile. "It's hard to sleep while everyone's out here talking. No one seems to go to sleep at the same time."

Not that there had been enough beds, but even if there had been, she knew they wouldn't have been used.

"We're all actually getting ready to vacate to give you some peace." Chaya stepped over to them as she spoke, her expression understanding. "If you need us, sweetie, call."

Isabeau nodded and she understood the message. They knew what she hadn't spoken aloud where her feelings for Tracker were concerned. She could see the knowledge in their expressions, the sympathy and concern.

"Come on, everyone, time to get out of here and let Isabeau have a little peace," Chaya said, her voice firm as she turned and looked around the room.

There were a few chuckles, a grumble or two, from everyone except Tracker and Chance. It took a few minutes, as everyone stopped a second to tell her goodbye and to call them soon, to assure her that they were there if she needed them.

Finally, the door closed behind Chaya and Natches, leaving her, Chance, and Tracker alone.

Isabeau slowly let her gaze fall on Chance once again.

"You may as well talk to your brother and fess up," she told him, ignoring his shock as he stared at her. "Trust me, the Mackays always know more than you think they do and expect far more of you than you expect of yourself, but when he's tired of waiting on you, he's going to hit you in the face even while he's telling you how much you've hurt him."

She'd learned that in the stories she'd heard of Natches as she grew closer to the family. He was the youngest, the most scarred of the three cousins. He was also loyal to a fault, temperamental, incredibly protective, and such a male prima donna that it wasn't even funny.

"I'm not his brother." Chance's voice hardened. "Trust me, Isabeau. Not his brother, Rowdy's, or Dawgs. I've answered that accusation more times than I care to count. Even from him."

She tilted her head and stared at him. She'd heard many times how Chance looked like Natches, walked like him, reminded others of him, on and on. They were related. . . .

"I hope you know just how calculating these Mackays can be," she sighed. "No doubt, Natches has already found a way to get your DNA and run it. He already has his answers, Chance. I'd just hate to see him hit you. He packs a punch for a man in his fifties, I'm told. And he doesn't object to a fight."

She ignored the way his eyes narrowed on her, and she let her gaze go around the living room, aware of the way Tracker watched her, his gaze intent, though he remained silent.

"I'm glad Burke decided not to rent the house out," she said softly, her gaze touching on the few pictures of her and Burke that she knew were in place before her mother's death. The furniture had been updated, floors redone, and the house kept in good repair. But it was obvious even when she'd moved in that no one else had lived there. Isabeau had felt the house's loneliness, even if she couldn't see it at the time. Sometimes though, she'd even sworn she could catch a hint of her mother's perfume on the air, or the scent of the cigar that her father would occasionally enjoy would drift in from the front porch.

"You sure you don't need more rest?" Tracker asked as Chance made his way from the room to the back door.

He stood on the other side of the living room, dressed in a pair of dun-colored cargo pants and a matching shirt that buttoned up the front. His dark brown, nearly black hair was a little shaggy, brushed back from his face but still softening the hard planes and angles of his face.

There was a scar on his left cheek, a thin, nearly faded line she found incredibly rakish when paired with his bronzed flesh and bright blue eyes.

God, he would make beautiful babies, she thought. Handsome, tall little boys and wild, beautiful baby girls.

It wasn't hard to tell his powerful body was all muscle, his shoulders wide. The arms he had crossed over his chest fairly bulged with strength.

This was the alpha male women swooned over, fantasized about, panted for, and dreamed of touching. And for one incredible moment in life, he'd held her.

She knew he blamed himself for her injuries, for the fact that Bill had nearly succeeded in killing her for good.

"It wasn't your fault, Tracker," she told him, knowing she alone carried the blame.

Those incredibly sexy lips quirked with knowing amusement.

"You know, princess, every time I left your side, you managed to get that pretty butt in trouble," he grunted. "You don't stay put very well, you know?"

To that she couldn't help but attempt to grin, only to regret it even faster as the movement pulled at her bruised flesh.

"Yeah, Dad used to say the same thing. So did Burke after I went to the ranch." She shrugged.

Her brother had been fond of the fact that she refused to stay in her room and play the embittered victim. He'd told her she had spunk, just like their mother.

"Burke must be really busy," she murmured then, looking at the picture of the gangly little boy her mother had possessed. "I would have thought he'd be here by now."

For a moment or two at the cabin, when the dizziness and blinding pain had been the center of her focus, she could have sworn she'd heard his voice. It must have been wishful thinking, because he wouldn't have left her if he was there.

"He's clearing up details with the family," Tracker stated, causing her to look back at him quickly. "Bill was a crackpot, but he was into quite a few criminal activities as well," he told her. "Drugs, gun sales."

"He said that was Mac's business," she told him, wondering how much of what Burke's uncle had said was the truth.

"Honestly, I don't know if it was Mac or Bill, but it's something your brother's trying to clear up. He's called several times though, as has your sister, Mac, and Mac's wife, Fiona." He rubbed at the side of his face, his expression turning quizzical. "I talked to Kenya. You sure the two of you don't share blood, Isabeau? Because I swear that girl reminded me so much of you."

Amusement almost had her smiling again. "We used to dare each other to do things that we knew would drive Mac and Fiona insane and force Burke home from wherever Mac had sent him. So I might have had a little influence on how she turned out."

"She threatened to hire someone to castrate me if I let one more single bruise happen to you," he snorted. "Someone needs to let her know how little you follow orders. I told you to behave yourself before I left."

"In my defense," she pointed out, "you did leave me unsupervised."

His eyes narrowed. "Angel and Duke were in the house, baby. With four men outside."

"Yet no one stopped me." She gave a little wave of her hand and forced back a smile. "Unsupervised, Tracker. Shame on you."

Was he fighting a smile? She could swear that was a smile threatening to tug at his lips.

"You're bad, princess." That grin quirked his lips as he shook his head. "Other than being hardheaded and stubborn, how are you feeling?"

She shrugged. "Like someone's punching bag?"

He shook his head at her.

"She looks like one too." Deep, filled with affection, and far too somber, another male voice pulled her attention from Tracker to the kitchen doorway.

Burke.

Her brother stood watching her, dressed in jeans, riding chaps, and a T-shirt beneath a leather vest. His black hair was short, his dark brown eyes piercing.

"Hey, stranger," she greeted, those tears she'd been fighting rushing up to clog her voice as she gave him her standard greeting.

His expression tightened in pain, his arms lifting, spreading for her, and she couldn't resist the invitation.

She walked into his embrace rather than running as she would have otherwise. The bruises really wouldn't have liked her for running. When his arms closed around her, the hold was incredibly gentle, though she tightened her arms around his back despite the twinge of pain.

"I'm so sorry, Isa," he whispered at her ear. "I'm so goddamned sorry."

It wasn't his fault. She knew he wouldn't accept that though, just as he hadn't accepted it so many years ago when she'd awakened in the hospital, hysterical and terrified.

He'd saved her then. He'd been there when she awakened, he'd done everything possible to care for her, to protect her. He couldn't

have known about Bill, couldn't have suspected, she knew that. If he
had, Bill would have died a long time ago.

"I'm fine, Burke," she promised him, feeling the tension, sensing
the heartache he felt. "I promise. I'm fine."

Easing back, she had to stare up at him to meet his gaze.

Her brother was just as handsome as she'd always thought he was.
Though, like Tracker's, his expression was hard from whatever life
had thrown at him, his gaze wary. Emotion was something her brother
was never comfortable with, Isabeau knew, and tears would have him
searching desperately for a way to make them stop.

"Don't you cry," he growled at her as she blinked back the wetness,
"I don't have cowboys here to sing to you or that damned horse you
love so much to haul you around."

"Dante," she murmured, almost laughing. "He loves me."

"He does indeed," Burke assured her, glancing behind her to
Tracker. "She's the only one he'll let sit on his back."

"I'm the only one that doesn't weigh more than he does," she
sniffed at the declaration. "Your cowboys are too big. He's delicate."

"He's a draft horse, Isabeau," Burke argued, incredulity coloring
his voice and his expression. "He's taller than you and weighs almost
fifteen hundred pounds."

It was a familiar argument, and one that had kept her surprisingly
grounded over the years.

"He's a baby," she reminded him.

"A baby monster," he grunted, and she could finally see the humor
and amusement on his face that she heard in his voice.

The monster loved her though. He always knew when she was
walking to the stables, and he'd call out to her. The sound of his hoofs
hitting the ground as he raced over the pasture had always made
her smile.

"You know he's taken up with Kenya while you've been gone." He eased one arm from around her and, with the other lying at her back, walked to the living room with her. "She's been riding him for you."

Isabeau nodded. "He's always loved Kenya. She was just too scared of him to go with me to the stables."

Dante was one of the few draft studs her brother bred with the wild horses they would round up yearly. The foals sold for an astronomical rate once his cowboys broke and trained them. Dante, though, didn't care much for men, but he'd loved her from the day she'd heard him whinnying in the pasture and thought he'd sounded so lonely.

"She's doing good with him," he promised her. "Come in here and sit down with me. I can't stay long, but I wanted to see for myself you were okay."

He took her hands as she sat down, and he eased onto the cushions beside her. Patting them, he stared at them for long moments like a man tortured.

"I wanted to stay at the cabin with you the other night," he said softly, causing her to stare at him in surprise. "I came in with Tracker, but he reached you first. And he wasn't letting you go." An understanding smile tugged at his lips. "I couldn't be there when the sheriff showed up, Isabeau. I'm sorry."

She nodded hesitantly, remembering what Bill had told her as well as the information Tracker had given her on his reputation and suspicions against him.

"You're going to get hurt," she whispered. "Whatever you're doing, Burke, it's going to get you hurt."

Drugs, guns. She couldn't believe he'd be part of that world.

"Sometimes, the choices you make are because you simply can't live with the alternative," he sighed heavily, staring back at her. "And once made, they're not so easy to renege on, baby sister."

She stared into his eyes, and in them, she saw things she feared were only wishful thinking. He was her brother; he'd made a deal with the devil to protect her, but that didn't mean he'd keep that deal in the spirit the devil demanded.

Doogan, a former assistant director of some clandestine office or another, admitted to knowing her brother. Zoey had told her how he'd helped Burke and several other friends when they were all younger. Tracker told her how he'd met up with Burke several times in his guise of John Black, and how adept her brother was at ensuring no one knew he was also Burke Weston.

A bad person didn't know the people he knew and go to those extremes just for the hell of it. He was playing a part, a very dangerous, very calculated game, and she was terrified for him.

"I should have been home more," he said softly. "I should have talked to you more, but I want you to know, nothing mattered to me but your and Kenya's safety. In protecting the two of you. You're the innocence I lost a long time ago, Isa. Preserving that is all that matters to me now."

"I know that, Burke." She nodded slowly.

"Whatever you hear or may have heard . . ." he began.

"Doesn't matter," she promised him, feeling his fingers tighten on hers for a brief moment. "I trust in you, not in the appearance of you that you give others." She wanted to cry, to sob for the boy he must have once been and the betrayals that brought him to the man he was now.

He was working with Doogan, she knew it. No one had to tell her, or hint at it. Her brother wasn't a criminal. But he'd let people think whatever it took to ensure other criminals were taken down. That was the man she knew sat before her now. She'd never believe otherwise.

"I may not be able to visit for a while again," he breathed out roughly. "I'm going to be busy."

And Kenya would be without him or Isabeau.

"Send Kenya here," she told him, ignoring the initial rejection she saw in his expression.

"Look, the Mackays around here terrify criminals," she told him. "And there's so many agents and former agents skulking around this county, there's no way she won't be protected. But she'll be with me, Burke. She won't be alone. And she won't feel like we've deserted her."

And Isabeau knew she and Kenya both had felt deserted several times.

"Do it, Burke," Tracker advised, moving from where he'd sat on the other side of the couch to face them. "The Mackays love a challenge, and she's about the same age as their daughters. She'll be happier here than in Texas."

Burke's expression tightened for a second before he gave a sharp nod. "I'll consider it," he promised.

"I'm sure Doogan and Zoey will agree," Isabeau told him knowingly. "Discuss it with them too."

For a second, her brother simply stared at her, his gaze going over the bruises before meeting hers once again.

"You're too damned smart," he sighed. "And even blind, you saw more than I ever expected."

And that was all the answer she needed where her brother's conscience, his values were concerned. And it was probably the closest he'd ever come to admitting to what she knew had to be the truth.

"I have to go." Regret creased his face, filled his voice. "Doogan and Zoey slipped me in here, but my men are waiting outside town for me. It's a long ride back to Texas."

"I love you, Burke," she whispered, rising from the couch as he stood beside her. "Don't be a stranger."

"I love you, Isa." His hold didn't tighten on her; instead, it lingered before he finally drew in a deep breath and released her. "Stop getting into trouble," he sighed as he drew back. "I'm getting older, girl, can't handle all that stress."

Before she could come up with a suitable retort, he turned and quickly strode to the back door.

Isabeau listened to him leave, her head lowered, her gaze locked on the floor rather than allowing herself to watch him go. If she watched him leave, she knew she'd cry. And Burke didn't need that. The stress he was living under had to be tremendous as it was.

Besides, if she cried now, there was no way she'd hold her tears back when Tracker left as well.

She watched him follow Burke's path to the back door, where he checked the lock, his tall, strong body so very enduring, solid. She was going to miss that.

She loved him.

She wasn't falling in love with him. Falling in love implied she'd had no choice in the matter, when she knew that wasn't true. She'd known the moment she heard his voice, the way it struck a chord of trust inside her, that a part of her belonged to him. She would have never trusted him otherwise.

To say fate had a hand in it, she wasn't going that far. Instead, it was like her soul recognized him, and had opened up to him. And once opened, there was no way to close it. And now that part of her belonged to him forever.

"He's living a very dangerous life," she whispered as Tracker turned and walked back to her, his expression quiet as his gaze met hers.

"Yes, he is at that," he confirmed.

He stopped in front of her, his hand lifting, cupping her unbruised cheek, his thumb caressing the corner of her lips.

"You could have destroyed him, and no one would have blamed

you," he said gently. "The fact that you didn't makes you a very unusual woman, Isabeau Boudreaux."

That statement confused her.

"Why would I do that?" She was aware of the way his thumb brushed her lips as she spoke. "He's sacrificed his life to protect me. He's put himself in danger, ruined any good standing he'll ever have if he's ever revealed. And that's a secret that can't be kept forever. Can it?"

His expression didn't change. It was somber, heavy with whatever thoughts he was thinking.

"I wish I had met you sooner, Isabeau," he whispered, bending his head, his lips pressing where his thumb had lingered moments before.

She held her breath to keep it from hitching, to keep the sob from rising in her throat.

"I would have been much too young for you," she whispered when he drew back.

She couldn't stare at him, couldn't let herself look in his eyes. She turned away from him and drew in a hard, ragged breath.

"I thought you were leaving in the morning," she said, because she knew, she knew he was leaving now.

"An emergency came up," he told her quietly. "Ramble's father's in a tight spot right now."

She nodded. "Family," she whispered, turning back to him and forcing herself to look up at him. "Be careful, Tracker. Please, take care of you."

His lips quirked, though there was no amusement to the curve, and it couldn't really be called a smile.

"Stay out of trouble, princess." He brushed the backs of his fingers against her cheek, lingering at her jaw.

She nodded.

Hell, he was leaving her unsupervised; if she got into trouble, it was his fault, not hers. Now, wasn't it?

"I have to go." His hand dropped away from her cheek to his side, though she could see how his fingers curled, nearly forming a fist.

"Tracker." She stopped him before he could turn away from her, fighting the tears, the pleas, whatever she thought it would take to bring him back to her. "Don't forget me."

"Isabeau," he promised her. "It's simply not possible."

He turned and walked away from her, never looking back. Isabeau watched him leave the house, her gaze remaining clear until the door closed behind him.

Tears filled her eyes then, spilled down her cheeks, and she let herself cry. This one time, she told herself, she'd let herself cry.

TWENTY-THREE

One Week Later

From: Angel Calloway Mackay

Re: News from home

Our once blind schoolteacher is living her best life, I believe. Pictures enclosed. Honestly, I've tried to warn her that Mattie Watts has had years of practice at this type of behavior, but Isabeau just laughs and waves away my warnings. It's good to see her focusing on having fun though. I think she's not been able to do that very often.

Tracker sat by the campfire, the scent of overcooked coffee filling his senses as he glared at the screen of his phone.

Isabeau line dancing at a bar, beer in hand, a smile on her lips. That smile didn't reach her eyes. Others may not see it, but he did.

The second picture was Isabeau in a bikini that had his blood pressure rising by several degrees. Damn her. She looked like peaches and cream perfection as she stared back at the camera, un-smiling.

He snapped the phone closed. Angel couldn't know what she was doing to him. She couldn't understand each picture was like a dagger digging into his chest.

For now anyway.

It would ease, he told himself. He just had to give himself time, and it would ease.

Two Weeks Later

From: Angel Calloway Mackay

Re: Duke's Birthday

Pictures from the birthday bash. Duke was pleasantly surprised, and a good time was had by all.

Pictures enclosed, goddammit.

Several of those pictures included Isabeau. In one, she was danc-ing with some hotshot Mackay cousin who thought he was God's gift to women. In another she was sitting with Annie, Laken, and Bliss Mackay, staring off over the lake. Dressed in one of those little sun-dresses she was fond of, her toenails painted cotton-candy pink.

Damn, he missed the sight of those pretty little toes.

He missed Isabeau. He ached to feel her against him when he went to bed at night, the memory of her tucked against his naked body a comfort as well as a torment.

He felt like a part of himself was missing and nothing was eas-ing it.

Closing the email out, he propped his elbows on his knees and stared into the flames, but it was Isabeau he saw.

Wiping his hand over his face, he admitted to himself that she was never far from his thoughts. Hell, never far from his thoughts? She stayed in them 24/7.

He missed her. He hadn't missed a woman like this in his life. Not to the point that she dominated his thoughts even while he was on a job or on a mission. Hell, he missed her too damned much.

Three Weeks Later

From: Angel Calloway Mackay
Re: Uh-Oh. Where's Burke

Of course, there were pictures enclosed.

Tracker's hand tightened on his phone, his teeth clenching as he stood in his parents' front yard in the island paradise they called home.

Where was Burke? Fuck, what was her brother supposed to do? Lock her away? That wild little hellion needed her ass paddled, not a locked room. And his hand was itching to redden that cute little ass of hers.

"Fuck!" he cursed, rubbing at his temple. He knew there was a headache coming and he was blaming Angel for it.

Isabeau's hair was falling from the ponytail she'd pulled it into, wisps falling over her face as she stared in surprise at the camera from her place on the ground, flat on her ass where she'd landed after wrecking a fucking dirt bike of all things.

She wore jeans and a snug white T-shirt. Across the shirt the words *In My Defense, He Left Me Unsupervised* glared back at him in large black letters.

In his defense, it was the most miserable three weeks of his life. He'd missed her every damned night and day, every hour, every minute he'd been away from her.

He'd left her unsupervised.

No, he'd plain left her, but he got the message.

She was trying to live. She was trying to have fun and find her life, but he saw the loss in her eyes that he saw in his own whenever he dared to look in the mirror. The same loneliness.

He had left her unsupervised, the words claimed. So she was living her life on her terms, good or bad, secure or unsecure. There was no one to care, as far as she was concerned.

"Hey, Tracker, Maria has dinner ready," Chance called from the back of the house. "It's enchilada night, man."

Enchilada night.

Fuck, he didn't want enchiladas.

He wanted Isabeau. God only knew what kind of trouble she'd end up getting into if she was left unsupervised much longer.

"I have to pack." He stalked past Chance, ignoring the surprised look on his face. "If you're coming, get ready."

"Let me guess, Kentucky?" Chance called back after him. "You're gonna get my ass kicked, brother, if we keep hanging around Somerset."

"Yeah, well, talk to Natches, it might put him in a good mood if you're honest with him," Tracker advised him. "You do it, or I will. This has gone on long enough."

It was the same warning he'd given his sister about her mother, Natches's wife. Take care of it, or he was taking care of it for him.

"Bullshit." Chance stalked behind him. "It's none of your business."

"Wrong." He came to a stop and turned on the other man, furious. "I won't be leaving Kentucky, Chance. I'm done with this work. The cousins can have it from here on out. If I were you, I'd do the same."

"Retirement?" Shock creased the Mackay dark features and filled those Mackay green eyes. "Hell, Tracker."

"Retirement." Tracker nodded. "Now get ready to fly. I'm going home. . . . You can do whatever the hell you want to."

TWENTY-FOUR

THE LAKE PARTY THE MACKAYS HAD INVITED HER TO WAS in full swing. One of those impromptu little barbecue things that slowly turned into a full-scale music and food revelry. They never got too wild, because of course, this was the Mackays, they were family men, and they didn't tolerate it.

Everyone knew that.

The parties were still parties though. In a wide clearing at the lake's edge, a band had been set up under a large gazebo, their lead singers belting out the most popular country and a few of the rock tunes. They weren't bad either.

Isabeau had thrown a strappy cover-up dress over her bikini. The ankle-length light cotton was split to the knee, the bottom half a light, lacey see-through weave. It flowed over her breasts and dropped to her ankles in a loose flow of material she found extremely comfortable.

Sitting on the deserted dock now, listening to the music and conversation that drifted to her, she propped her chin on her up-lifted knees and stared out over the serene darkness of the lake.

Little waves lapped at the floating dock, around it and against the rocky beach. A counterpoint to the music that filled the night beyond her.

She should be out there dancing, a beer in hand, laughing and mingling with new and old friends. But all she really did was watch the crowd, always searching for one face, for one man. And she was going to have to stop doing that. She was only tormenting herself, making the ache worse.

She'd changed since Tracker had left, but for the better. She went out with friends, made new friends, met with parents of upcoming students, and was in therapy to deal with the nightmares of the recent attack as well as her parents' deaths.

It was working out, she told herself daily. She was gaining a perspective on life that she found almost peaceful. A perspective on herself that she liked.

She had managed to actually gain weight in the past few weeks as well.

She enjoyed going out and trying new foods, eating the barbecue fare to be found at the lake parties, and late-evening coffee and carrot cake at the local diner with Mattie and a few of the other teachers starting the new school year in a matter of weeks.

She wasn't all skin and bones anymore, and she liked the way her body had filled out and developed a more voluptuous shape. She was a teacher, she told herself when she'd gone shopping for new clothes the day before. She wasn't a mercenary or undercover agent. She liked cooking, feeding friends, and she liked the new curves she'd begun developing.

She didn't like how lonely she was though.

"You should be dancing, Isabeau." It was Natches who found her.

She watched as he plopped down across from her, resting his back against a metal support to the handrail, much the same as she was.

He handed her one of the soft drinks he carried and, once she accepted it, popped the top on his own and drank from it as he watched her.

Isabeau looked out over the lake again, wondering what he wanted. Natches was always sticking his nose in someone's life, she'd learned. It was simply part of his nature.

"I hear your sister's arriving next week," he commented when she didn't say anything. "Make sure you bring her out for Bliss's birthday party. We'd love to meet her."

Isabeau's lips quirked. "Another stray, Natches?"

He chuckled at the description. "Hell, Isabeau, if I didn't have Bliss's friends to watch over, I'd drive her away for sure. Think of it as helping your friend out."

She shook her head; that was about the truth.

"You hear from Tracker since he left?" he asked before she could reply to his former statement.

Isabeau looked down at the can of soda then set it aside and shook her head. "Should I have?"

She rather doubted he called and checked in with former clients very often.

"I was just curious." He shot her an easy smile. "How are you doing? That therapist working out?"

"Everything's fine," she promised him, giving him a smile with her reply. "And the therapist is great. Thank you for recommending her."

He nodded back at her, sipped at the soda again, then leveled his gaze on her as his expression firmed and became demanding.

She wanted to roll her eyes but didn't dare.

"What, Natches?" she asked instead. "I came out here to find a few moments' peace, not to be psychoanalyzed by you."

He was good at that too.

"Tracker's a fool," he said quietly. "But most men are, I guess. Doesn't mean you have to hide and wait for him."

Was she waiting for him?

"That's not what I'm doing." She shook her head in denial.

"You go out with friends, but you don't date," he said gently. "You've turned down every request made by some very eligible men in the county. Our esteemed sheriff, Shawn Mayes, just to begin with."

Isabeau shook her head. "I'm not ready to date."

Even her therapist had mentioned the fact that she wasn't dating yet.

It just didn't feel right yet.

"Angel says you don't ask about Tracker either," he pointed out. "Won't discuss him or stay around when she mentions him."

She stared back at him. "What's your point?" she asked.

He blew out a hard breath. "You're in love with him, aren't you?"

"What I feel for Tracker is my business," she told him. "If I won't discuss him with Angel, what makes you think I'll discuss him with you?"

He shrugged at that. "No reason, I guess. I was hoping someone would know when him and that dumbass brother of mine are coming back to town though."

She couldn't hide her surprise. "He claims he's not your brother."

Natches laughed, a sound filled with amusement and maybe a little anticipation. It was kind of scary, actually.

"Definitely a brother," he sighed. "I was there when the DNA was run. Little bastard isn't as careful as he thought he was. He came through last year after being wounded on a job. I managed to acquire one of the bandages he disposed of."

He sounded so satisfied with himself that Isabeau had to fight a grin.

"He's afraid you're going to kick his ass," she offered.

"Well, of course I am." He laughed, his green eyes filled with mirth. "He's had years to get honest and refused to. That alone would get his ass kicked. But he's played games with me instead." He shook his head. "That ensures it."

Mackays were damned scary, especially this one.

"Come on, little girl." He rose to his feet and extended his hand to her. "I'm not comfortable with you sitting out here by yourself. No need to tempt trouble."

He wouldn't let it go, she knew.

"I need to go home anyway," she sighed, accepting his help rising to her feet. "I'll tell everyone goodbye first."

"Good idea." He nodded, letting her precede him. "They'd worry if you didn't."

She made her way across the beach and back to the clearing where everyone was gathered together. There was dancing close to the gazebo, the picnic tables laden with food, and dozens still enjoying the late summer night.

Fall would be here soon. Winter would sweep into Kentucky; the lake parties and warm-weather activities would end. The cycle would slow, school would begin, and cold weather would keep everyone closer to home.

At least Kenya would be there soon, Isabeau thought. She wouldn't be completely alone.

Natches said goodbye as they neared a group of her friends, his smile faintly chiding before he gave her a brief hug.

Maybe she should accept one of those dates she was being offered regularly.

No, she thought instantly. Not yet.

Not until she could sleep at night and not ache for Tracker. Not until she could leave the house and not watch for him, wait for him. Once again, it was a cycle.

"Leaving us?" Angel stood with her husband, Duke, and surprisingly, Tracker's parents as she neared the far edge of the party.

The Calloways must have arrived after Isabeau had left to enjoy the quiet of the lake. She knew they'd been talking about a long visit after learning Angel was expecting her first child, but she hadn't heard they would be arriving anytime soon.

Isabeau stopped and smiled back at her. "Time to go home," she told Angel. "It's getting kind of late."

J. T., his blue eyes so like Tracker's, watched her intently. Tracker looked like his father. Tall, broad, his facial features more defined with age.

She looked around quickly, wondering if Tracker was there.

"It's so nice to see you again, Isabeau." Mara Calloway, with her short dark hair and lively features, shared a few of Tracker's looks, though they were much softer. The shape of his eyes, the heavy lashes.

She pulled Isabeau into a quick hug, then stepped back and stared back at her fondly.

"It's nice to see you again," Isabeau greeted them, though her chest was tight and the need to ask about Tracker nearly overwhelming.

"We hoped to see you while you were here." Mara tilted her head curiously. "We've worried about you."

Isabeau nodded, forcing herself not to check for Tracker again.

"I'm doing good," she assured them.

"You are still teaching, then?" Mara asked.

"She actually applied to teach second grade rather than high school as she was originally hired to do," Angel threw in. "Second grade, Mara. Mini demons."

Mara's laugh was fond as she shook her head, but her gaze stayed on Isabeau.

"Children that age are a handful, which you'll soon learn," the other woman stated.

"They're full of energy and imagination," Isabeau said instead, unable to hide how much she was looking forward to it.

Mara nodded at that, as though she'd made up her mind about something, and stepped closer to her husband as his arm went around her.

"Curious and unstoppable," Mara chuckled, casting the small mound of Angel's stomach a fond look. "I can't wait to hold that little one, and for Angel to know how very exciting motherhood can be."

"I'm learning." Angel laughed. "Tracker and Chance need to find a nice girl and settle down so there will be little ones for mine to play with."

Isabeau shot her friend a silencing look. A hard one.

"You'll do fine, and your baby will have plenty of Mackay kids to play with." She looked back to the Calloways. "I'm heading home now. . . ."

"So soon?" The question sounded from behind her, causing her to freeze, her heart to trip, her breathing to hitch.

Isabeau jerked around before she could stop herself, his name on her lips.

And there he was. Still as tall, as broad, as devilishly handsome as he was the day he left.

"Tracker." She whispered his name.

"Hey, princess." He reached out and brushed back the hair that had fallen over her cheek. "Dance with me?"

Dance with him?

She looked out and saw couples coming together, a romantic tune beginning to fill the air, the beat slower, sensuous.

To be held in his arms again would be both heaven and hell.

She drew in a hard breath, fought her tears. She'd cried for him once. She wouldn't let herself do that again.

"No." She stepped back, ignoring the way his expression tightened. "No, I have to go. I have to leave. . . ."

And she wasn't waiting for him to convince her, or for her own desperate heart to force her to do otherwise. If she made the mistake of letting him hold her, then she'd make the biggest mistake of her life.

TWENTY-FIVE

THE HEADLIGHTS IN HER REARVIEW MIRROR FOLLOWED her home, then the Harley turned into the drive behind her.

Isabeau laid her head on the steering wheel briefly, teeth clenched, fighting the need to scream out in frustration and longing.

She should have just danced with him, she thought in hindsight. But she never would have thought he'd follow her. Show up at some point later or catch her at the diner, but not actually follow her.

Who did that anyway?

Evidently Tracker Calloway did.

Throwing open the door, she hopped out of the pickup and shot him a wary glance.

"You should have stayed at the party," she told him before turning on her heel and stalking to the house.

Yeah, she was pissed. When he'd left her, she'd been hurt, her heart broken, but over the long, lonely weeks, that broken heart had raged, spent too many nights alone, and now she was pissed.

He had walked away from her. Just walked out the door as though she hadn't mattered. And maybe she hadn't. He'd left, hadn't he?

He didn't speak, but she knew he was following her. She didn't hear him; she could feel him getting closer by the second until he was right behind her as she unlocked the front door.

Stepping inside, she deactivated the alarm, shot him a fulminating look as he passed her to enter the house, and resigned herself to listening to whatever he had to say.

He was obviously determined to say it.

Closing the door, she locked it automatically, kicked off her sandals, and turned to face him.

God, he was so handsome.

What she wouldn't give to—

The thought was cut off as she suddenly found herself in his arms. One step. He took one step, snagged her around the waist, and pulled her to him. One hand locked in the hair at the back of her head, pulling it back as his lips covered hers.

And she was lost.

Deep, hungry kisses, voracious with male lust and impossible to resist, stole her senses. Her lips parted beneath his, met his tongue, submitted to his hunger as well as her own.

A gasp left her as his hands slid down her back, gripped her thighs, and lifted her. She curled her legs around his hips, crying out as his erection wedged between her thighs.

It was so good. Her clitoris instantly swelled, became so sensitive she swore she was going to explode in seconds. Her breasts became heavier, her nipples desperately hard.

She pushed her fingers through his hair, holding on to him, feeling the warmth of him sinking through the pores of her skin. Every cell she possessed sang out in pleasure, rioted, demanded ease.

"Tracker," she gasped as her back met the bed and he pulled away from her.

Forcing her eyes open, she watched, shocked, aroused, desperate for him, as he began tearing at his clothes.

"Get undressed, Isabeau," he practically snarled as his shirt hit the floor. "I've waited too damned long. I'll tear those clothes off you if I have to."

She was moving before he finished speaking. The beach dress was tossed aside as he went to work on his jeans. By the time he kicked off his boots and slid the denim down his legs, the bikini joined his clothes on the floor.

Tracker didn't say anything as he watched her, his gaze going over her slowly. She was naked, waiting for him, and he was just watching her.

"Why are you even here?" She tugged the thin duvet over her breasts and would have re-dressed if he wasn't between her and her clothes now.

"Because I'm fucking crazy?" The mocking answer only made her angrier.

Great, he was there because he was fucking crazy.

"How romantic," she snarled back at him, ignoring the little quirk of amusement at his lips. "Be fucking crazy elsewhere, Tracker," she demanded, too tired and too hurt to deal with whatever his "crazy" entailed.

"But I like being crazy with you, princess," he drawled, dragging the duvet from her and tossing it to the floor, leaving her naked once again.

Rolling her eyes in disgust, she tried to ignore that he'd wrapped his fingers around the heavy erection straining from between his thighs once he dropped the cover.

"Your crazy is not any of my concern," she enunciated clearly. "I very much appreciated your help when I needed it, but I'm certain I can handle things from here."

"Appreciated it, did you?" He was laughing at her. The bastard. "Well, I have to say I very much enjoyed helping you. Some parts of it, I excessively enjoyed."

Oh, did he now? She glared up at him, aware that she'd only become more aroused and the head of his cock was so thick, so hard, it appeared bruised.

"What precisely are you thinking?" she demanded when he remained quiet.

"Now you even sound like a princess," he quipped, giving the hair over her breasts a quick, playful tug.

"I want you to leave. Now," she snapped, indignation flooding her. "I am not in the mood to be mocked by you, Tracker."

Especially him.

"Not going to happen." He grinned. "You're sweet and naked, and I know you're ready for me. And, baby, I intend to have you."

"Not if I shoot you," she snapped.

Damn him.

"Let me suck your nipples first." His tongue flicked at his lower lip. "I've dreamed about sucking those pretty nipples again."

Isabeau blinked up at him.

She simply couldn't help herself.

Sheer astonishment held her speechless, unable to believe what she'd just heard or the sheer devilry in his gaze.

"Come on, baby," he cajoled, his tone gruffer now. "All I've thought about is how pretty your nipples are and how sweet your pussy tastes."

Oh, how she hated her body at this moment. Immediately her

nipples hardened further and became more sensitive, her pussy spilling liquid heat and her heart pounding at a frantic pace.

"Tracker . . ." she began.

"I'll let you suck my dick." His tone was husky, enticing. "Baby, you can suck any part of me that you want to put your mouth on."

Isabeau's breath caught. She meant to lambast him furiously, to tell him exactly what she thought of his high-handedness. Instead, her pussy clenched and the burst of sensation that struck her clit came far too close to ecstasy.

"God, Isabeau, the look on your face is going to cause me to come before I even touch you. And that's something I've never come close to doing until you."

His tone was graveled, heavy with lust as Isabeau fought to drag enough oxygen in to make her brain work.

"Let me touch you, Isabeau." His voice was a velvet murmur as his fingers stroked his hard flesh. "Just a little bit, then I promise we'll talk."

He came down beside her, pushing her slowly to her back once again as she stared up at him, uncertain how to handle him at the moment.

"We should talk first," she protested weakly.

"Fuck, you have the prettiest breasts. The most beautiful pretty pink nipples." His breathing was rough, erratic, as he cupped them, his thumbs raking over the tips, drawing a smothered cry from her lips. "Let me suck them, baby. Just for a minute."

He lifted the mounds his hands cupped, framing them with his fingers, stroking them, creating a firestorm within her senses.

"You can't just come back whenever and do this to me," she moaned, her fingers fisting in the sheet beneath her. "Please, Tracker."

"I have every intention of pleasing you. So, so good," he crooned. "Sweet, sweet Isabeau."

His lips brushed over hers in a feathery caress, lingered, and within seconds became greedy and hot. They slanted over hers in a kiss that pillaged and possessed her senses.

What did he do to her?

How did he do it?

He'd hurt her, broken her heart when he'd left her, and within minutes she was writhing beneath him, desperate for more than just his kiss. Once he touched her, anger was forgotten, betrayal became hunger, and nothing mattered but the chaos of pleasure overtaking her. She'd never imagined the ecstasy to be found in a man's arms until Tracker. Until his kiss. Until his possession of her body.

She had accused him of being crazy, but as her hands sank into his hair and she arched to him, Isabeau admitted she was the crazy one. She was crazy, and the incredible, exquisite pleasure she found in his touch just might be addictive.

He was like human catnip. One taste was all it took for her to crave more and more of him. Just one touch of his calloused hands and she was willing to put aside her anger, for the moment, to have his touch once more.

"Beautiful Isabeau," he crooned as his lips released hers to smooth along her jaw, then her neck. "You make a man drunk on you."

His kisses moved to her shoulder, then lower, to the aching tip of one swollen breast.

"And I do love your nipples, darlin'." The sexy, erotically dark voice had her breath catching. A second later, the heat of his mouth surrounding the sensitive point had a thin, muffled wail escaping her.

"Tracker . . ." She arched, desperate to be closer, to push her flesh deeper into his mouth. "Oh God, it's so good."

His teeth raked over the tender flesh before his mouth covered it again and began sucking with firm, deep draws of his mouth.

Sliding her hands from his hair to the bunched muscles of his shoulders, she felt her senses becoming engulfed by the wildfire exploding through her. His naked body was warm against her.

"How good does it feel, baby?" his voice rumbled with a sexual demand too irresistible to fight.

She wanted to answer him, she needed to, but had no idea how.

"Talk to me, Isabeau." The sensual demand had a moan whispering from her. "Come on. Tell me how it's good. Let me know what you want me to do to these tender nipples."

"Anything," she sobbed, though there was the distant concern that giving this man carte blanche might not be a good idea.

"Anything?" he questioned her, his voice enticing. "That could include many things."

He sounded so wicked, so sexy.

"You're going to end up destroying me," she whispered.

"Never, Isabeau, would I hurt you," he breathed against her lips. "Unless you want me to." She felt his grin a second before he delivered a heated little nip to her lower lip. "Don't you know, princess, pleasure and pain, like love and hate, are the most intimate of friends."

Burying her fingers in his hair once again, Isabeau fought to hold on to her senses. Not that she had a chance of retaining even a semblance of reason.

With his suckling mouth, wicked tongue, and nipping teeth, he showed her a sensuality she hadn't imagined. First against the tender tips of her breasts, then on a heated journey to the damp folds between her thighs.

Isabeau hadn't imagined she could ever be aroused by an edge of pain or that she could get wetter, hotter, than she'd been before with him. That he could find a way to push her pleasure higher or make her burn brighter.

But when he spread her thighs and laid his lips to the slick folds there, she found out differently.

Tracker's lips moved to her clitoris and at the same time he pushed two fingers into the gripping muscles of her vagina. Rubbing, stroking, his fingers found a sensitive, too-responsive nerve-laden area just waiting for his caress.

Her knees lifted, her thighs falling farther apart.

"Tracker," she gasped on a strangled moan. "Oh yes, please . . ."

Hips writhing, she tried to thrust closer to his tormenting mouth, only to find herself restrained when he gripped her hip with his free hand.

His tongue raked over the engorged bundle of nerves his mouth covered before he drew on it with devastatingly sensual pleasure. His fingers rubbed inside her pussy, caressed and moved against the slippery flesh. Sensations tore through her, whirling in an ever-tightening chaotic rapture.

His tongue was a wicked whip flicking around the swollen bundle of nerves his mouth held captive. The fingers buried inside her alternated between deep thrusts and destructive caresses. Perspiration coated her body; the need to orgasm had gasping cries falling from her lips.

Pulsing, desperate flashes of sensation rippled through her, throwing her closer to the chaos amassing inside her. She could see the sparks of color edging at her normally darkened vision. She was a second, one breath from orgasm, and he released her.

His fingers, his mouth were gone, and he was kneeling between her thighs, his hands pushing her knees back as he guided the engorged crest of his cock to her pussy.

The first thrust of his hips buried the engorged length only partway inside her and sent a bolt of the most incredible sensation tearing through her. It was like a flashfire. His cock stretched her, invaded her with such shocking sensation she found that edge of pleasure and pain.

The second thrust buried him fully inside her aching vagina and sent her careening into an orgasm as unexpected as it was destructive. Stars flashed across her vision, pinpoints of light in the dark landscape of her vision.

And he wasn't finished with her.

He pounded inside her with hard, powerful thrusts, his cock impaling her, stroking so many points of ecstasy that she became lost in the sensations and the rainbow of color gathering just beyond the darkness.

Coming over her, his lips covered hers, his arms sheltered her, his body stroked against her, inside her. The iron-hard length of his cock penetrated her, stretched her, destroyed her until she exploded again.

Ecstasy crashed over her, claiming her with a savagery that stole her breath until she was left wasted beneath him.

That easily, the hurt was gone, and as he collapsed beside her, gathering her in his arms, she wondered how long it would last this time.

When would he leave again? And how much more was it going to rip her apart?

As she lay against him, the feel of his heartbeat beneath her cheek, his fingers idly caressing her spine, she knew this had to be the last time. She couldn't make a habit of it. It would destroy her. And she wasn't much into the destruction of herself. It seemed rather pointless to her.

"Why are you here, Tracker?" she whispered against his chest, hating the thought of his warmth retreating, no longer surrounding her once again.

No words could ever express how much she'd missed him, needed him.

She felt the heavy breath he took as his fingers caressed her spine, stroking against her flesh with heated pleasure. A languid, gentle pressure that soothed rather than aroused.

"I'm here for you." His quiet words resonated inside her. "Because I love you, Isabeau."

She sat up slowly, certain she had to be dreaming.

"What did you say?" she whispered. This couldn't be real.

The low light she kept burning in her bedroom shed just enough to see the somber, intent expression on his face. To assure herself she was really there and that she wasn't dreaming.

"I love you, Isabeau," he said softly, staring up at her, a hint of a smile at his lips now. "I came back because I couldn't live without you another day."

Her lips trembled, tears filled her eyes, forcing her to blink back the moisture so she didn't have to look at him through a haze of emotion.

"You love me?" She had to be sure. Certain. *Oh God, please don't let this be a dream.*

He reached up, his palm cupping her cheek, his blue eyes filled with so much emotion that she didn't dare believe.

"I love you, princess," he whispered again. "I told the cousins they could have the business. I'm out of it. I want you, Isabeau. A life with you. A family with you. All the things I was certain could never be mine. I love you."

"Oh, Tracker, I love you so much," she cried, her lips trembling, tears falling from her eyes now as she touched his face with shaking fingers. "I love you so much."

He pulled her to him, wrapping his arms around her, holding her to his chest as his lips touched hers, his gaze holding hers.

He loved her.

She hadn't dared hope, hadn't allowed herself to dream that he'd come back to her. But the hopes and the dreams had still lingered.

Right here, in his arms, sheltered by his love, she let herself believe.

EPILOGUE

April

THE MAID OF HONOR LOOKED LIKE A PRINCESS.

A barefoot princess dressed in chiffon, lace, and tulle, holding the skirt of her sapphire-blue gown up to her knees as she danced in the middle of the dance floor like a sensual little nymph.

Long chestnut waves of hair spilled down her back, and her laughter-filled blue-green eyes sparkled with fun as she and the bride rocked out to a rousing country tune.

Chance Grogan stood in the shadows of the ballroom, his favorite place to be, and watched as Mattie Watts danced, laughed, and somehow managed to keep him distracted from his self-imposed task of watching the crowd for any threats.

He kept forgetting what he was supposed to do, for what he couldn't help but do.

Watch the girl.

She was a hoyden, a temptress, a pain in the ass, and far too reckless for her own safety.

"Her brothers will kick your ass." A far too familiar and unwanted voice spoke behind him.

This was what she did to him. No Mackay could have ever slipped up on him if that woman didn't mess with his mind. But there was Rowdy Mackay, amused and too damned nosy as he eased in beside Chance.

"They can try." He gave a dismissive shrug.

Her brothers had nothing to worry about though, because he didn't intend to do more than look.

"Maybe Natches will take care of it for them," Rowdy suggested.

Oh, that fight was going to happen eventually, but it would have nothing to do with Mattie. And it wouldn't happen tonight.

"Tell him to let me know when and where?" He really wasn't interested in this conversation.

Rowdy's chuckle was actually amused, but Chance decided he'd be offended by it later. When Mattie wasn't dancing like a living flame and holding his attention.

"When are you leaving?" Rowdy's voice was curious, seemingly unfazed as Chance continued to ignore his presence.

Chance forced himself to appear relaxed, unconcerned, but he had to admit, he was getting damned tired of this question.

"When I'm ready." He should have already left months ago; instead he'd found one excuse after another to stay.

Rowdy sighed at the answer, and to be honest, Chance hated treating this man like the enemy. Too many times the older Mackay had tried to be a friend, and each time, Chance had insulted him.

He was a good man. Hell, him, Dawg, and Natches were all good men, and Chance knew he was anything but a good man. He wasn't the monster his father had been, but neither was he anything like the man standing beside him.

"Natches managed to get his hands on some bloody gauze you used when you blew into town a while back behind Tracker. He ran the DNA on it, Chance. We know. And Natches has known since he first met you. Hell, we all have." The statement had Chance freezing inside.

Emotions he'd never allow free ripped past the door he kept carefully closed on them. Pain. Regret, broken hope, chaotic rage.

Pushing them back was never easy, but he managed. Holding his breath, he forced every ounce of it back, deep, locking it away for a time and place when no one else could possibly see it.

"That's too bad," Chance murmured, true regret building inside him now.

He'd have liked to hang around awhile longer, be a part of Tracker's and Isabeau's lives. Maybe remain just in the periphery of the Mackays. And maybe even Mattie's.

"You're family, Chance," Rowdy said then, the regret that filled his voice almost releasing the hoard of emotions demanding to be free. "A brother . . ."

"Wrong." Chance straightened from the wall he'd been leaning against, gave the girl a final look, then turned to the Mackay determined to ensure Chance left the county immediately. "I'm nothing to any of you, Rowdy." He faced the elder Mackay with mocking amusement rather than the regret that filled him. "Something all of you need to accept."

Rowdy stared back at him, his expression somber.

"Wrong answer," the other man told him. "You can't run, and you can't hide any longer. Won't matter where you go, someone will have your back, just because they owe us. . . ."

"No one will know. . . ."

"Wrong again," Rowdy assured him. "Once me, Dawg, and Natches pull in all the favors we've accumulated over the years, it won't matter where you are, what you do, we'll have eyes on you. Might as well hang around here long enough to figure the rest of it out."

"Figure what out?" Fuck.

The hell if he needed more to figure out at this point.

Rowdy shrugged. "Oh, I don't know. We could start with why Homeland Security caught a hack searching for information on you specifically and your ties to the Mackay family in particular. Whatever you've been running from is about to catch up with you. And this may well be your last chance to defeat it. Here. At home . . . Let us help you, brother. . . ."

Photo © Jenna Underwood

Lora Leigh dreams in bright, vivid images of the characters intent on taking over her writing life, and fights a constant battle to put them on the hard drive of her computer before they can disappear as fast as they appeared.

Lora's family and her writing life coexist, if not in harmony, in relative peace with each other. Surrounded by a menagerie of pets, friends, and a son who keeps her quick wit engaged, Lora finds her life filled with joys, aided by her fans whose hearts remind her daily why she writes.